BACKED AGAINST THE SEA

BACKED AGAINST THE SEA

WANG WEN-HSING

Translated by
EDWARD GUNN

East Asia Program
Cornell University
Ithaca, New York 14853

The *Cornell East Asia Series* publishes manuscripts on a wide variety of scholarly topics pertaining to East Asia. Manuscripts are published on the basis of camera-ready copy provided by the volume author or editor.

Inquiries should be addressed to Editorial Board, Cornell East Asia Series, East Asia Program, Cornell University, 140 Uris Hall, Ithaca, New York 14853.

ISSN 1050-2955
ISBN 0-939657-86-4 cloth
ISBN 0-939657-67-8 paper

ACKNOWLEDGEMENTS

Among those people who have read portions of the draft translation, I would like to thank especially my wife, Jennifer, for her patience and good humor. My thanks also go to the author, Professor Wang Wen-hsing, for graciously consenting to the translation and for discussing a few points which remained in doubt during preparation of the drafts. Christopher Lupke has acted as editor, and a very informed and engaged one. Beginning with the title of this translation itself, he has offered numerous valuable suggestions. The work of translation was supported by The Council for Cultural Planning and Development of the Executive Yuan of the Republic of China, Taipei, through its program of sponsoring the translation of important works of literature, past and present.

Since its publication in 1981, *Backed Against the Sea* (Pei hai ti jen) has been received and read in a variety of ways, a number of which are represented in the articles collected in the journal *Modern Chinese Literature* (September 1984). More recently, the novel has been placed in the context of contemporary Chinese literature by David Der-wei Wang in his study *Fictional Realism in Twentieth-Century China* (Columbia University Press, 1992) and has received extensive analysis in Yvonne Sung-sheng Chang's forthcoming book *Modernism and Nativist Resistance: Contemporary Chinese Fiction from Taiwan*.

Edward Gunn
Ithaca, NY
June, 1992

A NOTE ON THE TEXT

The Chinese text is well known not only for its strong and idiosyncratic language, but also for its unconventional use of a variety of graphic systems, including simplified as well as traditional Chinese ideographs, romanization, the Chinese phonetic transcription (Kuo-yü chu-yin fu-hao), and odd punctuation, not to mention erratic spacing. These are all suggested, if not equaled, in the translation by various devices, including the use of the International Phonetic Alphabet. Wade-Giles romanization has been used; if nothing else it should serve as a reminder of setting and milieu. Notes for some of the many allusions in the novel have been appended at the end of the text.

January 12-13, 1962

Damn! this rat's ass rat's cunt rathole! It fuckin' sucks! Fuck it! Fuck this! Eat me, eat my meat, -- scum suckin' homopansyfaggot son-of-a-bitch suck my cock! bite my crank! Dogshit! Not worth dogshit! not dog's ass! not dogsnatch! dog pelt! dog claws! doglegs! dogpricks! dogteeth! dogpaws! doggie dick! dog shit! shit!

How in the hell did I end up here? How in the hell in this fuckin' dead end hole? I was doing all right in Taipei just ten days ago. It might as well have been eighteen hundred years ago now. It seems like Taipei and everything in it is history -- In terms relative to this small fishing harbor, Taipei may be likened to such heavenly bodies as the moon in its vast, vast distance. Hardly anyone even realizes there's this pinprick of a place on the island no more than five hours from Taipei -- four by train and one on foot, it's a walk that does your legs good all right. The thing that bothers me is that I may never be able to get back. It's a place you can put your feet up all right it's okay for that, sure, for that it's a fine place. It's nice enough the way they've got a Christian church up there on the mountain slope -- and whorehouses and tea parlors squatting around the village down below. So there it is: Heaven above; Suchow and Hangchow below. The place I'm staying now lies along a low rise that looks pretty dwarfish next to that mountain if you sneak a peek at it there poking up between the church and the whorehouses.

Fuck this endless fuckin' rain. I figure it's been raining from the first day I got to this dump and every day since; the hills and the ocean around here were pathetic enough before it started raining, and if it goes on raining they'll be so pathetic the place will collapse from sheer embarrassment. Oh, fuck the hills, the gray ocean, the sky; fuck the sunless days of plopping rain, and pitch-black nights, and this whole place, this whole earth, the entire human race and every

1

society in it, every culture, system, economic structure, and money -- right, fuck the money, and every one of those rich people, and everyone in the past, everyone in the future, fuck all my ancestors and all my descendants, and, oh, fuck me!

I sound like a dog barking, yapping, right, just like a dog barking bowwowwow, a totally meaningless bark, that floats right off deep into the night where it can't leave behind the single scrap of a scintilla. But I still want to let some of it out, I want to let my throat rip just to shout it out. How I've needed to do just that these past few days. That doesn't mean I want to write a memoir, does it? I suppose I'm just about at the age where you want to write a memoir. Ha, so I've got that affliction of old age, too. I'm not going to write a memoir, absolutely positively not going to write one of those things. To write a memoir, first of all, you have to be famous. -- It seems only famous people have memoirs. Tough luck, I didn't make that leap to fame in time, so now "time like an ever rolling stream" has taken my youth with it, and I couldn't grab it back if I wanted to. It's a congenital defect. Even if I made up my mind now to shut myself up for a decade to write out a memoir, it would be no use. The memoir is actually a pretty odd form of writing, since it doesn't rely at all on whatever effort you're going to put out, but on all the effort you've put out before you write -- It's a lot like cashing in your entire life insurance.

And there's another drawback to writing memoirs that's a drawback for any kind of writing as well: Once you've got pen in hand you can't go on pouring out all the inane things you want to -- consequently the pen is used to obstruct thought, not to generate thought. So what I've got to say now I'm saying purely for just myself to listen to only, -- no, no, even I don't want to hear it. I just simply want to talk, no, not talk either, I just want to bark it out some.

It's dark, and not just inside this room. It's a thick black pitch outside too. There's an air vent about the size of a square of beancurd in here somewhere but I can't even see where it is. I can't tell where the room ends and the outside begins. I can't even feel where the walls are. The last stub of the candle just went out. I'm the sort of person who particularly hates light. Even during the daytime when I'm in my room I usually like it good and dark. And when it's night time I like it dark even more. What I detest the most are those evenings when it isn't quite dark and it isn't quite gray. Nights like that when you can't tell what color it is irritate my eyes the way it feels so bright it's dazzling. And then whenever I'm alone talking to myself privately then I want it the darker the better, that's how I like it. Maybe the reason I can't stand being around light is most pertinently related to the fact of my having just one eye, just a left eye? Could that be the one and only reason, that one eye can't stand as much light as two? Let's have another slug, ... can't feel where the bottle container is, just about knocked it over. I don't even use a glass, just twist open the cap and chug it down like Parathion insecticide. Whew -- I bet Parathion goes down easier than this, the wine of the masses, Taiwan T'ai-pai.

Fuck this mother-humpin' freakin' place, this dogpatch fishing harbor. There may be hills on three sides covered with dense plants and trees, but this harbor's like a shiny scar from some fungal infection on a bald pate, a patch of sand that doesn't support so much as a blade of grass or a leaf. It doesn't even have one of those tall cocoanut trees you see all the time to show the place is under the flag of Taiwan. The place is simply a desert, it amounts to a desert in the middle of an oasis. And speaking of deserts, this is a place that truly deserves the name. There's not a drop of drinking water in the harbor itself. Never mind that it fronts on the Pacific Ocean with all the surplus excess water you could imagine, in that whole boundless ocean of salty brine, there isn't a spoonful you could drink. Don't bother imagining taps with running water. The drinking water for all the houses in the harbor is spring water run down from the hills through bamboo tubes. It all flows down from places drawing on clear streams, sources still located in the prehistoric stone age, who knows but one day, it's hard to say, we'll be eating meat raw maybe? Hasn't it been almost a month or more I haven't seen any signs of fish around here? And as for the next few months it doesn't look like there'll be much hope of any more of them swimming through. Just now this harbor is dead quiet. A few people on foot are scattered around on the pale gray cement dock. Altogether there are no more than about 20 motorized fishing boats grouped together sleeping soundly side-by-side. Occasionally two or three sampans slip in and out silently sculled by sea hands under the same old gray emptiness. The sky in this place is unusually weird, each day the same sky, every day the same sky. From morning to night it's all uniformly the same dreary gray; the only difference is between day and night: days are pigeon gray, nights are pitch black. Taken together the entire population of the harbor is no more than 500, about half of them rely on fishing for their living, a hundred plus actually go out to the ocean to do the fishing -- all unemployed -- and some 200 dependents of fishermen -- also all unemployed. But they say when the fish come in this small harbor can hold nearly a hundred boats -- most of them coming in from other ports all in one mass and then they say over a thousand people stay here. But the situation now is grimmer by far. Not even 500 people. And what is the name of this place!? **Deep Pit Harbor.** Perfect, just perfect. Likely there's an unspoken **symbolic** significance to that ------; or, is it pure realism? Either way seems right. An exceptionally rare "authentic" example. It's truly a pit, with mountains on three sides. The one cutting us off behind in particular is so tall it's awesome, reaching up deep into banks of clouds and mist. This colossal mountain stretches around behind where the mountain on the left rises. If you look up from where the harbor is,

3

you can see on the face of the tall one a whole lot of armpits and haunches squatting from mid-slope on down. Then higher up the slope is ringed by the coastal road cut directly into it -- that road slithers up over the chest of the mountain to the right of the harbor. The tall mountain in the rear to the right of the harbor looks just a little tiny bit like some reservoir dam. If you raise your eyes from the harbor to the sharply rising hills that form a screen to your immediate right you see rolling straight down the slope a swatch of soft green grass like the cloth surface on a billiard table with some forest green small round trees looking like so many beads which to the eye simply seem ready to roll down that grassy slanting slope, where at its base so so many of these small round trees are packed closely in clusters. The face of that hill on the left hand side reveals a perfectly squared off gravel landfill, bordered on both sides by dark green shrubs that look just like bundles of rolled up carpeting. This patch of sand cleared for tilling and gardening is furrowed row after row like one of those washboards you rub clothes and socks and stuff on when you wash clothes. Beyond the mountain on the left a deep blue solitary peak rises erect even higher and more prominent. Again and again you can see small solitary clouds rise up and throw themselves on it. It looks they're committing hara kiri. The mountains ringing this village one after another are just like a fat mother cradling the harbor, and the small fishing boats bunched together at its edge the very image of a swarm of fleas sheltering in those like billowy, sour, fat arms -- no, armpits -- of hers. And surprisingly, it's almost impossible to discern even a single Japanese-style dwelling in or around the harbor. The Japanese were here once for sure, but they haven't left behind any buildings -- maybe they saw for themselves a long time ago that this place wasn't fit for human habitation? Never mind for the moment whether this place is habitable or has anything else to distinguish it, this is a place without a past, without a trace, a shred of historical background, no matter how you put it. Its **present** consists of that filthy, rundown, hodgepodge of shacks beneath the belly of the surrounding hills. With the exception of the "Ma Tsu Temple,"[*] all houses alike are made of wood planks nailed together, or are just even cruder thatch-straw huts. Now, to pick up where I left off, if we make a more thorough survey of the housing in the neighboring hills, then there actually is after all a western style structure. Of course in these parts it's pretty much a spot of red accent against a vast green canvas, so to speak, constructed out of genuinely "solid materials" like steel frame, concrete, and glass, and that's the church the Roman Catholics have. It's as though, knowing perfectly well that it shouldn't disturb the perfect harmony of the general squalor preserved beneath the surrounding hills, it lies prostrate far off, midway up that peak off to the left.

How much longer am I going to go on hanging around here like this? I'm at the end of my rope in a pretty "desperate situation" where the only thing I could depend on to make a living for a while is to take to the ocean and try to net some fish. I knew all along this dim prospect would be an exercise in futility, but I never imagined that if you wanted to go after fish there wouldn't be any and all you'd be left with is just a lot of cold sea air in your gut. It looks like I'm just going to go on living here flat broke, until I've landed some fish. It's like this: There's no place left to go that makes any sense, and going back to Taipei is out of the question. Whatever else you may say about this fishing village it still plays a valuable role "security" wise. I absolutely **can't** go back to Taipei. The cops there are waiting to bust me, just over some minor thing at the "Wanli Emporium." That's nothing, really. But "Blackface Tiger" is another story, he's trouble. At this moment he's in Taipei looking hungrily to catch me -- he wants me to pay up everything "you owe me" in no more than one week -- what I owe according to him, that is -- 15,000. He said that my one remaining eye was his, and if I still wanted it for myself to win back fifteen grand fast at the gambling table. It was just my goddam lousy stinking luck to run into "Black Face Tiger." That maggot Wu Hsiao-mao damn him he's even worse. That asshole Wu Hsiao-mao, if I ever run into him again -- haah. That time for a change I didn't have my act together and I got screwed up bad. Before, I just screwed up. This time it was clear they were ready for me, and planned the whole thing out in advance to set me up. Once things got going I figured out that everybody in the place had something up his sleeve, and my one thought was: discretion is the better part of valor. Only they had me there with no way out. All I could do was what they wanted -- "Play what you feel like for a while." So I played and in no time at all I went right ahead and lost six grand. No question about it, they'd teamed up to take me for a ride. I'd heard how people got slaughtered this way, and now it was happening to me before my eyes. I could see that if things went on this way I'd lose my pants, so I tried to get my brain in gear. I couldn't resist trying a trick or two, but before I'd even made my play they turned the tables on me, right away they jumped me and piled on. Okay, okay, fine -- so this time it was my own stupid fault I got myself into this mess, but I'd already said it: "No problem." I was going to cough up everything I owed this time, but Blackface Tiger got together with Ku Lao-ssu, Wu Hsiao-mao, and Hsü Lao-ch'i and they cooked up something about giving back what I "cheated" them out of a few times before, a century -- three centuries -- ago, because they -- that's Ku Lao-ssu, Wu Hsiao-mao, and Hsü Lao-ch'i -- they said they were all his sworn brothers. Can you believe it? On top of that Wu Hsiao-mao like the scum bag he is put the entire responsibility for all the money he'd lost to me of his own free will on my head without owning up to it himself at all and said he didn't owe me a thing. You tell me, have you ever heard anything to match that for shameless indecency? That time that worthless tramp Wu Hsiao-mao was soused out of his mind like the stupid pig he is, so I didn't even have to bother pulling any tricks and he still lost nine times out of ten. I only had my mind set on "income" and to tell the truth I actually didn't get a chance to do anything. The friggin' result was that after losing all that cash he still wouldn't admit to losing it, and afterwards Wu Hsiao-mao, weasel that he is, kept coming around to my residence to ask me to return it -- needless to say, of course he didn't get it back, and he kept inviting me out to play another three hundred rounds. I thought, "Not bad at all, this is one more fat chicken I'll cook for dinner" --- How was anyone to know that this time he hired "Blackface Tiger" out of the Palace of Hell to preside over the game. It was only then I knew I was getting taken for a ride. How was I going to win back a sum like fifteen thousand for him? Money! Easy come, easy go. I'd already spent it 'till not a trace of it was left, but not a scrap. So it's come down to this, this time, like before it comes down to "discretion is the better part of valor." Now as for the "legal case" involving "The Wanli Emporium," my relations and neighbors couldn't rise above their petty-mindedness to see anything with their own two eyes beyond local cash or American greenbacks! They actually accused me of borrowing capital from them on the pretext of opening a business and swindling on the sly and so on and so forth -- enough, enough, enough, I say, enough, all I did was just borrow a little now and then from friends. When did I say I wasn't going to give it back, you know, like, see? Besides, wasn't it just no more than just a few bucks, a small sum? Damn if it didn't come to any more than at most just some small start-up expenses, about four thousand. I just needed enough to stake myself to one game, and in that game thousands were changing hands all the time like, you know. If I have to pay it back then I'll pay it back, no need to make a big deal out of it. And even if I did honestly have a ball and spend the money, so what, it didn't amount to anymore altogether than coins like "Little Miss sugar sweet cheeks" about as big as a piece of rat shit, right? Isn't that what neighbors and kin are supposed to do, assume the responsibilities of "the obligation to circulate capital loans" among their own kind? But hardly two months went by before they got all excited as monkeys over something, I don't know what. They got on my case as quick as slapping a dog's butt, pressed the panic button to "ring in the court" hearing. What kind of kinship is that? Is that what you would call neighborly? Is that any way to treat a person, to go as far as that? Ah? Is that Fair? Ah?

Really people like them are all hatched from the same egg and poured into the same mold. It was the same way with that screwed-up episode at the South China Publishing Company over a year ago. They got so uptight you'd have thought their asses were on fire. They got so frantic you'd have thought they were in a hurry to a funeral. And what was so inexplicable was that all I'd done was to borrow the miniscule sum of 2,000 from the funds in the insurance vault. How does that amount to anything. And I never said I wouldn't return it, you know? That limp dick wimp of a manager actually told me, the way he speaks

6

Mandarin in that Yangchou accent, his face all sallow, his voice trembling as though he was going through a malaria attack, he stammered along, saying, "you... you you... you tell me if you haven't dishonored the venerable Mr. Yao... you stole money... tomorrow..... tomorrow don't show up for work ----" I was scared he was about to pass out -- "We deal with matters on the principle of compassionate lenience in punishment. In this case we are not expecting you to return the funds, nor will we press charges in court. The issue is finished and done with. We have especially allowed you a way to help yourself to make a new life... From to- tomorrow on you may not enter these offices again. You may not come to work." Could anyone have it this good? Leave me a way to turn over a new leaf and make a new start in life just especially for me? No need to return the money? No criminal suit! And no lawsuit! I began to wonder how and when my luck had taken such a turn for the better. And just at that moment I saw through the whole thing: They weren't leaving me a way to turn over a new leaf out of some humane compassion; the reason they were doing this, the real reason was that they intended to suck up to Venerable Yao, so in that case it would be too awkward to make things difficult for me and leave them having to explain what had been going on. And now, at present, based on deeper consideration and observation, even that still isn't the crucial point; rather, it's that they're afraid of me, someone like me, they were scared because they didn't know whether I'd get even with them one way or another. Now that's what was really going on. Venerable Yao, that old geezer, that bastard son-of-a-bitch. He has a sawed-off body that makes you think of the five foot runt Wu Ta-lang.* He's always constantly taking a sitting position more often than standing upright, for the most part -- so he's good at covering up the fact that he has hemorrhoids that way, and at the same time he shows off the best part of his body (which is that his torso is comparatively long), so when he sits down he looks quite tall, he almost looks taller sitting down than standing up. When he's sitting all you see are those two long, drooping eyebrows of his, that make him look like a seal. His cheeks are so red they look like a pair of bricks. And if you ever go near him, please don't forget to keep your distance so you don't catch a load of that stinking breath of his. No sooner did I set foot inside the reception room of his office and was about to explain to him what this was all about than he started in before I had a chance: "Don't say anything, not a thing. I know all about it, I know it all, so just leave, leave, this minute! And don't come back anymore don't come here --- !" "Uncle, please listen to me, please listen --" I was just about to come up with a reason to go on with the conversation. "Don't bother. I couldn't put any trust in a single word you have to say from now on. You are a person who cannot be given credence. And what's more you're an irresponsible **ingrate**. I've done everything possible to help you from the start -- helped you get transferred helped you get your medical

7

certification, then I helped you get a discharge, and helped you to find a way to make a living. I never thought you'd turn on me like this and **betray** my **generosity**, and that's exactly what you've done after all. In a second you wiped out my reputation. Do you know what other people are saying about me right now? Do I have any credibility left after this? Is anybody going to dare believe me from now on?! You tell me!! Who can I make introductions for after today? After this who can I help anymore? All right -- now get out of my sight, now!" The old man was just turning around to go back into his office when Ah-hua the maid just happened to bring in a hot glass of tea and set it down on the tea table in front of me. Old man Yao he was so pissed his nose rose high into the air and he stood there stock still. I bent over, lifted the cover off the tea glass, and moistened my lips with it -- but I didn't actually drink any. I spat into the glass. I set the glass down, looked up and with perfect composure I said, "True -- Uncle -- this was all my fault, **I let you down, I wronged you.** After all this the way things have turned out I wouldn't dare ask anything more of you. I was only hoping that you would leave me some way to start over, only wish that I, that to help me face my relatives and neighbors, you might please for --" "If you don't want others to know something, better not to do it in the first place."

"True, Uncle, true. But you must forgive those in adversity, forgive those ----"

Just then Ah-hua the maid shufəld her way in flipfləp flipfləp; this time she offered me a cigarette.

"Never mind that -- what sort of person do you take me for? You think I go around gabbing about other people's faults like some common, ignorant womən?" With that he suddenly wheeled on the maid and said, "Hey, will you stop constantly coming in here all the time, okay?" Then he turned back to face me: "You don't have to worry about that -- whew! I can't be bothered keeping track of your personal affairs -- now are you going to get out of here?" I did, I walked out right then and there, right out the door. The old man may have said he wouldn't be "keeping track" of my "personal affairs," but he repeated the whole story! He was the one who publicized the "Wanli Emporium" incident all over everywhere, so they say. Although he didn't say anything at first, when they started asking him he spilled it all the whole thing non-stop like rice out of a sack. And that hypocritical, two-faced bastard had the nerve to say that I'm an ingrate. That old double-crosser, he could stand there talking away about how he's helped me, but I brought a few gifts to his door, too, didn't I? Haven't I fuckin' run errands all the time the past few years and done all sorts of things for him, isn't that right? That time before when he once, illicitly fronted for some businessmen buying cement, for a commission, that got him in hot water bad -- what was so sterling about that? He had me going out in the middle of the night paying off all the key officials. But after everything I'd gone through to pull him out of really big jams and tight squeezes, how could he forget it all, every single thing? So all along it was he who's the ingrate, who uses people and then throws them away. That prick of a scheming, double crossing snitch, stick it up your ass!

That "Medical Certification" he talked about -- I really was <u>sick</u>! The way he talked about it you'd think it was like it's just as if I got it all totally because of all he'd done as if it was all his doing. Unbelievable! Absolutely unbelievable. After all the pain and mistreatment I went through, he was the one who wound up with the rest cure in the beautiful scenery it all went to him everything. What I was suffering from was a genuine case of a bleeding ulcer, outright, pure and simple! The blood was gushing out like a stream, just gushing out so I looked like a heroic martyr who'd sacrificed himself to save the nation! But, wouldn't you know, I had to have a certification to certify I was sick -- and they wouldn't give me a certification. If you went back over all my medical problems to have them examined and ranked on a scale, most likely only my gastric hemorrhage would count as something really impressive, whereas none of the other problems I have would qualify me to get in line to be seen. Even my right eye when it went bad wasn't enough to get me accepted to qualify for getting "elected" and all, like, you know, like. And when it came to my bleeding ulcer I had to first have "certification" -- it's just as if a baby had to have a birth certificate tucked in its tiny fist when it first comes into this world whining and crying before it could be recognized as **born**, otherwise it just plain wouldn't be born at all. That old weasel if he ever helped anyone out with anything at all for sure it was himself, that's all -------- I was the one who had the gastric hemorrhage --------- he simply helped himself to the benefits and the property rights all went just to him.

Along with this ulcer at the same time I've suffered from several other illnesses. I've had this intractable chronic old respiratory problem. -- My illness would suddenly act up late at night then and I'd start wheezing like a bellows, *shushu* like that. Thank Heaven -- it was late on the very first night after I arrived here that my sickness started up -- that breathing sound of mine -- reverberating around in a place like this under the vast sky overhead where all you could hear is the faint sound of ocean waves -- this breathing sound -- *shushu* -- it blended right in with the very breath of the tide in nature itself, each echoing the other. I also have a hemorrhoid that's over twenty years old. With qualifications like that it outranks my respiratory problems by a long shot, so I call it "old first"; the breathing problem didn't start 'till after I came to Taiwan -- it's "old second"; I got the bleeding ulcer four years ago -- it's "old third": -- In one year alone it can act up any number of times and when it does then before long it oozes blops of blood down below there. When the hemorrhoid comes on like that you can't sit and you can't stand, much less walk -- and it even hurts just to lie down, unless you stretch out flat out on your stomach. But then even this prostrate position has certain drawbacks, since quick as a wink it gives your prick a hard on in short order. Still even when you take times like these they don't amount to the absolute worst; when it comes to the absolutely worst of all times that's when I start having trouble breathing at the same time. When it gets to times like those even lying flat down on my stomach doesn't work. ------ You oughta see me then at times like those when I look like a stray dog cornered by a whole crowd of people around me. I thank Heaven -- **thank Heaven** -- I haven't had twins like that since I got to this "Peach Spring Paradise."* If I did then I'd have to say that calls for a round of applause. Given this instance, moreover there being no fish, it would indeed of necessity be termed "triplets," would it not? Still, you can't trust in Heaven too much -- it, Heaven, that is, it just may be waiting for just the most opportune moment to strike. So in that case it would be appropriate to express deep appreciation to Heaven through a truly elegant piece worthy of the name, like "Serial Homicide of Mother and Children" -- triplets, give it a subtitle like "One corpse and four lives" -- all of them all together each stretched out stiff and still on the birth bed. -- Now you could say that really is what they call a "clean sweep."*

Wherefore depart I not? -- Seriously, why don't I go someplace else?-- Because there's nowhere to go. -- Whatever else you can say about this place for good or ill, I can still have a wait. After all, the fish may return, who can tell? The other fishing villages in the vicinity are all each down to four or five sampans each. Even if there are fish, that doesn't necessarily mean there's work. A move to Kaohsiung would cost a lot no matter how you travel. What's more, you only have to wait another week before the mullet season will be just about over around Kaohsiung. ------ So it seems as though Deep Pit Harbor is the only spot in the entire world left to live in. Once I wound up here I couldn't remain "unproductive," simply trying to get by from day to day without some gainful employment, could I? I thought of applying what I had already acquired in the way of special skill: **gambling**. But the **poverty** around here is so bad people are at the point of pawning their pants, so who's got the money to gamble with you? Consequently, on the third day after I got here that day I started up and set up a stand as a fortune teller ---- I learned a thing or two about palm reading a long time ago, but after a while I got to feeling I couldn't believe this evil, so I dropped it and never took up studying it again. But this time I came prepared for what I was going to do; in the bottom of my bag I'd packed some old dog-eared manuals for reading palms and the like. I've been cramming daily now in order to like "sell what I've just bought"! The truth is when you start palm reading there isn't any one right way, no orthodox method. Since what you're saying is all a fraud anyway it's all the same whether you make it up yourself or not, it still won't be a bit inferior to any other method. But then, after all, you feel so, so much better if you've got a book to follow. No matter what the topic is, you always feel so much more relaxed when you speak, much more, if only you can get hold of some book to base yourself on that you can rely on every step of the way. It just about makes the case that you ought to have a rough draft first, even when it comes to bullshit. -- The fact that when I got to the point that I was at my wit's end with no way out I switched tracks to take up a gimmick like fortune telling amounts to saying that when you're down to your last cent being broke turns into "wisdom" ----- Never in my wildest dreams did I imagine a trick like being able to turn poverty into "divine prescience." A -ha-ha -- so that's it --eureka-- "poverty purchases prescience," that's what it's all about! As a money making proposition, fortune telling actually doesn't bring in very much (where could people here find the spare cash to go have their fortunes told? -- still, I've since found out that once people have some extra cash they're more than happy to expend it upon fortune tellers.) No matter how you talk about any kind of fortune telling as only amounting to a few cents here a few cents there even so it has some good points of its own, no doubt about it: to sum it up, it's worth something more than being flat broke. Since I wanted to set up shop as a fortune teller I needed first of all to pick out a "vocational epithet" for convenience sake. It was then that I styled myself with the title "Lone Star" -- the hidden meaning behind this was that I had only one, single eye! -- A lot of people have never imagined that having only one eye could be such an amazing advantage. It tends to generate within people a greater, deeper belief in you, most likely on the presumption that it's in order to look into their pasts to read their futures that you're one-eyed in the first place.

Where in the world is all this rain coming from? Just listen to it *hua hua hua*, pouring and gushing so hard you really have to see it to believe that it -- this rain -- could be coming down as hard as it is. You'd be amazed that heaven can hold so much water, bursting down on you before you know what hit you, what's the point of it all anyway? This stupid dump is so absurd in every way that even the way it rains around here doesn't make any sense: It'll be a normal, fine drizzle one minute then flash flood a cloud burst, the next, stop all of a sudden, and then go back to drizzling again. Thank Heaven himself, it hadn't yet started raining this ferociously up to that moment the day I arrived in this harbor village, it wasn't even drizzling yet. They say that up to the moment I arrived they were getting drenched with the downpour of the season, and right after I settled in here this misty drizzle started in again. It was a good thing it was a great thing it didn't rain a drop of anything at that particular moment -- by that time I'd already had enough troubles and my fill of annoyances. The train I took went only as far as *Jui-ho* (---- the Highway Department bus line also terminates at *Jui-ho*) -- and beyond Jui-ho there are no other means of transportation to this harbor. Ordinarily you have to wait until the fish start running before there's some privately owned transport ------- and even that runs only once a day round trip. You can't even find a pedicab anywhere. I was loaded down with a bedroll and a broken suitcase, so the only thing I could do was try to carry them. One person couldn't shoulder that load, it took two. So I went to look for someone to help me carry them and paid him twenty dollars. With the stuff on a carrying pole the two of us shouldered the load to the village huffing and puffing. Once we carried the stuff into the village I realized why there weren't any pedicabs -- to begin with they couldn't make a slope as steep as that going up hill, and once on the way downhill it looked like they might not be able to stop before flying off the edge of the cliff. Better not to have any pedicab three-wheelers around, a lot better. Better not have any of those stupid-looking junk heaps. Those three wheelers dart all over Taipei thick as flies, altogether the most ungainly, revolting things you've ever seen. You take the guy scrunched up in front to be an ox or a horse, and the one sitting up behind in back sits paralyzed like a bump on a log, why the whole thing bears a striking resemblance to a cartload of cow dung --doesn't it? Besides the difference in three wheeled multi wheelers between Taipei and this place, there are some other things here that aren't the same as in Taipei. One point that is easy to spot is a strange thing I noticed as soon as I got here: there isn't a woman here with even so much as the looks of a cat. Only later did I learn that women with any sex appeal at all are packed up and shipped off to Taipei, the whole lot of them sold off to Taipei. It's true, just the way I'd always heard, that once you set foot outside the city of Taipei itself, no matter where you look or how hard you look, you won't find a single woman with any looks to speak of ---- it's really that way. All the best watermelons, best bananas, best oranges, the best chickens and ducks, the best pork, the best beef, and the best women are all shipped off to supply Taipei. And another difference, (this one I didn't discover until the third day after I'd arrived here) -- the place has no cops! Thank fucking Heaven -- this is a paradise after all. You won't run into enē repression from them here. You can do whatever you want as open and free as you like. Cops don't get around to a hick town like this until the fishing season is getting underway, and even then only one comes just once for a day (probably he gets a free ride in one of those hires), but for the rest of the year you could say the place is left to itself, falls outside any jurisdiction, and the only reason for detailing a cop here is to keep order among the fish, not among the people. There's another difference between here and Taipei and that's the businesses -- naturally so, the businesses here are all small shops with no exception, and without exception they don't have any fancy lights, any artsy interior decoration, atmosphere, what-have-you, so forth, and such, but just what's practical -- not bad, either, for genuine goods at fair prices. There's about twenty shops in this location, a string of one-storey wooden row houses one after the other all bunched together propping each other up out back of the Ma-tsu Temple. By and large business is pretty slack, a dearth arising from the influence of the fish not running. It's no different than the way a decline in the national average per capita income affects the liveliness of internal commercial transactions. The first shop on the right as you face the harbor is a grocery store, but it survives chiefly on selling gold foil coins, incense, and candles, and all the other sundries are of secondary importance. Religion is such a big business in a spot as tiny and isolated as this one -- it reminds me of a store selling religious articles for Roman Catholics in Taipei on Chungshan North Road, I think, anyway the grocery store here you could say is the religious articles shop for this place. But the proprietor of this "religious articles shop" is a thin, brittle petty shopkeeper who moved here from Chu-tung who's so obsessively greedy and parsimonious that he has no match for sheer mean stinginess. That day I went over to his shop to buy some paper and ink (he was so afraid that the sheets of stationery might stick together) he took every last sheet of ten-column stationery I bought and rubbed it between the filthy black fingernails on the tips of his scrawny index finger and thumb. That ten-column stationery is thin to begin with, so by the time he'd finished fingering every sheet the edges were ruined. And then, when I paid him, he rubbed every bill just the same way -- as if he couldn't wait to find out if two bills had stuck together. Located directly behind the "Ma-tsu Temple" is an herbalist store, "Shen Nung's Hundred Herbs," something like that, but this little stall of a drugstore actually is a true rarity. In these parts it functions as its public health institution, and its public hospital -- and a major general hospital at that, with a registration department, a billing department, dispensary, emergency clinic, outpatient department, and operating room, all making use of the latest managerial policies, and adopting management methods completely open to public inspection totally above board. A square metal sign in the shape of an herbal plaster hangs under the eaves at the entrance with a black disk like a sun printed on it. This metal sign amounts to its red cross, I suppose. -- Once I saw with my own eyes a young man sitting inside the shop facing the street, his jacket pushed back up exposing his torso, his hands on his head, his face contorted unbearably into an expression of pain and anguish, getting his spine massaged gently by this marvelously gifted reincarnation of P'an Chüeh, the ancient Warring States physician. It was all there for anyone who came by to see, as plain as day right there in broad daylight under the bright white sun. -- and yet the weird thing was I didn't see a single soul who stood by to watch it. Then there was this other time I saw a guy with his back to the street sitting in the pharmacy, open up his belt and ask our great "national champion" to rub some medicine on his private parts. If you count them up the biggest number of small businesses are the brothels and tea houses selling sex, followed by the restaurants and stalls selling food. The total count is: brothels, 4; tea rooms, 3; food stands, 5. Since the biggest number of shops are for eating and whoring

13

it's pretty evident that eating and whoring genuinely deserve to be recognized as the most important things in life, second to none. It seems as long as folks here can get in their eating and whoring then nothing else matters too much. Hence it is further evident that eating and whoring fully comprehend and constitute the utmost of all pleasures in this world. Yes, it's true, that once you've got the pleasures of food and sex you won't eat your heart out over gardens and western-style homes, gold or greenbacks, cars or swimming pools. . . . so the gratifications of food and sex really make them the most affordable of all desires. Why, you could even say that food and sex are the most genuine and straightforward pursuits of happiness in terms of democratic principles of **"People's Civil Rights,"** accessible to rich and poor alike, enjoyed alike by rich and poor, or possibly to a grātər degree by the poor than the rich, you see. Now with all these spots to spend money there naturally has to be a location that can offer funding too -- and this isn't a place where there's any way to strike it rich so that means taking out a loan and robbing Peter to pay Paul -- in other words pawning something. There's just this one place that has a monopoly on the vicinity, and that's next door to the general store I mentioned, known by the appelation "The Concerned Gentleman's Pawn Shop." There's nothing you can compare that to for sheer transparent hypocrisy -- but what's really interesting is that fully half the shops, except for the pawnshop, brothels, and tearooms offering sex, apart from these, those other shops don't have shop signs or names. No doubt that's because only the ones with a little style, something that passes for class in this region, have name designations. The names of the brothels and tea rooms were more than enough to turn your imagination loose, names like House of Spring Fragrance, Garden of Spring Delights, Little Miss Peach. . . . Rainbows, and such, lots of them. Of course the implicitness of transparent hypocrisy is just as ludicrous here too. That, after all, is the way it's been all along. It's hopeless to expect things all to turn out perfectly just the same way each and every time.

Given that perfection is unattainable in this locale, you should also find it in your heart to indulge the trash littered everywhere hereabouts. The amount of trash heaped in this place wherever your eye strays, from one end to the other, is truly unrivalled. So much that to look at it you'd think they actually breed it here, or that the town is actually a stockpile of trash merchandise inventories. Strange, but the closer you get to the ocean here, the môr trash you find -- I was at some seaside places once along the shore north of Taipei -- Chin Shan, Pa-li, Fu-lung and the like -- to take in the grand sights of nature. Well, was I in for a jolt, whew! Everywhere I looked the entire seashore was buried in a mindless orgy of trash, trash, and more trash. -- Really, I can't understand why the ocean doesn't make a determined move to march forward firmly, scour the whole mess and roll it away in one sweep? And the entire countryside of Taiwan looks the same way too, everywhere you go, there isn't a village that isn't filthy dirty. Who's ever described the villages as beauty spots who's ever been to one? **Natural beauty; rustic scenery; rich, unspoiled atmosphere**, and the like. **Unspoiled atmosphere** really just means **poor**. It's fair to say that the origins of all romantic feelings are formed by the same sources, and that's ignorance.

Speaking of ignorance, as I see it, probably no form of ignorance any place on earth can surpass the ignorant superstitious veneration of Ma Tsu here. People in this forgotten corner, one and all are superstitious beyond belief. Big, important problems or trivial little ones, it doesn't matter, they'll take them one and all to the Ma-Tsu Temple, light incense, clasp hands, and then get down on their knees, bowing and scraping for some guidance. It doesn't just stop at asking Her whether it's okay to go out fishing, but even if they can go down to *Hua-lien* and on top of that, even whether it's okay if they visit *Jui-ho* a day or two later. They have to ask Ma-Tsu to make up their minds for them and give them instructions for all of this. And that means in these parts everything down to the most ordinary activities in the lives of people here are all firmly in the grip of a lump of clay they call the statue of a bodhisattva. Still, as much as the common villagers who hang around this harbor believe in Ma Tsu above all else, devotion to her doesn't keep them from serving a whole range of ghosts and spirits (even when it comes to that foreign bodhisattva with the prominent nose and blue eyes the people around here throw themselves at his feet when they pay a visit -- that Roman Catholic church up on the ridge is a good example. The foreign bodhisattva has always seemed like a quiet type, in fact he's never offered any guidance to anybody -- and after all the saddest thing is he actually can't tell anybody a thing about how to get their lives in order.   ) When it comes to worshipping bodhisattvas you know it's really true that the more you believe the better off you are, you know, that's the whole advantage of superstition: Superstition gives you so much freedom to enjoy believing whatever it is you want to believe, to indulge yourself completely in freedom of worship so you can believe totally in something, whatever kind of weird spirit it is. It is precisely this which should be regarded as that wherein rests the principal reason whereby I, having established myself as distinguished in professing to read fortunes, could occupy a position and maintain my place. In a place like this I'm probably right up there as another one of those bodhisattvas they're so keen on worshipping -- dare I say it, a living bodhisattva? Make no mistake, it's really true that it makes no difference how many bodhisattvas you have here, just let one of those, those Islamic Moslem types that goes around shouting "Allah, Allah, Allah" set themselves up here and build a mosque and all, some people here would have no problem at all joining up to worship there too.

Islam may well be even more suited to being transplanted to a little place like this since a year could go by here without so much as the hint of a piece of pork. The principal daily fare for the locals is fish that's been dynamited and then pickled till it's pure salt. Say your body is a temple, even the food vendors provide it with at best nothing more exciting than things like fried rice noodles, sliced yellow radish on glutinous fried rice, red-stewed pork trotters, or salted duck eggs, and that's about it. On the whole these things are utterly tasteless unless you pour on heaps of monosodium glutamate. The walls of these food stands are all covered with the same eye catching red strips of paper pasted everywhere and it's amazing to see what sorts of fancy new and different dishes make an appearance there, like Chang-hua meatballs, sesame chicken, fried airplane, and sashimi. But when you start asking about dishes like these that's when you find out they don't have any of them at all. It's quite possible that once upon a time they really did have them --who knows? Invariably underneath the item sashimi there is a notice in large, bold print proclaiming -- "current price." Now of all the clever inventions modern times have popularized this mystifying phrase "current price" ranks at the pinnacle of fashion -- probably it's roughly in the same class category as the sack dress -- I have no idea when something like this blew ashore on a godforsaken coastal sandspit at the end of the earth like this place. Speaking of "current price" suddenly reminds me that, in addition to the worship of the four great idols* Francis Bacon once hauled out, there ought to be a fifth: "current price" -- people who've managed to avoid being hoodwinked by that scam are few and far between. Even the richest people people are so intimidated by it they don't have the nerve to order it, yet nobody actually realizes that if this current price turns out to be expensive it still couldn't be as expensive as all that. Who knows, maybe it's even cheaper than the other items on the menu ---- it's not impossible that the current price might dip one day, just a chance? Once it suddenly dawned on me -- a joy as if I'd discovered some great law of physics governing the universe never before discovered in history -- so off I went, spirits soaring, full of enthusiasm, just as if until that day I'd never before truly tasted the precious, incomparably sweet flavor of freedom, just like that, head high, dressed to the teeth I strode into a handsomely decorated, and by all appearances, mid-size restaurant establishment. The young girl who brings you your tea and a hand towel started in asking me if I wanted to eat some of this or that and so on. At this point I raised my chin slightly to survey what they'd posted on the walls (as always it was the same garish red blather and even the same 20 to 30 or more dishes), until I found the general outlines of where they had "current price," and pointed to it: "I'll have that. What's the current price for that dish? Expensive, iz it?" I could never have anticipated her response: "We're sold out of that today." I thereupon pointed out another slip of paper marked current price and said I'll try that! "We're out of that, tōō," she said. Now this was a young little slip of a country girl, a menial with a face full of freckles and blinking eyes. So I took my glass, which was covered in a greasy layer of dingy, grayish film, and rapped the table, asking, "just how long ago did you sell out? Has it been a year since you ran out, or did you just now run out of it?" "We just ran out of it yesterday. We'll have it tomorrow," was the reply. "Well, you can tell your boss for me you'd be well advised to change that 'current price' you've got stuck up there to 'not priced,' that'd be more like it -- since you can't buy it anyway even if you've got the money." After that incident I didn't have enough interest to try out another restaurant, so even down to today I still don't understand just how they current price the "current price" after all. And in reality the things they sell in this harbor, like fried rice noodles, sliced yellow radish on glutinous fried rice, red pork trotters, salted duck eggs and the like, aren't at "current price" -- instead there's a truly unbelievable "fixed price"! Honestly, that's the way it is, -- all these things are two yuan for each dish. I mean they're too lazy around here to even write out the names of the dishes, they just scrawl them on these long, thin strips of white paper (I've no idea why they don't use red paper in this case) in these birdlike, childish hen scratches and paste them on the sides of their gleaming, galvanized tin-covered stoves, each stall just like the next one. "Every dish, two yuan" -- interesting. The idea really deserves to be recognized as a step toward the founding of a new era in economics: Prices are not to be determined by things; rather, things are to be determined by prices! Honestly, even supposing what is available here wasn't limited to these unappealing, unsightly, pathetic, pathetic, poor, paltry, paltry little dishes and had what it ought to have, the stuff would still be inedible -- just because, as a rule, all regional, local cooking, and especially what the common folk of the working class eat, contains too much oil and too much sugar. (It's truly like this, even something like red pork trotters is sweet as sugar.) I don't know whether it's because of some special taste or fondness they have or whether it's all the calories they need to maintain their strength and energy -- a lot of empty calories without any nutritional value? As I see it, most likely the cultural level of us humans, wisest of all creatures, is intimately connected with salt: Only human collective social formations which know how to prepare foods with salt are human social formations with a relatively high standard of civilization.

Wonder what time it is now. My Swiss watch, you know the make that has the "longest history," "the best service," and "the fastest," is so old the phosphorence of the Arabic numbers on the dial is completely worn off (----- I can only hear it now, can't see it.) Should I light a match to take a look? There's really no point. It's still early for certain, and the nights here are the longest, so long they probably make people start to wonder whether it's going to go on forever and never get to dawn, it's darker a whole lot longer in this spot than it is light by a long shot, you know, like a lot more, you know I think of all the places on this globe this is the spot where time is the shortest and fastest, and by my observations here everyday it's only about four hours from dawn to dusk -- on account of the hills on three sides -- and the mountain on the west side is especially high. They say you can't see the sun set from this location -- that's what they say, that is, because ever since I got here I haven't even seen the sun! -- Actually we don't have to prove it according to an "alleged" **fact** -- it just **ought** to be that way. Daylight disappears early, yes, and with it even that "crow" also disappears early with it! Actually though it isn't a crow but a lone, dark eagle, circling around on its outstretched wings. When you get into describing the particulars of this area it turns out to be such a weird place that it doesn't even have any birds at all of any description. Here you have a locale on the coast, but there's not so much as a trace of a single seagull. As far as birds of other kinds go, be they, be they yellow ones, brown ones, red ones, black ones, whatever, they are completely nonexistent, with the sole exception of that dark and dreary eagle, diving, darting, wheeling, soaring about as it pleases in and out of view. You see him day after day circling over the harbor non-stop ceaselessly, no matter whether it's rain or shine (excepting **large** downpours). Why on earth is there this one and only creature; **why not two, why not a pair** of them? One can only hazard a guess about the other and infer that it died of disease or possibly expired after hunters fatally felled it with fire arms. Had there indeed been another bird prior to this solitary fowl at present? -- After asking some of the long-time residents here I was surprised to find that no one had ever noticed. That bird wheeling around up there is short-necked and long-tailed with a wide wing span some 3 or 4 times the length of its body. In flight its wings hold steady in the wind, so that it looks just exactly like a large floating page out of the newspaper that's been thrown away to drift through the sky. Now, the direction, or rather, the flight path, it, this eagle, adopts is invariably one of perpetually circling around, as though it's strictly following the steps to some circle dance round and around. And before it gets dark at four o'clock this bird flies right straight back to its nest up on the peak. I can observe it through the tiny square aperture of the window in the room I'm living in. And I can see that it's just about practically even with the window when it dips and swoops down. There's nothing more than this peephole of a window in the room I'm scrunched up in because it was originally the bathroom of this room -- I've got myself settled down in a bathroom at present. The reason is that when I first arrived in this decrepit dump I made up my mind I wanted a place that would accommodate just one person only, only I looked everywhere with no luck -- until I just happened to come across a bathroom like this which for better or worse fit my needs exactly. It was just turning chilly and the fish weren't running, so there wasn't anyone looking for a bath and it was just taking up space, so they turned it into a rental for me, 150 yuan rent a month, 50 yuan every ten days. That really suits me fine. It's just my own peculiar inclination to insist on having something like solitude to live in, you know. There's really no way I could share a rented cottage room with those fishermen who come in from out of town, the way they live all thrown together with the landlord's family in one room, crowded together without any distinctions of rank or status, and when the fish are in there's several people piled in together sharing a few tatami mats, and like that you know. That's really what it's like, so I've got to have a place to myself, and it's got to be a dark, quiet place, you know. Honestly, I have to have a room like this to myself **everyday** -- (like someone who's worried himself sick over getting sick) -- to give myself over to the darkness and the quiet so that I feel better. Yes, people in isolation, in quarantine, in prison, in exile, they're all in the same boat -- but being **exiled** is just what I want! Being **exiled** actually gives me a feeling of being free and uninhibited, it's a great way to lift my spirits. In times past exile was another word for **persecution** or oppression. But today in the 20th century it may well have become another word for **freedom**. The room I'm living in right now is at the very tail end of the end of a long row of low one storey brick houses, just four paces long by two paces wide, leaving little room left for anything else except a very large bath tub that's been installed. Since there was no space left ouvər I wasn't able to put together -- pulling together some chairs and benches into -- a bed, because the bed space was taken up by the tub. So then I, uh, hmm, it looks as if down to today no one has ever before come up with something so ingenious as adaptive improvisation, that is so worthwhile, so totally beneficial that it would allow me to go ahead and sleep right in the embrace of the bath tub itself. So I hauled in a large door (still smelled of dried turnips, this because the door was used for drying turnips in the sun, you see like) and laid it over the top of the tub. As for what there was about it that still didn't seem like a bed, truth to tell, if there were running water now that would be something unbelievably ingenious, too ingenious for words, you know, I mean like, supposing it was set up like that, then whenever I'm feeling thirsty, I've got ice cold water running from the tap with just a flick of the wrist, and even when it comes to water steaming hot enough to burn your lips, I've got that to drink too. Suppose I want a bath, I've got a whole tub full I can splash in right here in my bed. Or if I want to piss, I can go **right here**, just run the tap and it's all gone without a trace, clean as if it were a flush toilet like, you know, I mean just like that. **That's right**, all tubs amount to "omni beds" there's nothing they can't do ---- that's right, say you die suddenly, then with all the mourning ceremonies, all the sobbing going on for the departed to accept our humble offerings and so on, then you can even use it for a coffin, and when it comes to that it will even serve as a grave, if you just seal up the top and sides with some wet concrete it'll work fine. It's simply amazing that no one's ever thought up such a great idea as this "omni-bed," so incredible that I'm announcing as of this moment I have exclusive rights from now on to this new model "Omni-bed"! But the thing is the water to this room is disconnected at present so there's no running water (the faucet taps have been pulled off and the spiggot plugged up with some filthy rags), all this evidently before I arrived, and I've no idea what the reason for it was -- a washroom without water, and on top of that there's not even any electricity (there's a wood box mounted on the wall where the electric wires have been sheared off and twisted into what look like short curly whiskers stick sticking out curled up, I suddenly realized it was the day I moved in when I went out they gave me no warning and sheared the wires off with a pair of cutters) -- of course doing that in itself stands to reason, that way they can save some on electricity. Right now they're in a state of economizing on everything, so even the genuine bathhouses don't have any lightbulbs. The only bath houses open now out of the entire lot are the first three rooms up in the front row of houses, and then only on Wednesdays and Sundays, two days a week, just in the afternoons and evenings; it's a rarity for someone to use them, customers are few and far between. And where else would they have the steambath rooms but right up next to my room. The night I first moved in I nearly jumped out of my skin when this staccato banging kicked on. It was about seven or eight that evening, I was in my room unpacking and getting settled in when suddenly I heard it loud and clear next door, this thundering roar and this earthshaking incessant vibration shook that room and the one I'm in shuddering so hard I thought they'd both blow up any second. I was out the door in a shot in sheer panic running for my life, my feet bare, my face pale as a sheet, I stood behind the door to the next room, craning my neck for a look inside: ha, outstanding, there inside lay a new world totally beyond any expectations, inside it was filled with something in the shadows rising and dipping, twisting and undulating: machinery. Yes, it was a mass of giant pipes and tubes attached to barrels of oil, greased a glistening black gleam, the bold, proud, imposing form of some impresssive "system," some of it spewing out steaming hot water vapor while the whole "system" itself went on in a chattering rattle whoomp -- thud -- chug -- lug -- whoomp -- thud -- chug -- lug --- shaking with a sadistic relentlessness. What's more there was this mystifyingly complex gadget of sci-tech magic that looked exactly like an electric meter, showing a needle rising and falling with such dizzying spins that you couldn't tell what direction anything was. And it had a small light, red as it could be, red like the eye of a mad dog crazy with fever -- this was the only room with a light. And besides that small red light there was a small dim one up in the ceiling. Here, of all the things you'd never expect, amazingly enough, was a "machine room"! No one could have imagined it! Here, I mean, I was living in a place like this of all places and even so there was this "room," a "machine room"! This room was set up to heat the water for the place. Most likely if not certainly this machine was put together piece by piece assembled by the bathhouse owner rilaiiŋ himself on his own skills, with<u>aut</u> relying in any way in the least on outside help, genuinely a clear sign of thoroughgoing "self reliance" and "independent achievement." It's impossible to have peace of mind living on the other side of a wall next to a room like that. I'm worried that some day when I'm not thinking about it, just honestly going about my plain and simple business unguarded and unprepared it'll blow me to bits without a piece left over.

Except for the bed (the door plank --) you could say there's next to nothing more in this cramped little room of mine but the four walls. There's next to nothing in the way of furnishings -- apart from a wood-backed square chair and a small round mirror hung on the wall. As for a table and chairs, I just have a chair and no table, so I usually use the chair for a table and sit on the bed instead. And I put all sorts of odds and ends on the chair, like just now, I've set what's left of a red candle and a wine bottle there on the chair. And then sometimes I use the wooden bed top as a table, that's when I get to thinking I want to write something -- a letter, for example, -- and at times like these I make all signs of it as a place to sit vanish without a trace. Thæn I light the short candle, stand it up on the flat surface of the chair, bring it over next to me, and then get down on my knees and kneel on the ground and write whatever it is I want to write, some letter or something, just like a schoolboy doing his lessons. As for the small round mirror, the one hanging on the wall, if you want to look in it during the day usually you can't see a thing; you have to take it down and move it over near to where the tiny window is located to catch the light to see into it. Actually even when it catches some light it still doesn't reflect anything clearly. The surface is spotted all over with grimy little specks, and it's such a small round mirror, so particularly small, that you can only see a few parts of your face when you look in it, like all it can show is a bit of the tip of your nose and upper lip, just that little bit. As for what I've got for the bedding these things are even less worth noting -- just a rancid old greasy grimy greasy grimy quilt, a thin one, as stiff all over as a thin, flat layer of Chinese pancake. And all the things I brought with me are hardly enough to list, just a few few odds and ends odds and ends easily counted. I only had this worn-out leather bag and the dingy luggage roll when I first moved in. The accessories which I possess (not counting a few items of clothing) include just one straight razor with a curved handle which I have had for a long time, a thermos bottle, all scratched up, banged and beaten beaten, battered and rusting inside and out, and besides these an aluminum toothbrush cup, an aluminum toothbrush cup you could use at the same time as a tea cup, and a wine cup, and even as a rice bowl if you happened to be without one sometime you could use it for that too. So this also counts as another "all-purpose" gadget. In general, when I think things have gotten to the point that they're as bad as they are today, then all sorts of things turn into all-purpose "omni" gadgets. I also own what used to be a lightweight, graceful aluminum wash basin, but it's gotten knocked about so much it looks more like it's a piece of tin foil, or something, like. Next, here's a toothbrush. This toothbrush has lost so many bristles that there's only about half of them left. Next there's an old face cloth I've used for a long time, so old the nap on the cloth has been worn smooth. The toothbrush, the old wash cloth, and also that toothbrush cup, all of them fit together inside the washbasin, placed there in one group. In addition to these there's the old watch I mentioned before and a thick, black fountain pen of mine with a tip wide enough so it offers no problems when you want to write out Chinese characters just like you would with a brush, you can write them one after the other in good block style. In addition, buried down in the suitcase, I've kept a stack of eight-inch erotic photographs made here in Taiwan. There are eleven of them altogether, used to be a dozen originally, but I lost track of one somewhere. With the exception of setting this assortment like of "spiritual sustenance" aside then, I still have some worn-out old books collected in the suitcase -- this doesn't include fortune telling books, they're my "material sustenance," my "noodles and rice" or what they call my "bread and butter" -- together with a volume of poems I've cooked up that aren't yet ready for publication. They're what are termed "new poems of the vernacular school" recorded in my own hand over the last decade or so. All the books which I've kept at my side and added to my suitcase collection up to today, all of them were either fished out of libraries or borrowed out on unlimited loan from friends whom I asked to let me "borrow them for a while" -- in sum, and I don't know why it's turned out this way, I have always treasured having them collected in my suitcase, and kept them with me no matter where I go, even though they're so worn they're frayed, and so soiled they're filthy. These most treasured books are comprised of Dostoevsky's *Notes from the Underground*, Nietzsche's *Thus Spoke Zarathustra*, Gide's *Fruits of the Earth*, and Tolstoy's *Resurrection.*[*] This is what the material possessions I have are like, simple and crude, but whatever else you may say about them they are more than useful enough to me for my use, and when I say "useful enough" that means they absolutely come up to the mark of useful enough so, I am deeply aware that the accessories of material life among modern humanity at present are unnecessary to the point of being superfluous and where it most especially has gone to extremes of conspicuousness is in the way Americans live -- why do they need to have so much of all that junk -- one person surrounded completely on all sides with enveloping rings of all sorts of trash like that. (-- it's as if the world is just one big seashore like what we have here from the look of it)   Generally speaking, on the whole two or three sweaters are enough for one person when it turns cold in the winter season, and a single pair of leather shoes is more than enough for an entire year. But now those Yankees with their deep-set eyes and prominent noses (I'm judging by what I've seen in films and the like, to be sure), when you open up their clothes closets what what you see inside them is like like so many kinds of wool clothes in every kind of color you can't count them all, upwards of a dozen thick wool overcoats, ten or twenty pairs of shoes, so much stuff it all comes tumbling out ka-flop like. And on top of that they're always incessantly even keener to gain possession of yet more kinds of weird machines of every description: televisions, washing machines, record players, tape recorders, slide projectors, film projectors, electric typewriters, power lawnmowers, freezers, streamlined luxury sport sedans -- it's as if they live their entire lives solely just to get these things. It's as if their purpose in life is to set their wills to **master** machines, once one is mastered then it's on to conquer the next load of machinery -- until finally you could say of such a person that once he's bought up and acquired everything there is, then his very self is enveloped wrapped in the heart of all those colorful enticing machines he owns, and by then his very own life is over, the soul of the deceased is taken away to the Realm of Separation while mourning for the departed soul of this hero begins oh woe oh woe accept oh woe these oh woe our woeful offerings sorta like you know. So the sum of what a person gets out of life truly amounts to this pile of ice cold machines, and of all of them the very weakest, the worst, and the least durable are people themselves. What a pity, what a pity, how **regrettable** it is that Yankees they really miss the mark, how they miss it, when it comes to understanding humanity, they can't understand "life," they make you truly sorry for them, it's astounding the way they use up life and waste it on "utility" -- oh, oh, life, life, how could it ever be taken as something to be "used": Life is something to be "**cherished**," life is something that should be savored leisurely at length. Life, in sum, ought to be for being human, not accomplishing things ---- that's what I personally have to say myself.

Hey, wait a minute, wait, just hold on now. The way that came out, it sounds, I don't know, it seems there's something a little odd there. Because if that's true then that must mean I'm supposed to be happy to live "the simple virtuous life," "to be pleased to experience contentment," to get by with just two or three sweaters and a pair of shoes for the whole year, happy to spend my life that way, right? No way, not me, absolutely not. I most definitely have my eye on fame and fortune and women, no mistake about that. Consequently that means I'm loaded with contradictions. I may know it's not worth it to make money my big aim in life, I may be **completely aware** right from the word go that it isn't something I have to have at all to begin with, but no matter what I just have to have it anyway, I just have to have it. --And that's what I am, a big, one big, big big **contradiction!** -- I am "contradiction."

Looking out from the square hole, the single dark hole, the sole ventilation window in my room (which requires standing on the balls of my feet and stretching my neck), I can see in a corner of the expanse of ocean, stretching

23

fairly far out from the shore, a single lone reef promontory, just so, as if it were a thin, bony arm with a tightly clenched fist reaching out along the serene surface of the sea. About every thirty seconds on average a wave sweeps over the face of the rock blotting out the sky, then fierce waves like these again and again pound this delicate, slender arm of rock (I mean when one wave is finished the next blow falls, you know, it makes me really wonder whether it won't go on, perpetually hammering away like this until the last day of this world of ours, until the last, final minute, or the last half-minute of time). Every time I watch this I can't help worrying whether this is the day it might be smashed and crumble away under those huge waves. Once the waves have hit this sole solitary stone promontory, then the foamy spray like clouds or fog or like snow, pauses in mid-air for a long moment, like a fishing net slowly spreading upward as it flies out flung toward its highest point, and only then does it pour streaming into scattering spray as it plʌndʒəz downward. Paths and pockets of snow white wave-carved lines wrap all sides of this one-armed fist-like promontory, just like annular rings and grain revealed in wood that's been chopped open. If we step out from this wooden structure which houses the room, formerly a bathroom, currently employed as a bedroom and concurrently for numerous other activities, we first encounter an empty courtyard where the woman who runs the place raises a flock of gabbling geese. Further on, close by the small side-path leading from the bathhouse, we come to the location of an old structure, burned out and completely gutted so that there's nothing left but a charred frame, like a black skeleton. This used to be a guest house for the convenience of travelers, a row of small rooms; hence, this was all originally a combination of bathhouses and hotel, a bath-inn, sorta like, okay. Last summer there was a howling typhoon with super gale force winds, it was nighttime then, when the wind gave the flame a helping hand and the place burned clean to the ground in no time flat just like that. The landlord and his folks all hang out there in that small house directly opposite the low row of bathhouses, across the open courtyard in the middle. In front of it, at this end of the courtyard is a tin-covered water storage tank. So the water for the bathhouses is drawn down from the spring water in those hills beyond by the bamboo tubing, flowing through this structure, until it spurts into a reservoir. This may well be what in general is commonly called "Soaring Springs" yes, bath water flowing from heaven -- **"Happiness falls from Heaven"** -- Yellow River water comes from heaven -- (The Heavenly River) -- The Milky Way -- *Niagara* -- **Marilyn Monroe** -- hah!* I'll have a sip -- no -- I've got something else in mind -- I'll have a, just one, in my pocket here. "New Pleasure Garden," sounds like the name of a funeral home, probably that's an association with plumes of mist and fog, what supreme satisfaction, like stepping up to a world of ultimate pleasure, dazed and entranced, a carefree immortal. ----------------- A cigarette after a meal, divine enjoyment. Matches. Where are the matches? Oh, on the chair.

Tobacco, and alcohol -- I take the two of them both together. And I like my tea strong, strong strong strong, deep dark steeped 'till it's bitter, tea leaves heaped eight tenths of the way up the tea glass. Everybody always talks about "smoking and alcohol," "tobacco and alcohol," but for some reason nobody talks about "tobacco, alcohol, and tea." Not that all three are completely alike -- why all the special lenient treatment of tea? Why does it get some special, unique exemption from vice? Yech. I don't think I should smoke the rest of this cigarette, I'm beginning to feel a little sick. Well, yes, that's the way it is, there's never any guarantee that whenever you smoke you'll always find it agreeable or gratifying. When it comes to smoking the best time when it feels the best is usually when you're working on something. At times like those after you take a deep, deep long drag and then slowly exhale it back out slow and easy, it's just as if all the strain and tension there in your body is eased on out right along with the smoke. But then if you like smoke one you know sometime when your mind's already in knots and you're feeling lousy, well then the more you go on smoking the more you get upset and you feel even more miserable. Actually even a three year old knows smoking's bad for you, sure, there isn't anybody who doesn't know it's dangerous, smoking, and all the same still just about everyone who smokes has still gone right on smoking anyway, and knowing it all hasn't had the slightest effect on them -- probably that's because they use the excuse that cigarette filters protect them and that way they maintain their habit -- nonsense like that is as "purely" as "out and out" ridiculous as charging into a hail of bullets and blazing cannons fearlessly imagining that you'll come through without a scratch since as long as you're wearing one thin shirt it can protect you! Sometimes I often think it would be safer if I didn't smoke the last part of it. But how do I measure a part? So many inches long? Or so much of a fraction? It's on account of this that every time I inhale the smoke into my lungs it's always a war of nerves, a battle with terror, and "terror" is what I inhale over and over again non-stop ten or twenty hours a day. But, to tell the truth, the real reason that I go ahead and smoke that last part when I should really just leave it is because I'm too greedy, that's the reason I do it, now that's the reason I do it, thæt. Every time, every single time I have a smoke I just can't resist smoking it right down as far as I can to the very last drag -- and all the time I'm thinking you've still got it's still there, you know there's still that filter, I can count on that great, wonderful, incredible, filter, that's my protection, that is. Then too, I could smoke less -- but do I smoke fewer cigarettes, is that what I do, eh? **No way.** I smoke at least, at the very least, one **pack** a day -- "Not much, less than two packs a day!" Then again, some people, people who're friends, I know well, see all the time, they smoke five or six packs a day, so much you can't even keep count, it's going on everywhere you look. I'm the same when it comes to wine and liquor, too, not a bit excessive once you compare me with these other people. The way these other people are used to drinking mostly they drink as much as they please at least every day, they all do, while I wait a good number of days, four or five days, before I sit myself down and tie one on. And that stomach problem I'd always had for so long didn't even bother me much any more, for the most part, anyway, sort əv. In fact my mind gets to where it's funny the way it gets into a state it feels, you know, dulled, dazed, dopey like. I really don't understand why it is that when people feel like doing something, say eating a little something or drinking a little something, they get so concerned about it they have to go look everywhere to find a reason for it. Actually all these reasons don't amount to anything more than adding a postscript onto the very end of something as if you were pasting on a tail or something, and desire itself takes off all by itself full speed ahead no matter whether you've got some reason or not, it's -- so, then, since that's the nature of desire itself, why, why bother looking for, why not just forget about finding some reason or other, and just think if there's something you want to do then just do it. If it's something you want to eat, then go ahead and eat it, whatever, you know, right then and there if you can then go ahead and eat, it, sort of like you see.

. . . Cigarette ash, give it a tap there, . . . tapped it onto the chair seat. . . Of all the animals only humans alone are capable of leaving piles of ashes, ash heaps, just humans, I mean you know. It's true. Have you ever seen like any other animal of any kind that leaves piles of ash heaps, hæv yōō? Right, only people dump "ash," the bits of ash people leave after they're finished smoking cigarettes, the thin, fine ash from paper after it's been burned up (the love letters burned up down to the last syllable --), coal ash, and even all the ashes that are all that's left over after a building has burned clean, clear down to the ground -- and then, then there are what by any reckoning would count, man's last ashes, his own bone ash. Right, in the end people leave a pile of their own ash remains, sticky greasy fatty and still seared clean, with a pungent odor. And it is people after all who are the only animals among all the animals who will consume "smoke." Really, what other animal of any sort of description have you ever seen where it'll like eat smoke like ju nou, rait? You know, I mean, has there ever been anything to match a thing like that?: "Mmmm! That smoke just smelled delicious --" "Wow, oh, when that car breaks smoke I just can't get enough of it it's sooo good."

And just because of smoking cigarettes like this, that's why it'll come to the point that people will find themselves with a shortage of energy, burned out like. "Burning the candle at both ends." There's one end that obviously refers to that, smoke. And there's another one, hah! That's it, right, the smoke has slowly steeped me slowly bit by bit and baked me into what I look like today. It's this smoke that's cured and aged me slowly bit by bit until I've now been fuckin' "baked to perfection"! Look at me, it's true, every inch of my body from head to tail has tanned completely into this dark soy sauce brown, so I look just like, ju nou, an aged, smoked ham or sᴧmthiŋ I mean I look so bad all over it's ridiculous, like some opium addict, and as for what you might charitably call my face it was so ugly to begin with it's even more unbearable to look at now.--

-- These last few nights I've been cramming to bone up on how to read faces for fortune telling, so on account of this I'm always taking down the small mirror that hangs on the wall to study my own face in close detail for signs of fate, and on account of this, when I was washing my face yesterday before noon, I approached the window and stood on the balls of my feet, and then took a long, loŋ break fixed right there sizing myself up for a long time. I held this little mirror in my hand far, way far away with my arm extended straight out, ah! -- The face that appeared in this little mirror reflected back at me it, it was this pale this white, fair-complexioned countenance scrubbed 'till it was completely covered in dense, snow white soap bubbles. And I had to keep on looking at my reflection in the mirror, looking up, then looking down, left, then right, all over, before I could see through to it -- I mean I had to rely on a powerful memory to add up all the different, separate impressions into one whole before I could do that. Then I turned my attention to my eyes in the mirror, my eyes of which I've lost the sight in my right one, leaving me with only my left ai. **"Eyes are the windows of the soul,"** oh brother, I thought, now what do I look like with just one fᴧkin' eye?!? I was thinking then how if I hadn't lost my right eye then I'd still have a set of "those flashing orbs," a pair of those "autumn waters," that might well be pretty good looking, ju nou, laik, wel -- not likely! When I took a really good close look at it, it was just black and white; the black part was jet black, the white part was grayish-white like, and then on top of that I've got a pair of long, curvy eyelashes, that sweep right up into points the way students in elementary school will draw a sun on paper with those radiant bursts all around it, like. Then I looked over my eyebrows, the way they slant downward slightly, a little bit like the character eight 八 . "Long, white eyebrows are a sign of longevity." They're long -- they're white! -- that's the white foam from all those tiny little soap bubbles. Well, in that case, will mine mean longevity? -- I asked. But I haven't the slightest idea. I'll have to wait until my eyebrows start to turn white before I'll know whether or not they mean "longevity." -- That's really brilliant! Keep on looking! Check out your hair. Now my hair is like hay, and it actually does have some frosting, sparkling white frostiŋ mixed in with it that does look, after all, like soap suds -- down around the ears just below the temple. Up top where I have this matted mop of dark hair, it's all speckled with strand after strand of coarse white hairs, really really ugly like I mean, what is this supposed to signify?! Is it a sign of good fortune or bad? The manual doesn't sei. On to the forehead -- I wiped ɔːf the traces of soap -- and a low forehead appeared covered with protruding bumps and undulating recesses. By any standard this had to be absolutely unprepossessing, right? I thought of when I was young and fresh and bright as a clear spring day and my forehead was fair, supple, and smooth just as smooth as polished marble -- and then the present, what I see in the mirror I mean it's a heap of gravel, a bed of crushed rock, this forehead, it looks as though the bone of the forehead had been crushed into a huge number of tiny, crushed fragments all strewn around. So, it's the forehead, after all, that's the window of the soul! I thought, no doubt about it, the forehead is smooth when a person's got a tranquil settled state of mind, and fragmented when like I mean a person's peace of mind has been shattered broken you know like. Moving on a bit further (no need to say this meant face reading) the hairline on my forehead is so low, so far down, that when I'm in a perfectly even temper and happen to glance up to look at it fuck, double fuck, mutha fuck muthu humpin' fuck I don't like it very much. As for my nose, let's get closer to the mirror there, a bit closer, wipe it off, there, now, it's too sharp, too long, and too narrow. When I look at myself I have this genuinely supreme loathing for it. On the sides there, left side, right side, they're too small, too bulbous, too flap like, these twisted ears are really just like a pair of snail shells or conch shells, you know, I mean they're a sight. Moving on down below to check out what's down there, wiping away a screening layer of whitish soapy film after I've scrubbed above my mouth lips thin as thin as they can be, not a particle not the least bit of flesh on them, basically no more than just a skär line for lips. And if when I get to talking -- I know -- the top of the corners of my mouth get filled with saliva and froth until this spittle is constantly spewing out a spray of droplets that take a leaping jump over onto the tip of the nose on the other person's face. (Moving away from it) I really don't like it, this face of mine in the mirror, I don't like it at all. It's so absolutely unlike anything you could call a face of "genius" even if at the same time I looked at it with the eyes of the ordinary, common everyday person, it would still be a pathetic sorry looking face it could never make it as the face of someone "destined for longevity or wealth." This thing that passes for a face, the feis of a beggar fated to starve in the gutter, this "camera fäs," this masterpiece, it looks like there's more than forty years on it to look at it, at the least over thirty, well over thirty, I got fed up with the sight of it long ago, so fed up I could burst, I could die, and with that I spat a wad of saliva in it (onto the image in the mirror), and then then I pikt up a chunk of soap again and this time right across that clownlike clownish feyce -- -- the one in the mirror over the surface of the mirror -- -- I dru: a yellow crisscross **X**. Not only do I thoroughly detest what I call my fäeis, when I close my eyes and try to describe my body, even then, I can't stop shaking my head I'm so completely at a loss for words to describe it I can't come up with any. These goddam fuckin' shoulders of mine are so indescribable they're uneven, one high, one low, and to match that I've got a pair of splayed feet that can only do a duck walk. When I walk forward, left foot right foot, it seems no matter which direction is forward, left, or right, they just go flapping along, smacking the ground like they had a mind of their own. Now, you know, if somebody watched me from behind at a distance or in front at a distance, he'd be certain to see that I don't walk in a straight line, you see. So, therefore, you can often see, in this village, me, slightly hunchbacked, feis forward, eyes front, in a bright brown plastic rain hat on the front of my head that doesn't even look like a hæt anymore, a beaten up old thing, on all sides, a faded raincoat, originally a sapphire blue, the kind that air force officers are used to wearing, and then the toes turned upward high up like a small boat in a billowing ocean rocking as if its bow was tossed in the surging sea swept way way up high to awesome awesomely breathtaking heights, on a pair of old black leather shoes with the outsides covered in chalky mold. That's the way I go around here, my hands buried deep down in my trouser pockets like and the raincoat, minus a kupəl əv buttons lost, flapping like a sail in the harbor breeze you know, I mean that's how I go around here in this hole in the wall of a town drifting on sleepwalking or something, who knows what! Say if I were to to take off the raincoat there you find the same old thin padded cotton jacket I wear every day, a dark, grungy thing, and also a patch of white shirt cuffs down at the far end of the sleeves. Cuffs are filthy too so the spots all around the edges look like the punctuation dots for ellipses. . . . And those old leather shoes of mine, they're in the same condition, too, not just moldy, even the shoelaces are "knotted intestines," an unfortunate turn of a phrase for tender affections but vivid anyhow when you look at how many times they've broken and how many times they been tied back together there are so many knots that they simply look like some sort of arrangement of decorative flowers lined one after another along the top of my feet. How I could use some quick money, some real money, junou, ai mi:n if ai kəd ol əv a sʌdn get rich I could change myself completely and heave all these filthy old rags sky high as far far away as they could go and then some, you know, <u>then</u> in the blink of an eye quick as a wink I'd be transformed into a new, a totally totally brand--stunningly--new new person, just like ah a new born cicada strips off that cicada cocoon and breaks out of it I mean way away way beyond beyond the blue you know like sorta. Well, so much for touting the philosophy of the virtues of simple utility, eh! Wow! I might come into a pile of cash overnight I mean it's not absolutely impossible! I've had lots of friends I used to hang around with when we were all broke it was all they could manage just to slurp to slurp down some thin watery thin rice watery gruel, then all of a sudden like a complete miracle out of nowhere for no reason at all they got rich, I mean rich you know.

Therefore I now know -- and it's only been in these past few years that I've finally made it to chapter one of this basic discovery -- "getting rich" is the kind of thing that works on people's minds the way an itch works on their bodies: It actually isn't really the way I used to think of it when I was still young: something approaching the supernatural, that was so distant and unreachable that it was unimaginable. Not at all, "getting rich" is after all quite <u>possible</u>, it really and truly can happen to "you" or to "me." Getting rich really could happen to **me, yours truly, numero uno, the old man himself,** just fall on me right out of nowhere. Those friends of mine, along with some of the singers in the nightclubs along the movie street that area in Taipei, they all struck it rich in two or three months. And the way they struck it rich it was so fast it was simply like winning the **grand prize** in the national lottery -- lots and lots of people could thank their lucky stars when their numbers came in, the incomparably lucky the hwuchya call it the big grand prize. And those singing stars in the clubs -- whoa! -- They had banknotes piled so high they couldn't spend it all no matter how much they threw around, everyday nothing but the finest of surf and turf to eat silk and satin to wear, and every day nothing but the best deluxe hotels and fanciest clubs, now ouvər to Hong Kong, now daun to Singapore, out all night and in bed all day, playing on as if there were no day or night! Fun! Fun! Fun! And <u>gambling</u>! Aaaand sex. -- ho, ho -- casual sex, wild, crazy sex, sex, sex, sex. You can think of them like human boomerangs beyond the force of gravity up in outer space, with nothing to hold them back or tell them which way is up or down, enjoying a freedom <u>that truly</u> deserves to be called "**freedom.**" You can only have freedom <u>after</u> you've got money. If you compare the scope of freedom in what I say and what I do here with the freedoms enjoyed in other places then I have far more, far, far, far more. In a hole-in-the-wall hamlet like this I can do <u>whatever</u> I feel like doing! **Steal, swindle,** even **mug** people! Any any fuckin' way there's nobody here to pay any attention to what I do so here I've got any kind of freedom you could name, any kind. But now what use is all this freedom crap when what I lack is money, moolah, and I've never had the <u>pleasure</u> of getting close to any mooloney. In fact, what I don't have is the utmost supremely important freedom that has all the others at its beck and call: **freedom of pleasure.** Now when it comes to freedom, I'll tell you truly that in my view the very most utterly and totally insignificant freedom is that worthless little thing the intellectuals who've studied overseas and gotten brainwashed by that culture of prominent noses and blue eyes in the West go around promoting called you know I mean like "<u>freedom of speech</u>." What do they want a thing like "freedom of speech" for anyway? Whether you've got it or not doesn't mean anything more than the hair on your æs. People like us, like us, you know real people, have our own "spiritual" freedom: <u>so whatever it</u> is you feel like thinking there's nothing at all to keep you from thinking it, nothing to hold you back, you see, hwutevə it is. Now compared with "freedom of speech" doesn't that take in a whole lot more, doesn't it add up to something more meaningful, a lot more, you know? Right now the status-seeking the contemporary the "modern" Western intellectuals today would just as soon dump "spiritual freedom" and go struggle in their single-minded their secretive conspiracy for "freedom of speech." Now can't we say that's a display of the grossest stupidity at its utmost extreme, putting the cart before the horse, kǝnfyōōziŋ cause with effect? "Freedom of speech" really doesn't even compare with all sorts of other freedoms, like the freedom to steal, swindle, mug, and like various sex offenses, that we've got right here where I am. Freedom of speech is "meaningless talk" it's just an "empty" kind of "freedǝm," can't match the varieties of freedoms around here for like "actual practice" in any way, can't match them for "genuine goods and fair prices," for "solid materials," or, say, for "usefulness and applicability." To tell the truth, taking it to a finer levǝl when we delve deeper to analyze more carefully and investigate investigate it, does "freedom" in and of itself itself have any meaning? Is it really a necessity that people need? Is it genuinely good? Actually I feel that before you have freedom you feel it's good, but then after you have it you feel it's about as insipid as plān, old ordinǝri boiled water after it's cooled off is tasteless, so you don't feel that there's anything particularly, you know, like "good" about it, freedom. Take say my recent discharge from the service as an example now: Before I was discharged I could hardly think about anything but getting out, but then when the day came my hitch was over, well I never would have imagined it, it was about as exciting as chewing a piece of wax, the whole experience couldn't have been duller couldn't have been blander. In sum, when I'm not free I'm unhappy, and when I am free I'm still unhappy. That's life, for the most part. And in particular more and more I've found that freedom actually amounts to an even greater "bondage." Once you're free you fuckin' find out there are more and more things you want to do, always more and more -- when you aren't free you simply put your everything you've got into fighting for "freedom" and devote yourself completely to just one, single thing. If you've got freedom though then life gets really complicated, there're so many things to do, there's dozens and dozens upon dozens of dozens of things, that you get so busy coping with them you burn out, you see like, and end up never getting anything done! My life after I was discharged is another good -- ouch -- burned the edge of my finger tip -- I've got a good memory for that too. I'm always doing that, I've burned that ridge on the tip of my fingers I don't know how many times, and all because of on account of that the tips of two of my fingers have been bǝrnd an opium yellow stain you see like opium yellow stain there, see. This leads to the fundamental source of the cause I like to day dream. If you you compare the two, daydreams turn out to be far more, much much more pleasant than dreaming at night by a long, long shot, a long shot, since, you don't have <u>nightmares</u> in the dreams you daydream -- I really just don't know why but recently at night I've had constant non-stop nightmares of the most terrifying kind so spine tingling, blood curdling, stomach churning that I'm left drenched in sweat sweat all over. Just last night I had this awful dream --

for some reason I'd been sentenced for a vicious murder, and I'd been completely tied up in big thick restraints of all kinds, and I was being led along a path step by step to the execution ground where they were going to execute me. The guy whose life I'd taken looked just exactly like some supreme court justice (and for some reason at this point everything suddenly changed into this huge, awesome court hall place you see like sort of) . . . then a second later I strained with all my might to struggle free, I felt my legs desperately shoving and kicking until they were so worn out I couldn't raise them and my whole body in an instant went numb all over, weak as a limp plant all over until again some new change that was taking place started happening and went on for a long, long time that went on and on and on I fell rolling from the very tip of a staircase and kept on going down as though it would never, ever, stop, but go on and on down, down, forever, on down. . . . .

What's it supposed to mean? I don't know. I don't have a **clue**. Fortune tellers with deep knowledge of the universe and astrological conditions ought to be able to decipher whether fortune telling is really reliable, you know I've still, I've still got "Dreams Interpreted" written in big bright characters over my now well-known stand as my own specialty,   ah, junou this face-reading scam, to tell you the truth, it really isn't worth dog shit. Those guys, the "philosophers of life," who write the books on face reading and the ones who read faces too, they're simply full of shit, each with his mystic babble like a "King of Fools." It's truly hard to fathom why there are so many willing servile wimps, worms who absolutely worship them and let them get away with being "tyrants." A "philosopher of life" of this sort generally imagines he's "**god**" putting on a show of how busy and important he thinks he is in front of everybody. Whenever he says "long fingers are lucky" then they're <u>lucky</u>; whenever he says "short fingers are unlucky" then they're **unlucky**. In sum it's entirely up to him to determine any and all the rules of the book covering absolutely everything -- and that's not all, not only that, he also doesn't even need to come up with any reasons, he can spout any nonsense he likes without having to tack on anything to back it up. That way he can spew out all kinds of hoodoo, yack away, yack, yack, yack, babble, babble, babble, babble and not take any responsibility for it. And most ordinary folks still look up to him with absolute awe, bending down, clasping hands and groveling to do his bidding as if he were some kind of deity. But as for him, why as often as not he'll just sit there high and mighty like with his own kind of "reason" like you know how! Take, for example, he'll say if somebody has a mole between his eyebrows, you see, that signifies that person definitely will die before reaching thirty, but the only reason for saying something like that is because this guy once saw somebody else with a mole between his eyebrows who died before reaching thirty -- or else like maybe he saw two people who had moles between their eyebrows to begin with and not long after that they died before they hit thirty -- but, but, hah, come on now, how can he, how can he know for an absolute certainty that the fact that someone died before reaching thirty is really truly because they had a black mole like that right square between their eyebrows? A black mole above the space between the eyebrows like that might very well, it's very likely to tell the year, the month, the day, the hour and the very minute when this person (-- make it two, that's fine by me) will take a ahem a shit. It's possible. And it's possible that the sign that actually indicates that there's a relative possibility of dying before thirty is indisputably, has just naturally got to be a red mole on this person's buttocks. (-- -- Oh, yeah, how come there's only "palm reading" and "face reading" -- why not the hips or feet, some form of "buttocks reading" and "sole reading"   ?) They also have another kind of reasoning: The way they tell it, if the tip of a nose is red that's a   **bad** omen, since the professional term for nose is *chung-t'ang*, the same as for the scroll mounted in the front hall of a home. So the reasoning goes, if the tip of your nose is fiery red isn't that associated with "a parlor scroll on fire" and so the house burning down sorta like, you see. Now, on the contrary, I think if your nose is red that's auspicious. After all, doesn't a red nose suggest a sanguine, healthy face, and doesn't that therefore suggest a "prosperous home"? These people they have a knack for "self justification." Once they spot they've made a mistake (like when some conclusion they've reached doesn't match up with a premise they've just made like you see, oh things like that happen so often I wish I had a nickel for every time I'd be a millionaire), they really know how to catch the breeze no matter which way it's blowing! One way is when they're finished doing a classified reading of each part of your face or hand then you have to have yet another reading on top of that, a "comprehensive synthesis,"   that's right, **a comprehensive synthesis**! That's the special trick these professional face-readers use when they have to make everything **match up consistently** after some mess they've gotten into. Even if all their rules were just right, perfectly correctly, completely believable, even then you have to reckon with thousands and tens of thousands of **"rules for reading,"** so even if there were such a thing as a genuine face-reading or palm reading, I doubt there's anyone who could do it, unless this person had a head on their shoulders with a computer in it for a brain, that's the ounli way they could keep track of everything. Or could they, could a computer do it?   Not really, no, these computers only have the **power** that **people** give them in the first place when they load in information so in that case how could anybody determine which rules are genuine and which aren't, you see? So, when you see palm reading and face reading in that light once you get down, once you really get down, to what the whole set up is really all about the only thing you're left with is "Heaven only knows." Like of all the face and palm reading methods I've ever read about, each and every one, there isn't one of them that can do more to blow your mind, spin you around 'till you can't tell left from right, front or back, north from south, none of them more than the annual status report method. Now I'm not saying I think there's something in all these different schools that's better, I'm not, because the others are all the same -- when it comes to reading palms and faces there are so many schools, such an endless variety of flavors, no matter who you are, any bumpkin you can name, anybody but anybody can indulge themselves and their every fantasy and form their own "school" of learning, and they come in such incredible numbers such a dazzling array that it's like you're back with the Hundred Schools of Contending Thinkers over 2000 years ago back in the Spring and Autumn and Warring States period. ------------ I figure that out of the whole lot of them the most inanely inconsistent of the bunch is the annual status report method. Even for this method alone there are three different sistəmz. On one of them you read from the highest point on the face down to the chin. Another begins reading on the left side with the ears, moving across the face to the right side ending with the right ear. And a third system reads across from the left ear to the right one, then from the topmost point of the face all the way down to the very tip of the chin below. Now, just which of all thi:z systems is actually the correct one after all? And besides these, moreover, there's still another one called the "cyclical repetition" system, where the reading gouz from the top of the feis crossways down to the chin. Now, if səpouziŋ someone's past sixty, beginning with the sixty-first year on to read each year successively down to the very last point on the tip of the chin -- now that's what I call "catching up with the times," something you could ardently and justifiably pronounce worthy of the title The Atomic Energy School of Face Reading. ---- By far the most common sort of people for readings a: ouvə sixty, and none of them can get a reading that will even go down as far æz their Adam's apple, junou, and since they've reached the end of the line with nowhere to go, why then nothing could be more natural than to "start all over from the beginning." Now to be able to believe sincerely in a cock-and-bull story like that doesn't just show sheer ignorance; no I believe strongly that giving yourself over to blind faith like that comes down to a form of immoral behavior. These people end up actually willing to believe firmly that when somebody gets rich it's a matter of things taking their fit and proper course, it's the way things ought to be, pure and simple, so by the same token, the suffering and hardships of the poor also seem like something perfectly ordinary that's just a part of the course of things and the way they ought to be. It's devoid of even the least trace of eni concept laik junou sei laik "compassion," "humaneness," "fairness," hwutevə. Something like this is **not just** a matter of **immorality** towards other people but it's also immoral in the most extreme sense of the term to the person'z own **self**, especially its opportunistic mentality of "gain without pain," or when confronted with some dire threat, its mentality of "leave it up to fate," "**go with the flow**," "take things one day at a time." Truly nothing can surpass the depravity of this attitude, and its obscene decadence for being so thoroughly and utterly unprincipled and so self-defeating.

Still, as unreasonable as it may seem, I do secretly wonder whether all this hoodoo about reading fortunes might not just be, just possibly be, right. Maybe perhaps it's not that I myself personally believe in reading fortunes, it's really more like, like I believe there could be a chance a **one-in-ten-thousand chance** that it's **true**! There's always that chance. So, to be honest, way down deep inside there's a part of me with a sneaking sneaking little suspicion that if reading fortunes turned out to be valid, if, I say, if,   then in thæt keis I'd say that's just "great." Just like ordinary folks! It's a certainty that everyone has an "**inner need**" that craves superstition well then, in that case, does that mean, well, that I'm, like, an immoral person, you know?   --   Yes, it does.   --

I am an immoral person. Actually if I had a chance to do an experiment like that that offers results and proof, actually it probably wouldn't matter whether it was "efficacious" or not or valid, I mean whatever the results showed I still wouldn't take the whole thing, for better or worse, I still wouldn't take it seriously. On the other **hand**, maybe, just maybe, it would suddenly show I have a special talent -- really -- maybe all I need to do is say whatever pops into my head, just babble on saying whatever I feel like saying, really awe people, and it turns out that I didn't utter a single syllable that **wasn't** perfectly **true**.

Still I know for certain for a sərtənti even if it could be verified somehow no matter what kind of verification was used to corroborate it, it shouldn't actually be taken seriously ------ because even if the results of the verification showed "inefficacy," even so like see, that still doesn't mean you could conclude that it's "**inefficacious**" -- you could only say it hasn't been put through the process of "comprehensive synthesis," so the conclusion would be that unless you you know you've **already** completed a "comprehensive synthesis," the results you obtain aren't a "valid reading." Conversely, on the other hand, if the results of the prediction if they're "**efficacious**," then by the same token that can't be taken æz bi:iŋ genuinely, truly "**efficacious**," since you still haven't gone through the stage of "comprehensive synthesis," like then then you really couldn't tell what is there that "is inefficacious" that's junou that's valid as a reading! But, perhaps, let's take a recent, a recent episode, a superficial one, as an example, an example where what was "inefficacious" about it was "really, truly inefficacious" -- for example: there was this guy who'd gone out to sea not long before a few days before to catch fish -- no, to "look for" fish. Now he already had an "<u>**omen of imminent death**</u>" like, so, this fisherman, this "lucky devil," had actually never had anything like "imminent death" happen to him like, so this serves as corroboration that the clearest, most obvious obvious prophecy is in fact actually something that is actually "inefficacious." I mean with like evidence, "proof," like this you can just go ahead and relax, you know what I mean, like -- but, but you still can't say for sure that under some kind of, you know, some kind of actual circumstances, like, it might be a "lucky sign" indicating "survival of a great catastrophe," that just hasn't been found before, that's all, so that thæt all this stuff that is "inefficacious" actually still isn't <u>truly,</u> <u>one hundred percent unadulterated "inefficacious."</u>

But no matter how much it goes against reason I'm <u>still</u> kwaiɔtli setting my sights on it secretly on the sly like waiting for the ultimate final results to be <u>inefficacious</u> and that <u>will</u> happen, it's positively **guaranteed** guaranteed to happen -- never mind how much however much the process of verifying it is unscientific -- because of that, every time I come across something suitable for texts on reading palms or faces, I pay special attention each and every time. If, if I like come across some relatively **say** distinctive examples, what I have to decide is to follow what the, what's in the "reading manual" -- of course, certainly first and foremost I have to first settle finally on nailing down one particular text to follow to the letter, decide decisively on one text only and not deviate from it the least bit, if you want to have any hope of being able to find some truly strong **evidence**. Each time I get an evidential basis even if it's still yet somewhat junou laik sortɔ questionable as usual -- just as long as we can suppose that the "evidential conditions" obtained are you know "efficacious" like sortɔ laik, you see, ------ then there isn't anyone who who wouldn't be delighted to treat the "great efficacy" we obtained as the the genuine, the authentic genuine "truth," you know, like and in that that instance it won't matter a bit whether the method adopted was after all correct or whether it was my own display of ɔv that "special talent." What's important is revealing at least that a "mysterious" force at work in our "world" has been witnessed, and that something like this verifies, reveals that a force determining fate which "settles all" and "decides all" really, **truly** exists in this gloomy gloomy dark vast bewildering vastness, and that can prove that in the great vacant emptiness of this universe there has all along been a "blueprint" and a "preliminary draft," and a "model" of some kind sort of, you know, -- just to be able to **know** these things is enough, just this alone is more than enough, enough to thrill people with a delight beyond anything to compare it to it's so so supreme, it's so it's so incomparable it it it iz.

And there's something else odd about abaut me that's **beyond** any appeal to logic, that's contrary to **reason**: I believe, very deeply, in the "life line" on my palm! -- I don't know why: -- For some reason it's my belief that I, myself, personally will undoubtedly have a particularly an especially long life, no reason to to doubt it. Actually, it's not for any unusual, remarkable reason, it's just plain just out of sheer "vanity" that I think so.   My life line is especially like, long ju nou -- and no matter what school of palm reading it is, they all agree that people with long life lines will enjoy longevity. Something like that gets me right square in my vanity, so of course I put some credence in it, you know, like. Actually there's a small "continental" or "insular" square part in the creases right at the beginning of my longevity line, and, well, so according to them, according to the manuals on palm reading, -- and this is something based according to the manuals --this thing they call continent or island is, like, it's unlucky, probably when I'm in the neighborhood of fifty or so.   But then I know this little island really doesn't signify anything more than that, that it just is an episode of some "minor little misfortune," something I can, something that's no cause for concern, I'll get around out of it -- that is I believe this square little islet actually is something I can get by, slip right past it.   I believe in this life line with all my heart, with every fiber of my being -- and as for the rest, the things like "face reading," stuff like that, I am completely and utterly **unconvinced**, -- ------ and that for no other reason whatsoever, mind you, but just like you see, you know it has never been been flattering enough to like to satisfy my v-a-n-i-t-y.

I don't know why, probably because of I mean you know something like its "mysteriousness" -- people who have their faces read and the face readers, the "philosophers," they both feel this, this like "mysteriousness." But what's actually most important, believe it or not, is for the philosopher, the face reader himself, to feel it -- he, he himself -- this business, this profession, well it doesn't matter how absurd it is in the end, because that's the only way it can endure.   The primary thing for any profession is that the the professional the professional himself must **believe**; no profession can ever go on and survive the loss of its own practitioner's faith in it, no sir, none, uh uh. By its nature reading fortunes as an occupation actually isn't a bad profession at all.   It seems like it's got such unrestricted freedom I mean it's unmatched it's so limitless actually you know. You can go to work whenever you please, anytime it suits you you can you can go -- go to work -- any hours you like.   As for that the profession of reading fortunes is, why it's really worth being called a full value, undiscounted **"free occupation"** sort of like.   My work hours everyday, that's when I read fortunes, my "clinic" time that time say, you see, invariably never begins before it reaches one o'clock in the afternoon.   I can pretty much say on a daily basis I don't get to sleep before late, very, very late, late at night, and usually sleep to just around about ten o'clock or so in the morning more or less before I get up, you see like sort of.   I always need lots and lots of sleep every night, I sleep for a long, long time, and I need to sleep so much I can't go without up to at least eleven hours per night at least, so when I do sleep it looks like I'm already dead already that's what it seems like kind of, you know, I mean ai mi:n when I fall asleep it's a slumber so deep and sound it's just a kind of misty grayish slumbər pearl colored pearly like. Sleeping like this, you know, for such a long time, isn't just a chance to cut down on the number of meals I eat per day, it's also a way to cut back on all that endless time during the day when I'm so unhappy, such a long time, too long, it is, you know. And it cuts out going out looking for a good time with a fʌkin' <u>hairdo</u>, looking for one of them to enjoy for a while, or otherwise like tonight, getting loaded like I am this evening, getting totally blitzed, and you know, have a good time getting drunk like this I personally sleep a whole lot, on average, an awful lot, usually. Not bad work, not bad at all; lots of time lots to sleep lots and minimal work hours besides.   Most other people, they have to put in at least eight hours work a day, while I only, -- only have to, -- work five-and-a-half hours a day. I don't start reading fortunes 'till one p.m., that's when I open the clinic everyday and stay open, clinic 'till five. I don't open again 'till 6:30, after I've had dinner, and then I clinic on 'till 8 p.m. After eight o'clock you won't find so much as a shadow of anybody around here (-- by seven people around here have already gone to bed, you know), so unless you want to give the local ghosts and spirits a reading after dark, as long as you weren't born a simpletən for life, you'll know it's definitely time you should close up shop and head home, you see, like. Like, I get home, and sit on my bed kaindəv kaindəlaik smoking cigarettes, lots of them, and after I've sat there a while like a bump on a log, it's getting on to 9 o'clock, and I lie down on the bed and kind of like sort of go to sleep, and that's that. Only, only I don't go to sleep just yet, what I do is I get insomnia, you know, like so I start in rouling over back and forth like, tossing and turning the whole time until it's nearly eleven before I can get to sleep finally, laik jə si:.

If there's anything that's kind of like, say, too bothersome about work like mine, you know, it's all that paraphernalia you have to bring with you so you have it with you when you set up shop it's just a bit too, too much, there's so much of it, so much stuff. It means getting dressed up to the teeth every time I start work, there's all this stuff that drapes over my body, buttons up my neck, hangs from my wrists, so much of it, and a square wooden soap box, a small bamboo bench, a bottle of black ink, a brush, a stack of bamboo pulp writing paper, a bleached cloth with my logo on it (it's also the table cloth for the table in the stall), and one lamp, acetylene. In addition, besides all that I also bring my "self-sufficient, self-sustaining, self-supporting" bottle container (a Hsien Pa-wang brand soy sauce bottle) I use for drinking water. It was only later, something I never imagined at first, I had a sudden inspiration -- so simple I was amazed that I hadn't thought of it before -- why not gather up this unlikely assortment of props, take the whole ridiculous mess over to the general store (the outlet for religious articles together with sundries) and put them there for safekeeping. After all, this absurd collection of knick-knacks originally came from this store in the first place! It's not often you get hit with an inspiration just as, as much as, quite as brilliant as this one, so then it makes you wonder whether it's because you were so smart this time after all, or whether, all along, you've always really been, you know, like, like really, really dumb.

Well then I spent a good bit you know quite a lot of energy looking around everywhere for a site to locate my set-up. And like most people opening up a business I didn't know where would be a good place. Later I finally took a cue from *feng-shui* geomancy, to you know to be "near hills and facing water," and set up in front of the gate to the Ma Tsu Temple, maybe roughly 60 or 70 feet in front. Græb the people who had no choice but to walk along the street to and from the dock -- that's geomancy, plus "business management." And stare vacantly, day and night alike, I light a luminous oil lamp with its smoky dazzle shining bright, and I sit in the endlessly vast deep darkness, looking distantly out uneasily on the domain of the deep sea. It's like you could simply say that I, that it, that I've lighted this lamp for someone or other, somebody, you see. Aaah-Mmm; probably this just looks like something that'll become one of the local tourist sites around the harbor like, you know. What I've got here simply amounts to a kind of theatre sort of, after all. Everything is here: the scenery -- there's darkness, mountain peaks, a stretch of ocean, and a glowing spot, and then there's a lead role here, right here. The whole thing looks, to me, anyway, like I'm acting out some play, you see like, that's what it looks like sort of. The whole thing looks completely unreal, it all looks as though you could just fold it up and pack it away anytime you felt like whenever you wanted to, it could just be loaded up and hauled away like it was all for some "social occasion," something like that, kindəv you know, like. That's the way I've felt about every other occupation I've worked at before, all of them, they all felt like some sort of "social occasion," so that everything I've done before, whether soldiering in fatigues* or at a desk job, it's never seemed in either situation like I was doing anything but acting out the role of somebody else like, you know, how that is sort of. What role is really my own "role," eh? I don't know what "business," "career" whatever I'm right for or I'm suited to --------- it seems that everybody, that anybody who gets anywhere in this society, has got to have some sort of "profession" like, you understand, like the "mark of existence" for any person amounts to nothing other more or less than than his "profession," just that. Is it possible for a person not to be suitably adapted to his career? Can it be that a person could have their own "mark uv existence" even if they don't have a career?

Fundamentally a stunt like "reading fortunes" only amounts to a beggarly form of panhandling, that's all it's worth being taken for, a game. At bottom it isn't basically a "profession," so it's no wonder when you take it up it's like acting out something for a while, not something that amounts to a "profession proper." I hear beggars in foreign countries depend on selling matches to get by; for Chinese beggars, on the other hand, it's simple, very simple -- set up a fortune-telling stand. So then, what do I have to say for how I wound up where I am today, except nothing better than just what a **beggar** I am!

Actually the special distinction that sets off a stunt like reading fortunes as possessing a "nature" removed and apart from the ordinary really is not in that which may be termed the fortune teller's "certitude"; to the contrary, it is rather in "expectation," the kind that's the way it is when you're waiting for a bus, that kind of expkteiʃən, like. I could wait forever all day -- five hours, six hours-- whatever, waiting just for some people to ask directions, and often no one would even come around the houl day, or just one, maybe two, at most no more than four (----------on that day--------....!), just like waiting for a bus, like I said, no different, junou so:təv. It doesn't matter how you cope with it, it doesn't matter what you do to pass an empty stretch of time as long as that, it's still going to amount to a total failure. Even if you intend to do a little thinking to think through "values" some, well, it's like, you see, you can't, you know -- all you can do is "wait," and you ought to be able to say that all that time, all that time, is yours, but then it turns out to be something that's absolutely not yours -- and that's the reason why, small wonder, not wʌn **"thinker"** has ever emerged from "fortune tellers" ever since they've been around, never has.

Most of the time I spend glancing or gazing at the endless sea at the edge of this vast ocean "commenting on reading fortunes," it looks pretty monotonous, the way it's invariably a monochromatic grayish blue bluish gray like. Now, then, along the horizon of the sea (uh-oh, this doesn't quite make sense) -- the horizon? Well, the horizon, the horizon looks as if it's extremely close, so close it seems to run along a line that's at most əraund əbaut a few hundred meters away for the most part, and it makes the ocean seem like a curtain screen that's been let down. So, then, the gray-blue cast along this horizon comprises the lightest hue of all, but the part encompassed just underneath this long, flat horizon is relatively speaking quite **dark.**

Thə sand around here, to be sure, is this dark, wet, dark, damp stuff, nevertheless though as soon as a wind blows up, it will sweep up all kinds of filthy træʃ that whip a person's face pretty painfully. It'll all bore right through your eyelashes before they can shut it out right into your eyes, like, you know, right inside, like. Small wonder, it's no surprise that there's a particularly large number of villagers around here suffering from eye ailments, and lots of people's eyes invariably look a blood red color like. Nearly everyone has trachoma, oh, ah, **no, no,** I take that back, trachoma isn't basically caused by irritation from grains of sand getting rubbed in, not that way, like, right.

People around these parts are so different from ordinary, normal folks, really, it's pathetic. You see them hanging out shiftless and dissolute around the dock, ju:slis and good for nothing, strolling around strouliŋ back and forth all day long day after day like they were just simply "robots." You can't help but start to wonder, like, why on earth, for what possible reason, did He, the Creator, endow them with brains, you know like? Those people thei just roam around out there by the shore on the flat surface of the dock where the poured concrete has dried into a hard hardened surface, with this vacant look of dread, dread, every one of them, all with their hands stuck into the front pockets of their trousers. It's been a long, long time since they've had any anything to put in to those pockets, so there they look with this vacant stare out past the harbor at the misty ocean, all the time waiting at the ready for the fish to form up and start running, then they can put those ape bones of theirs to good use and like really swing away and give them a good workout. This is a bunch of guys who've simply detached their brains and stuffed them down into their stomachs, you understand, like, that's what they are. And then, too, there are the w̲o̲m̲e̲n̲ -- I saw one on the dock, with her fingers clenched tightly around a sun parasol that was in tatters and moreover, old, in addition to that (she should have had a proper umbrella to use when it rains, that would be more like it, you know). Now the handle of that parasol, its grip, the whole of it in its entirety was gone, I never laid eyes on it, what I did see was that there was this screwdriver handle that had been inserted into the rod that forms the center part of the parasol. Aaw, no, now wait, no, no, no, day, I did bump into a young one, not necessarily all that good looking, ah but like, like she had a face on her remarkably gentle and benevolent, the kind that's "pure and saintly" that kind, the kind of young woman, the newlywed, the young wifely sort that prays to Kuan Yin for a son, that's what her feis was like, just like that, standing there on the shoreline by the sea, smooth and straight as jade, there next to the ocean along the seashore, looking intently, staring out at the distant sea. Cocking my fingers as I count I figure I've seen her, seen her altogether, four times. The first time I came across her it was on the day I settled down to open up for business, start "**reading fortunes**," and so forth, like, so it was just right right at dusk. The second time, that I saw her, it was just the next day, twilight time, like, I'd put it then pretty much about the same hour as that time the day before sort of sorta like, and her face still had that look about it, how can I say it, the exact image of "the warmth of goodness,"   "a spiritual radiance," just that kind of face. Well then, when I ran into her a third time, it was the third day in a row, and around the same time as on the previous two days -- I have to admit this to myself openly and honestly sort of -- I don't know like how it all came out how it hæpənd, like, this way, you know, really, you know it all happened so, so gradually, the ways my feelings changed, subtly bit by bit, toward her, this

41

woman, it was all so, so deceptive the way it ended up turning into this strong, physical, passionate lust. Oh, yes, eh-heh, I thought, it's because of all those bizarre, sudden, weird, weird enthusiasms middle-aged people get for the very first time after they've taken that plunge into middle age, as they say, for the first time. For example, aside from everything else, I've got this intense thing now for "doll-faced" young girls. That's her! I'm so stuck like this on these nice round baby fresh faces probably because I've now switched over to a new-found interest in "skin." -- Why is that? Is it like rileitid to the stimulation of a new order brought on after the hormones undergo a new sort of adjustment like -- ?? Anyway, the fourth time, as for the way that face looked like it belonged to a young woman, a perfect little Kuan Yin, -- ah-heh, -- that was an experience, that was one intensely memorable, one unforgettable experience.

During my business hours doing people's fortunes everyday, at thi:z times again and again there's been another person I can usually get to be able to see frequently, an old guy, a real geezer of a little old man who's got a small business hawking what would be amazing if it were more than at the very most two brands of cigarettes and lottery tickets, whom I could see at some distance (you have to put a hand up to the place there's bone above where your eyebrows are and shield your eyes with the flat of your hand to look over) from the place where I've been located at which is where I can look over to the place where he's been located. All day long he steiz there under a street lamp on this long, tall post, along the winding little path that goes up there where the public baths are in the hills, on the way to the bath houses, the ones on the hill up there. (The "stri:t" lamps around here are all covered with what look like these pointy, conical things exactly like like the straw rain hats the farm laborers wear out in the paddies, and there is this steel hoop around the botəm of the shade there, with a big, round, bulbous glass lightbulb installed inside the steel hoop, a big, round, bulbous glass one, like, well it's been a long, long time now since you could see a "street" "lamp" like that in Taipei, they disappeared there a long, long time ago.) This old man's named Liu, came ouvər from the mainland over here, like, so, everytime, no matter when it is, so long as it's me he comes over, as soon as he sēēz me, then, and this is without a single exception, he gets himself up all bent over, and gives me this big, warm smile while he goes on and on with these deferential little bows. Actually, I've only bought cigarettes from him once altogether. It's true his cigarettes, compared with other people's, are relatively cheaper cheaper than the ones other people sell kaindev, but since, later on on account of my appropriate and necessary needs in "foreign relations," I've switched over to buying them from the "sales agent for religious articles," that store, again. --   Old Man Liu, the old geezer, is there everyday, rain or shine, and on rainy days he brings two umbrellas, one he ties up to the cigarette stand so it's covering over that stand, and one he rests on his shoulders, right between the shoulder blades there. What a burden it is to bear, every day at least twice at the very bare minimum, you know, like it gets under my skin it's so irritating! There's only this one single route, no other, not a single one, and it's like he's got me by the throat the way he has a grip on my key transportation artery. And that's another reason why I don't have the fortitude, the nerve, or the will to go back and buy cigarettes from him again. Normally, if it's raining, and I have my big black umbrella open, then it's all right since I can keep my head down low, get it really down low, and cover up my face while I scratch my skin on the brambles next to this "avenue to success" he's got occupied astride as I go past him. But, if it's just gray out and it hasn't like started to rain yet, you know, then it's like sheer aggravation. Then there's nothing you can do but go through with it, you have no choice, you're stuck going along with him submissively exchanging greetings in this obliging way. Once I stood off in a little spot quite some, quite some distance away a good long way away from him and I looked him over for a while lukd him ouvə. I caught him just as he was happening to doze ----   (he often curls over into a ball and naps next to his cigarette stand there like -- but once you get up to about a hundred feet or so from him, he wakes right up -- it makes you wonder about this old guy, whether or not he's actually not really been asleep really all that time, or whether, maybe all along he's just kept his eyes half closed, like this, while he's sneaking a peek at whoever's coming by) -- this time I kept on looking and watching for a very very long, long time -- until I thought I could be 90% certain that he was actually fast fast asleep like, you know, and then I picked myself up lightly and darted ahead quickly to sneak past where he was. But that old coot, he wasn't a moment too soon, and not a moment too late, when just at the critical juncture, his eyes went on like lamps, they opened wide awake and the next moment he was on his feet, his face beaming away with that smile grinning from ear to ear, pumping his waist back and forth doing his deferential bows, so, once again I'd been puld in and snârd by him hook, line, and sinker. With all the dips and turns played out in this dance you could say it was simply a full-blown, full-fledged "manhunt."* Now it was for this reason that I tried going to work a bit earlier, around noon, and then in the evening return to "base" a little later. But, it was no use. I went out to work that day at noon (after all he had to eat, right.) but he was already, already sitting there waiting for me. It was the same that evening, he kept on sitting there just as long as I did (he had himself tucked away hidden in the dark. -- my god! -- it was enough to scare the deilaits out of anyone -- but wasn't he undər one of those street lamps along the side of the path?? Yes, yes, of course he was, but it happened that just at that time the, the damn light was off, the filament in the big, round, bulbous glass bulb in the street lamp had burnt out,) It simply seemed as though the old coot was deliberately waiting for me to pass by his stand first on my way back before he was going to pack up and go home himself. I waited, procrastinating until 8:30

that evening (and 8:30 is reckoned to be pretty late in a small place like this, indeed it's actually quite late, extremely late) before I closed up shop, and there the old sot was, still there. He was simply like a stone lion, crouching there forever, month after month, year after year. I had to kənsi:d I was beaten, I'd had it! I'd just take it as some trying, aggravating, vexing unpleasantness I'd have to face everyday. I had enough of this sort of thing as it is, it's really on a par with things like the erections that pop up every morning with the first light of dawn, the hunger pangs in my stomach after I've gotten up and haven't yet packed down some breakfast, you know, like the constipation that's as hardened as dried concrete each morning, the itching reddened sores between my toes when I'm under the warm blæŋkit alone in the middle of the night. . . . .
. . . .

To tell the truth, the first day I started, you know sort of **reading fortunes** here, I predicted what you could truly honestly say was a "major event." It was   an experience, an encounter, I'd never had from the very first day I came out of the womb, and you can say this about me, I've predicted kwait a number of things, I have, in my time. But never before have I had an experience like that, a personal encounter like that, not where I've made such a fool of myself right there in broad daylight in front of everybody. It's never been my experience to take it as my sacred duty to undertake the task of educating whoever steps into my school, no matter what sort of fucking low-life loser he is, no matter what kind of neanderthal, no that's not been my practice. Nevertheless, the way I read this situation, without the slightest sign of the least discomfort, steady as a rock, completely kəmpouzd, I think <u>probably shows I have the</u> makings of a natural born fortune teller. So first of all I drew a hexagram reading along the width of the skirt-hem on the stand's "logo cloth" (which we might as well also call the "table cloth"), and with a large brush I wrote "Expert Readings" across the top and across the bottom "Lone Star." Then down the margin on either side I wrote:

"Yin-yang Astrological Readings"

and

"Annual Status Reports"

Then on another piece of paper I wrote down the fees:

palm reading: 10 yuan
face reading: 20 yuan
divination: 30 yuan

44

Backed Against the Sea

date-time reading: 40 yuan
complete reading: 1,000 yuan

Actually the date-time astrological method really shouldn't be practiced in this area, since hardly anyone knows the correct date and time they were born. By the time you start taking an interest in what your fate is and begin taking up consulting spirits and hexagrams by then your mother's long gone already,   or else by that time you've already moved a million miles and left your home town far away a long time ago, I mean, like, like far away. When I started out reading fortunes on the first day, at first there wasn't a single person, as much æz I'd staked out a good location I still was at a complete loss to capture **anybody's** attention. It made me think that all these people seemed to have something against me, they all looked so solemn like they were suspicious, -- it wasn't like something like you'd see around Taipei actually, -- people around here had nothing -- to do, whereas in Taipei people are busy, yet the people in this pint-sized, rabbit-patch pin-prick of a place didn't have the time to spare, not like people are up there back up there in Taipei you know, like, they're always curious all the time about everything that goes on around them. So I was left with no choice but to "express myself in my own words" and take to barking away furiously all by myself out at the space around me where there wasn't a soul in any direction for a distance of some 200 feet, so that I simply sounded like a kind of schizo lunatic who's really lost it sort of, that's what I sounded like: I yelled at the top of my voice: "Hey, -- hey --- I, Lone Star, have crossed the ocean from the mainland to Taiwan. I studied under Reverend Chang at the White Cloud Temple on Mount Hua until I mastered the true teachings of the Immortals thoroughly, and now bring you my mastery of astrology, of geomancy, capable of revealing past and future, the ancient, the present, foreign, domestic all these things if you don't believe, then come and see for yourself, come one, **kum** all -- Hey, hey --! I, Lone Star, ..." I said the whole thing in the local Taiwanese Southern-Min dialect. Fortunately, I can speak it. In fact I've never understood how people can live here for fifteen years now and still not speak a word of the local, regional language, whereas with me, wherever I go, you know like, any place I go, even if it's for no more than a short rest somewhere for a week, I'll study it anyway. My Southern Min Taiwanese isn't much to speak of, maybe, but I stumble along in it since I think it's good form to try, and I can get by pretty well. As a result, people respond to me and I make acquaintances. And, it was effective when it came to advertising. People swarmed in, you know, you know, like hornets like, until they were standing three deep, three deep, that's how packed in they were, and at that moment, for some strange reason I've never figured out, never gotten to the bottom of it, without really realizing it I began to feel really satisfied with myself -- because, without **any** effort hwɔtsouevə on my part, like you know like I was chatting

45

away and pouring all this out on my own like, kind of kaindəlaik you know, like some "paragon" of articulate speech, the way I was going on like that. So then I began to address them, like a judge in court, like a priest enlightening sentient beings on the nature of existence, and then I, then the crowd gathered all around me began stirring, they milled around milling back and forth and then milled around some more, I tell you it was an impressive spectacle, it had everything, I spoke, I gestured, I moved, more and more 'till it was so lively I was like a **"revolutionary,"** and then at that moment I had a thought all of a sudden, how about if I added a few karate moves, a punch here, a kick there would work well (I did aim a couple of jabs at the sky, and threw in a kick -- but after that I decided I'd better not do that again since the shoes I wear are a bit waid too wide for my feet and one of them nearly flew off, came pretty close , you know, like, that time). It was too bad I couldn't also sing a couple of pop tunes then and there (I did do some opera, a bit from "Su San sent to trial"[*] in a high-pitched falsetto). After going on like this for quite some time, a helluva long time, though, still after all this time no one showed any interest in being a customer. After a while it began to look to me like the audience was running out of interest, and I began to worry out of concern, like, maybe, that "popular support" would soon melt away.   What to do? Now how was I to draw them in, what could I do to, like "entertain" them more, you know, like a crowd like that, you see? So I made an announcement: "All right, for today, for the first day, I "Lone Star" will now, right now, offer you an invitation, like, right now I, Lone Star, will **invite one of you**, one of you to step forward and "open the exchange" -- yes, *hey!* **Fate** has brought me from far away to be with you here, though as strangers we have not had the good fortune to meet before, now Lone Star invites one of you to come forward to have his or her fortune read without charge -- You, -- you! -- Yes, you! -- You, now here's a face that looks quite promising. Here:

> When people are in luck,
> There's a healthy yellow between their eyes.
> If folks are out of luck,
> They're bluish around their noses.

(When I wuz nearly half way through reciting this masterpiece of a five-word four-liner I switched to speaking Mandarin). . . . Well, as I was saying, I got the feeling from the space between this guy's eyebrows that he actually had something wrong with his liver -- there's this discrepancy between science and fortune telling. So I stuck to this line and talked on and on, anyway, like, you know, saying lots and lots of greit sounding empty junk, since if I was diplomatic the **first** dei and treated someone to the house -- soon I could rely on "fortune" to bring me "guests," the arts of **advertising** and of **fortune telling.**   Sure enough, it got results. No one walked away any more, -- people, there's no one who can manage to rizist listening in on the personal confidentials of other people. Soon one by one their eyes flashed nervously, their mouths hung way, way open   big as bowls and they took in every last syllable greegreegreedily, like they didn't want to lose a single single drop. Once I'd offered to treat one of them on the house, I couldn't just go on giving it away or I'd end up losing paying clients. Consequently, I rambled on gibbering gibbering inanely for close to an hour and seventeen, eighteen, nineteen, twenty, about twenty-minutes -- it turned out like always, like, you know, you know how it is, sorta, "once the banquet's finished -- the guests depart" ------ and I still hadn't even hooked so much as one fish, not a one, a one.

And so the next day I thought to myself I thought you've got to start in all over again with a fresh approach, that's what you've got to do, like, you see, that's what, like. ---- So I settled on new rates, took out a piece of white paper and wrote on it in big characters: "PRICE-SLASHING BUDGET-GOUGING, INSANE REDUCTIONS." I gave up itemizing things in detail anymore, and set the price of the whole ridiculous "complete reading" at five yuan!! To my utter disbelief still no one came! The way things were taking shape if they went on went on and kept on and on going along along like like this conconconcontinued on this way, I couldn't "slash prices" any further, and yet as things were going ai mi:n laik there wasn't anybody wasn't anybody coming around they were so scarce no no one had come by the whole time hardly. However, few as people were, I did later get my fill and more of local esteem, I made quite a neim for myself, quite a reputation. And all this because of the day I kaindəv kaindəlaik played "the blind cat who struck a mouse dead," -- Heaven only knows how I got it right, you know. Now I've become quite a "celebrity" -------- but even if you are a celebrity you can't make real money off it, and I still don't get any business, still not one iota, no business yet. That's the reason, that's why "reputation" is an "empty" thing -- and it's why a fortune teller is, why it comes down to being, an artist.   That day was truly something right out of the zodiac, an "auspicious day" of the ecliptic path if ever there was one. In one day, I had altogether four people that day who came for consultations. First one came, then three more showed up. Two of the three who came later, -- it was still afternoon -- these two showed up together. One of them had a pretty hefty a pretty strapping framework, just his expression looked like it seemed very sort of disheveled and tousled, a look of bebebebewilderment, and a pair of great big great big eyes, slanted a bit fiercely like. He had on some underwear of white material (--white?--), he had stout, round arms like two overstuffed, fatty sausages, and a chest that bulged out bulging like two big, round, thick discuses. The other one, by comparison, was quite a lot   younger, looked like he was under twenty about, somewhere only in his teens more or less, and wore a something like it was a brand new bright red thin nylon wind breaker. The one in the white (--white?--   ) cotton underwear came up to me very meek and anxious and meek; he gave me this deferential smile of respect by way of a greeting; and he said, "I'd like, . . . a, ... I'd like, a reading, please." It's quite common for people who want their fortunes told to take their deference to take it to an extreme, very, very much so. "Fine, fine. No problem -- how about, how about like the two of you getting or having your reading together, like, you know? It's cheaper that way -- together" (sort of the equivalent of a   wholesale   price). The young one, the one in the screaming red jacket, smiled bashfully, skipped bæk a step, and excused himself, "--Aw, I I couldn't do that." "Don't be nervous, there's nothing to worry about -- It'll be fine, you know, absolutely fine, just be brave ænd itəl all be over in a minute, I'll have it done for you right away, in no time like you know -- it'll be fine." I kept coaxing him along to lead him on. Like a surgeon leading somebody on until, until that person demands "operate! Operate!"   like that sort of. "Try this first if you don't believe me, try, just look at you! Come, come, come on, come on, step over here just a bit, there, now, now if you let Lone Star take a good close look I guarantee, Lone Star gives you a guarantee, we won't find anything wrong, no, not a thing, nothing here now."   But then, wow! Red veins transversing pupils, bluish veins, what's more, below the eyes -- this was a person close to **imminent death**! Between the thickets of eyebrows were some bristles of reddish hair. This afforded not the slightest room for doubt that this person was definitely doomed to death by fire, such was unquestionably, undoubtedly thethethe case the case. He had an inescapable date with eternity! Now, now, nau, nau I mean under the circumstances, being such, like this, then, well, should I, how should I, announce it, you see? Should I prevaricate, or should I tell the **truth**   ?   A major clash of conflict raged within my conscience.   Conscience!   "Hmm. . . . Hmm. . . . It's a bit. . . . it's a bit. . . . Things are never absolutely perfect for anybody, you know. . . ." I didn't spell everything out for him. I mean, not the whole thing, I "exercised restraint," skipped over those things sort of for the most part kind of, and, with courtesy   . . . . "The best thing, for the next few days, the best thing for you would be to take a little extra care with things, all of them, the important ones and the little ones, whatever it is, treat it with a bit of caution, caution in everything, yes, that's it, be more be much more kɔːʃəs a bit, that's it

" There, now let me make a mental note of exactly how he actually appeared and tuck that quietly away in my memory silently so that I'll be prepared to bring it back out as corroborating evidence. -- I've memorized in detail all the signs of appearance I've recently come across that I can use for confirmation. -- And this case ju nou was not, in fact, the sole and only distinct exception.

When I went on to give the youth in the red jacket, "young one," a reading, why, this guy, -- in the red jacket -----, of course he was even more unwilling to let me go on with it. In fact, I laughed at him to myself, secret secretly, -- his facial signs were the best and the most remarkably outstanding inininin in the entire community, in fact, you see, like.   That eye catching, bright red loud jacket he had on, complemented perfectly his cheerful auspicious face that boded such a magnificent future, they were a pərfiktli perfect match. How come? How is it someone could have such a face -- in a poor, rundown, dirty, little fishing cove ?   Make no mistake, he had to have like come into to this locale from someplace else outside like, you know, or, itititit could be he was on the verge of leaving Deep Pit Harbor like a shot, ready in an instant to plunge ahead and make his way up and on to better things, yes he was someone like that, one or the other, like, you know. He turned away and walked off toward the dock, that way, like, I mean, even his back looked real, real good, the best, just the very best, those big, round, ripe, I mean thththose those buttocks! "Full buttocks are lucky!"   Indeed, the bigger the buttocks, the larger they are, the more they make you think of the big buttocks girls have,

the   better   they   look   .   In fact, even when it came to those pants he was wearing, why, those too, I mean they had a "distinctive look," I'd say they did, cut so snug and trim they were really out of this world, absolutely the very best fitting Western-style pants, the best, best in the entire, I mean the whole, Deep Pit Harbor port area, like the best. Everybody else, like wears those, you know those baggy pajama pants, you know. Except that these trousers I've got on, you know, like they're like his, too. They're an exception. The ones I'm wearing they're the very latest, by far the most popular in Taipei last year, and this year too, up to now: peg pants. They look like two mysteriously long, slim and slender, sleek, sleek snug tight tubes wrapped like hoops around a pair of ti-twiggy-thin legs that could pass for real long, real long lean bamboo boat poles, and the bottoms are cut so high they're even, I'd say, oh, a good 2 inches and more above the shoes. This is the height of fashion in streamlined pants, but even so, they're hopelessly filthy, and like look, these round spots on the knees and the seat are at the point they've been worn down to the point that they're shiny inuf to see like to see your own reflection in them sorta, that's how much.

Along somewhere between around about an hour or so tototo two hours more or less, something like kind kind of like that, after I did this reading sort of sorta like like, you know, this middle-aged guy, of say, going on about 40 like, came around, a small little shrimpy sort with a black baseball cap stuck on his head on top there with one of those huge, enormous duck-bill visors for a brim -- most of the fishermen who work the ocean around here they all like squash these duck bill baseball caps down on their heads and go around that way, -- but over two-thirds wear theirs so the brim is like squeezed together and held in place you know with a slip of bamboo, that's one way, and as for the few others, left over, this remainder, the rest of them wear their cloth visors to brim the front of the hat kaindəv sorta like that, see, -- anyway n'n'not one of them had a visor (a cloth brim bill visor) that compared wiwiwith this guy's in <u>size</u>. Underneath this duck bill down below was a wee thin pointy little triangular face with a faintly yellowish ivory (-plastic?) cigarette holder dangling by the tip end at the kórnər of his creased mouth, and a face towel wrapped thickly around his neck. "Eh-h-h . . . . . errrh. . . . ." They're always in a pretty humble state when they come around to my stand, "I, I wanted to, to ask you about something . . . . see if you'd do a trigram for me, check things out. . . . ." "You want me to do a trigram reading for you? What do you want to look for?" Hwut he wanted to know was whether it would be advisable to go out onto the ocean for fish the next day, or whether in fact it would turn out to be inadvisable. -- He was "captain" of a fishing boat. ----   I learned who he was later, you see. Trigram divination --- ahha --- not that thing, damn that thing,   I was more than a bit nonplussed . . . . what I know about trigram divination is pretty elementary, since it takes about as much expertise as a mɑːstəri of the eighteen martial arts. Over the last few days while I was short on clients I'd been boning up and **cramming** on this a lot, in the Comprehensive Guide to Fortune Telling, the Appendix to the Encyclopedia Britannica, I'd given it a good going over. And I knew perfectly well, I knew it was humbug, even more humbug than face reading. The important thing there is, outside the features you're reading, you've got to relate them to all the other things going on, all kinds of things. Now as for <u>trigram divination</u> you've got to sort through your extrinsic reading, all things, all <u>present environmental stimuli</u> that go on around you while you're doing the divination, they're regarded as extrinsic -- now just what are you supposed to do about that? I mean, how many millions of things are going on in the universe, in creation, from one end of it to the next? Still, well, give it a try, I was ready to junou to try it out, all right -- no harm done, right? -- Well, I mean, like, no matter how it turns out, you know, trying it out doesn't <u>cost</u> anything, now, does it?   I had already gone ahead and tried out a prediction the day after after I'd set up my my practice here, and tried divination to do, like, a weather prediction. Right then the sky had just turned completely overcast, and I drew on these features, the weather, I used them to carry out, do this, you know, like experiment, sort of (-- at the time, I was convinced that the U. S. Space Flight Center was at that very moment conducting ən əxperiment in deep space flight to launch a man-made satellite into outer space -- two major experiments, one East and one West!). What I calculated the way it came out it, it would be a fair day, a very, very fair day, mmmmh, hold on, let's hold on here and check this. So I waited there quietly looking up into the heavens for something wondrous to happen. Pretty soon out of nowhere it started in with a drop, a splat, then splattering and splashing and a torrent of rain roared down like pouring, like I mean gushing, and then on top of that it was backed up by a deafening roar of thunder, (that was simply, it was just just just about about almost nearly almost nearly an impossibility, practically   -- winter thunder!) Well, with it pouring out like that, you see, you see I was so humiliated the only the only thing to do was pack up my stand and make for the Ma Tsu Temple where all the bats, the flying squirrels, whatever, they, they like to hide out there and like just wait the rainburst out in there. That's why this time when this guy wanted me to do a trigram divination I was really sorta pretty much non-plussed like, you see. I did go ahead and like do the like divination for him: It is not appropriate   to   go   out   to   sea! Nevertheless, the last time I did a trigram divination I was so bad at it it hadn't worked, so this time should I make an explanation that was the opposite, that was just exactly the precise exact opposite of what I'd predicted and make that my explanation? -- As things were going that's the only way it would work out to be like to be **efficacious**.   But, I didn't have the nerve -- you could ignore everything else whatever it was, as long as you just took one look at the sky, the way it was covered densely with miasmal clouds, and the ocean waves were already gigantic enough, each one after the other looking like sort of sorta like sheet after sheet of wind-curled blackened cabbage leaves, that's like what it was like out there. And it'd rained hard, hadn't it, just then just a second, just a moment before -- so, then, it seemed that for a boat caught hanging around out there on a storm tossed ocean to capsize in the open sea like that wasn't, I mean, it wasn't something that **could not possibly happen**, you see, like, you know. And, anyway, I was also quite delighted with sort of, like, this sort of opportunity to try the whole divination over again, test it out kindəv again like, you know, test like test the experiment once more, really delighted to. And so I did, I did my experiment, I tried it tried tried it all out again as a test. So I did it again once, and this time it came out it read going out to sea is "not appropriate."

A touch of sadness appeared on his face. But he was a brave man and he was still going to go out to sea anyway, ---- just after that he asked me to do a reading again, to read his face, like, you know, like, for, what course his own fate was to take. --------------- Very well, then, my good child, once you've made up your mind to do something, whatever, like it is nothing can alter your determination!   Fate, it's something already laid out and fixed for good, it is, is. It was the boat owner, a nephew of his, he wanted him to take the boat out onto the ocean to see whether or not they could find any trace of fish,   he tould me that like later I mean,   then abruptly he he just like turned like away junou sort of away and without turning back broke off and left just like

51

that just as free and easy as he pleased. Then I began to do a reading of his face. I have always held to the idea that to read a man first read his face!!"* - - - - - - But he wouldn't offer his face to me, no, so like I, for that reason I, that's when I first raised a hand to pick up the his hand, sitting opposite to me. It was actually just to spare him the effort of raising his own hand, I made every effort to spare him the effort of raising his hand!   But, he, the person being read, his face was, like it was like just a little bit too small by just a bit, like, and it was covered up so much underneath that large duck bill brim you couldn't see it, not at all hardly. I asked him then to take off the small black duck bill brim black cap with the big broad duck bill visor. The black cap with the big bill shade came off, -- to reveal a head like a calabash, not a hair on it, clean as a whistle everywhere, totally hairless.   I couldn't understand what that was all about, you see. I switched to reading his palm --------   A-h-h-h-h-h! There, along his "travel" line, square perfectly square, as plain as clear as plain as it could be, was a distinct "island" like that. Clearly this, it, like, was foretelling, you know, I mean, -- if you believe (and basically you have to believe) in something like "palm reading" -- someday in the future he would have a virtually unavoidable encounter with disaster on a vɑ:st sea of gathering gloom. But, what this bad omen was indicating wasn't anything like I mean imminent -- it wasn't a sign of any calamity that was imminent.   So in that case, with that in mind, should I present things to him according to this sort of, you know, like? Hadn't I already said that his boat -- just before when I did the trigram divination -- hadn't I ɔ:lredi said that it was facing a disaster on the seas at any time now? If I did tell him then that would give rise to a contradiction, wouldn't it,   between the two,   I mean   the former and the latter? So, like, then I mean which one, of the two, which one should I   revise? The boat's or   his,   the   man's? Since I'd already done the boat's first   so then that left me with just the man's to revise, you see, like? And, well, if I didn't change his, like, well, I mean, you know   it would be exceedingly "embarrassing." -- --   As long as one came out right,   it didn't matter for now whether it was the boat's or the man's, naturally if there were a mistake it would reveal my own failure as a "fortune-telling artiste." ---------   --**Damn**, like, like once yours truly gets **angry**, I really get **angry**! So what if there is a contradiction, fuck it, like you know fuck your old lady's mutha fuckin' cunt, you,   you, you goddam you I'm telling you "You'll live"! I'm making it so "You'll live" "Live," asshole! -- --   I mean once I said "it is inappropriate   to go   to -- --   sea" he may well have already made up his mind, you know, not to go to sea, precisely with the idea in mind that by doing this he could, you know like this wei, avoid, ai mean an extremely dire fate.

　　Right away **another** one came to me, like when things come they never come alone sort of, when it rains it pours like you know, see. Like this face full of filthy, dirtyfilthy bristle pocked pocked all over pocked with this stubble.

Oh, what the, what, I didn't have one iota, not an ounce see of patience left none at all none see to "**read--divine**" a patch of some dick's prick hair like that, see.   You're "**dead**!" This time I decided to "kill him off," and that's just how I   announced my verdict, like, see, and "   dead   soon,   " "dead soon,   in three days,   within **three days**!" When he heard that he was sorta, see, you know, he got I mean angry: "Fuck you, you mutha fucka! -----. . . ." Look at that, just look at how as soon as fate started to, like you see, to sorta   go against him, right away on the spot in an instant he immediately started right in wanting to "screw" fate like that, see, like you know what I mean, -- that is, he wanted to fuck him over -- -- the person who had undertaken to decide which **critical exegesis** was most appropriate to like to to like **explain** best the lines on his palm -- -- wanted to fuck him over and **his old lady too!**   "Mutha fucka, fuck you, fuck you, man, fuck you!" To begin with I threw it back at him without budging.   He spat on the ground, spat over and over again, like, all this saliva, like. To avoid bad luck -- most likely. As soon as he was done spitting he turned to walk əwei, so it looked as if he was not going to pay his "diagnostic fees." "Damn muthafucka, goddam muthafucka, fuck you you goddam muthafucka fuck you, man, fuck you" I went on like before, on and on, swearing at his back laud and clear like the whole time,   I didn't have the guts to rush over to grab him ænd demand my money   . That would only stir up a crowd, kick up a fuss, and I'd get the worst of it from him, better to avoid all that.

Once that frenzied burst of rage had burned itself out, well then, then I kind of started to feel that I really regretted it, how I'd let myself go, you know, I regretəd it more than anything. I had no business telling him "**you will soon be dead, within three days**," not so bluntly like that -- after all, what if, if he **didn't** die, you know   ?   -- That way I left myself   no   way out, I was just like burning my bridges behind me as I went, sort of, you see.   You see, that's anger for you, in just a single moment all that fire is enough so that it can can just about burn out the entire system.

The next day -- it was in a drizzling rain drizzling so fine it seemed ju could be simply breathing it sorta like, I mean -- I was undənēth the rain eaves of the Ma Tsu Temple there you see, when I saw the "boat captain" going pæst the front of the temple not far off there -- this time he was headed like on his way down to on down to his boat, see, like and like always he was still wearing that soft black duckbill cloth baseball cap of his with the big duckbill eave like up front, carrying a small container of flammable fuel. There was a tall guy with him, the one with all the whisker stubble, the one more than likely to end up cremated that I'd done the duet with taking turns trading some basic vocabulary singing our ABCs sorta, yes, you know like that one. The two of them were shouldering a big thick bamboo tube pipe like with a thick fishing net that was draped over it piled on top and trailing sort of translucent wintry powder threads translucent like. The wind scale on the ocean was too strɔŋ that morning so it wasn't 'till afternoon before they got underway and **went to sea** -- afterwards I like heard someone else say so, I mean, like, see, that's how it was sorta. Out in the misty blurring gray blurring misty drizzle I caught a flash of the young guy in the blazing red nylon wind breaker, far in the distance near the end of the dock. As night approached I heard two people as they went buzzing like past my (by that time I'd already moved back out again to my regular spot in the brɔːd, oupən, empty area outside the temple building) fortune telling stand say just at that moment that, that a fishing boat like had run into trouble æt sea not far out from port, like, you know, see, see, see. I was right! (My excitement!) My divination really worked! But, hold hold on, hold on now, since that **"captain"** since he was on the boat himself too, then it was ninety-nine percent certain that he'd met his doom, oh, oh, that meant I'd done, you know, like my face reading it was a **big mistake**! No, no, no, <u>look</u>, just **look** at who's walking over? There, in the dimness of the solitary lamp in the evening gloom, there was the "captain" coming over slowly up towards me there, like, you know I mean. So there, he **lived through it**, see, laik. Still, this stiff, wooden figure of a man, stiff as wood he could in fact really be, like, well, a ghost, sort of, you know, couldn't he, see? At that moment I even wanted to go up and touch him, give him a touch the way Doubting Thomas touched Jesus with his fing his finger, you know, like that. He came over -- the ghost -- and turned into a completely, a totally real, real true, actual true real person, -- see the way he still was sort of firm and solid like, hadn't actually gone translucent or something, like. What's more, he still had the same big, broad eaved bill cloth black duck bill baseball cap on his head that he'd worn when I'd read his face and before when he'd gone over to the dock. It hardly seemed likely there'd be a ghost for the cap too, like, you know, not really. And he like, like he started <u>speaking</u> to me out loud, you see, and, and he sounded <u>very</u> **rational**: --

Out on the ocean the boat suddenly encountered like strong winds and and pounding waves -- a huge wave struck them, and the boat listed badly, three of the crew went into the drink in an instənt, two were missing without a treis, the other was pulled back on board after a while, already dead. Only two of them survived, like and, and he was one of them, I mean, like. And not a bit not a bit of what what he said not a bit of it didn't sound reasonable like junou. My reading had worked! really, really **worked!!** He said so too, that the reading I gave him had really worked. -- So, then, the three dead men, like,

-- -- who were they -- -- -- -- -- -- ? -- -- I lost no time asking him right away then and there. One of them was none other than the very guy I had done a reading for the big burly big one, wearing the white (white?) underwear with the slanted eyes that had that slanty eyed, bəbəbəbewildered like that look you know, that one.   Wow,   did my face reading ever work! He knew about that too, so when that ill-fated, poor, luckless drowned devil wearing his white underwear, when he went on board, he'd tould him then and there, he'd said: "You've got to be extra, extra careful."   -- But -- if the guy in that filthy dirty underwear was fated to lose his life in a fire, then how come after all he drowned that way like that in the water like, see? I marked that reading down as a big failure! I went on to ask him then ask about the one with all covered with beard stubble, that one, what had happened to him, you know like? The guy with the face full of a dense spread of thick beard bristles that one, he also was <u>dead</u> and gone too. Once again my face reading proved to be even more effective like you know. (I was perfectly capable of figuring out that stuff about the "truth behind facial patterns" without even bothering to read faces, -- now that's really what you call a **heaven sent**, natural born <u>**special**</u> <u>**talent**</u>, I mean, it is, you see, like!) He also knew, knew all about it, -- Stubbles had told him all about it on the boat. --   He'd cursed me like royally I mean, like   "He cursed you too!" So was the other one, the one I mean who like made it out alive, was he the youthful that "<u>young man</u>" who wore the red windbreaker? I wanted to ask about this person, this youth in the thin red nylon sheer jacket, did he or didn't he, I mean, like go out on board you know the fishing boat.

"He was on board."

With his head bowed the large, broad eavebill of the black duckbill baseball cap completely covered over concealing his face entirely.

"Then, what happened to him   ?   " I was feeling like the most intense enthusiasm as I asked this asked him this I mean.

"He's   **dead**   " head hung low.

"Oh!" I let out a sigh only because his face nevər did get a proper reading, one that showed it worked. -- But it didn't matter at all -- nobody knew about that face --   he <u>didn't know</u>!

"He was. . . he was my oldest son." The broad hat bill screen of his duck bill baseball cap like was raised upward, this time it rose very high laik, see, and the glare of the oil lamp shown right square on his face -- there wasn't any sort of iksprefən on his face like.

"No kidding?" The way I said it it sort of sounded like I was was saying something like: "Oh! So, it was you, <u>you</u> won the grand prize of 200,000 yuan in the National Lottery,   **no kidding?**"

"Yes, . . . he was, . . . he was my oldest son," his big, broad shade bill screen of a duck bill baseball hat was once again lowered, down like, see, you know.

If there's one thing I know, it's -- finish whatever you start out to do, don't leave things half done, -- I made up my mind I was definitely going to, like, look up, you know, the, that other person who'd like survived, see, and then like I was going to see whether or not I'd already given him a reading, and if I had sort of then whether the reading was correct or not correct? The next day I finally found him, the guy who like had survived like, you know. In fact, it turned out I hadn't æktjuəli see like read his face before. It was interesting -- when I asked him about the boating accident he actually it was so much for him the tears came rolling out of his eyes, and to my amazement he wasn't happy at all that he'd returned alive -- he raised his left hand, all wrapped up in a ball of grimy old grimy cloth, to show how like he'd lost one of his little fingers. If you can believe it, it didn't matter to him that he'd been able to hold on to his life and get back safe, not at all, he was sobbing away   all because of how he'd lost like this little finger of his. When the wave struck, just at that moment he was standing next to the hatch down into the boat's hold where it was this cave pit. A bamboo chest covered in clumsy lead gray tin sheeting to hold tools and implements and whatnot was swept down and there was like this sharp knife that spilled out. That cutting knife sliced his little finger sliced it clean off right just at the base, the base just like that. I asked him then, I like said to him: I wanted to like, see, read I mean his face -- for free --   an after-action report, as a "great fortune teller of unrivalled foresight and foreknowledge after the event." I found like nothing when I checked his face,   switched to reading his palm then I mean.   But his left hand, you know, itititit was all like wrapped up so it so ititit, see, um like ræpd up so, you know. So I started in unwrapping that tattered old bandage -- what was important was that it was crucial that what I had to see was that spot over there on the side there, that's the corner where we'll like like glimpse you see the "secrets of heaven," glimpse a tiny speck of heaven's vast store of knowledge. I slipped it off some. Does it hurt? No. I slipped off some more   --this is what we call "dispelling clouds to see the moon,"   just a speck of understanding.   Ahah! Sure enough, along the upper part of the lines on his palm there were all these blackish speckled spots -- that, now that seems to indicate that he'll run into some serious troubles at some point in his life.   Then, that's it! Since that's right then I'm right! Hold on again, just a second, are those black things, are they speckles after all or, like could it could itititit be, you see, some black flecks of dirt that weren't washed out like? So I picked up his hand and rubbed it a bit like you know -- --   it was dirt!

So,   what conclusions could I draw from this reading of a face? -- None! On the other hand, everybody else had reached a conclusion: I was famous! Instantly Lone Star became one of the "Living Immortals." I'd made a name for myself that had the whole village in an uproar -- that's fame for you, like, I mean, you know itit, like, see, even if my readings didn't work out -- somebody with blue under their lips as an omen of death didn't didididn't like drop dead, you know-somebody like that -- it wouldn't make any difference it itititi wouldn't like you know matter you know like, I mean, you see like: subsequently subsesubsubsequent to the episode of the grand "efficacy experiment" and like thatthethereafter   , like, all these people started coming around for me to <u>cure</u> their <u>illnesses,</u>   Now then it's not likely a "Living Immortal" wouldn't know how to tototo cure <u>illness</u> is it? It was then, in order to preserve the "excellent name" I'd achieved only after so much exertion, exertion and trial and tribulation, see that I sort of let myself you know like go ahead and treat them, you see, tried out some <u>cures</u> for them. The only trouble I had came from the "herbalist's stand." I have this to say for the "herbalist's stand": For him this was something without a doubt that was truly and absolutely, truly "serious" -- a serious life and death struggle for him. So he came after me, thethethe, that son of a bitch, he, he, wasn't going to give me an inch not an inch to get by the way he accused me vehemently of practicing **"black arts** medicine," calling me a "warlock," a **"shaman doctor"** of witchcraft --

Immediately after this like calamity or so anyway kind of I mean not long after then there was this kind of see this aftermath like of what occurred with "disposing of the corpse." The "captain" had brought bæk what were the precious remains of that luckless child -- from the first he'd endured every sort of difficulty and exerted every effort before he could recover him from the dangerous waves like that I mean, see then only then to find out he was already gone like I mean you know he was dead -- and then he'd gone to all the trouble and made every effort to preserve the body and transport it back, you see -- it itititi so it so it was a surprise when his boss, the bankroll, (who came over from Jui-ho) got so mad he hit the roof and kept on going, wouldn't accept this. The boss thought this would bring him a lot of added burdens for the like the funeral arrangements, and without any good reason at all he added needlessly to the grief of the relatives. That reminded me of an item of a, man, it was a piece that appeared in the "fringed column" like human interest sort of sorta like section of the paper that I'd heard about like in Taipei once before like, so, you know. The story was that there was a big company in Taipei that was announcing it was hiring drivers through a competitive test. The oral part of the text was just one question "If you hit a pedestrian while driving, what should you do?" Everyone who answered that you should stop and wait for the police to arrive on the scene to handle it, like, ddididididn't get hired, you know not a single one of them! -- Only one person only one answered this way: "Go ahead, step on the gas and drive over him, since you might as well go ahead and crush him to death, like, you know, see -- that way you'll avoid endlessly paying out hospital bills -- death compensation and funeral expenses actually you know

they're really much cheaper by a long shot, much I mean you know like --" ---
This one individual drew great admiration and had the good fortune and great
privilege of being selected for employment.

Finally,   after they'd talked him into it, the boss pretty much
gave in and agreed to take responsibility for handling things. He bought an
ordinary "economy class" coffin and had it brought in from Jui-ho. Hwail they
were waiting for the coffin to arrive the body was arranged laid stret[d stretched
out in front of the door to his house. For some reason, I don't know, I mean,
like they left the head thæt pärt exposed, and everything extending below itititit
the part where the head was like I mean that was all covered up underneath a
grungy, rank, worn-out grimy piece of tea colored thin straw matting that had
been used for sleeping on.   Most likely it was the one he'd used to
sleep on like when he was, you know, alive I mean ititit was that one probably.

While he was I mean like exposed like that out there you know, up to
the day they put him into the coffin, I mean I did not have the nerve to go past
that spot there   -- I, ah, I admit,   if there's one thing one thing I
can't stand more than anything else it's the it's the faces of, you know, dead
people. As old as I am today -- it's sort of what I've said all along ever since I
understood what was going on around me wasn't just a kid anymore --I've
never so much as even once like once I mean seen a dead personz face, just seen
stiff rigid hands and legs and feet sticking out straight like from no closer than
50 yards or so, a good maybe some fifty fifty yards or more. This time there
was **no** cause for an **exception** either   -- I limited myself to "spiritual
contact" and never did "get acquainted face to face," just "spiritual contact."

Some distance away, a good distance, a good, long long distance (at
least 50 yards or more   ,   ) I could hear the thin soft soft moaning of a
woman in mourning, most likely she was the like y'know wife I suppose of the
dead man -- -- -- strange,   I didn't hear something actually "intensely
painful" in the sound of that weeping really, what I heard sounded well, like I
mean, it was "sexy" like, you know. The next day the coffin was delivered to
the front door of their house, -- it was bizarre -- there were these rhombus
shaped red paper strips pasted on either end of the coffin: on one piece of paper
there was the character for "longevity" and on the other they'd written like, well,
like you see the character for "luck."   Truly as a people we truly are a
people with an extraordinarily an amazingly high level of culture when it comes
to how good we are at särkæzəm and ridicule.   To put a label like
"longevity" on a person who's no more than thirty-ish you know lying inside
like this long, narrow box that's shaped like a trough, sort of you know, see --
to call his getting drowned in the ocean: "luck."

That nearly, it almost virtually amounts to like I mean nearly nearly telling
the dead man you know: " -- -- that was really well done the way you died

"After that, after he died -- at first -- I didn't know where people around here buried the dead. I mean like I'd never seen a cemetery or anything like it like it before on the feis of the hills in the neighborhood. The whole time since I'd come into like this place I mean I hadn't spotted any of those tombs you see on the road among the hills and valleys that are all modern streamlined, built with concrete and steel frame to have this semi-sərkjulər arc shape like I mean, that look like well what they look like is, you know, I mean they look like they look like a "loop" you know like an IUD like.   Then in that case was it possible that people in this like remote, I mean, such a such an isolated little fishing village would they would they actually wud they like bury him at sea maybe like?   Or, after somebody's died, then would they like I mean bury them in the dry gravel along the sandy beach outside the edges of the built up area of this tiny little primitive hovel this həvəl of a harbor?   It was only later on,   all on account of this guy like you know,   that I found a place like this at the foot of the base of these hills around here, with the graves all in an unbearably tumbled down jumbled mess al ouvər al ouvər, and they hadn't arranged anything according to yin-yang facing the sun or away from it, and what's more like none of these you know graves none of them were aligned to I mean tototo face the same you know direction like, see, like, and these tombs none of them looked like I say like you know the contraceptive things like IUD loops;   these were empty mounds that looked like row after row of waves swelling up on a sea of green grass like like more like breasts.

The day after all the commotion and everything over the episode of the of the disaster at sea, -- in the harbor there, -- I immediately lost no time going to see I mean that ill-fated motorized **"vessel of doom"** that had been marked for disaster, the *Good Luck II*, just before it was was about to set out like to sea again, see, like. This was like the only boat in the harbor area I mean like that had it its its motor like running, there like there it was like turning over like ready to go with this pale white cigarette white like pale blue smoke spouting out, sputtering up above the boat,   and then some "crewmen" (newly recruited and assembled) dressed in dark, dark rain gear and hats like that were walking back and forth over and over again back and forth up top ətəp on the wood deck, you know like, and this like I mean this wake of water like a path trailed out in a triangle at the stern of the boat where it I mean the more it trailed out the bigger it spread, slowly pulling gradually away gradually it steadily left the shore behind chugging away. It didn't raise like even so much as a stir of eni kind among enibody in this harbor town, and I didn't see enibody from around here who turned out to give to it the least offer of eni attention. I recognized him standing back there in the stern, his hands on the helm like, that man grasping the handle of the helm was in fact none other than the man called the "captain":   that short little, prominently visible prominent body, along with (since he hadn't put on that rush weave conical rain hat of his) that soft black duck bill baseball sun cap that was so easy to pick out with the broad, waid uaid sunshade visor front. It was only just the day after the "tragedy --" in that man's family of his, no more than that, his having just then lost his son like having just died like that, and still, on account of "survival," on account of "money" he like I mean he didn't even have any time to mourn this loss, this bereavement, like, you see. And even then his fate, the fate of his own future was all written down in the lainz of his palms, I mean, you see, that he would meet with a fatal calamity, on the ocean -- that day only two days before when I'd read his -- and read their -- those men, you know, who were on the same boat with him -- read their palms, I'd told them, like then -- wasn't he even a bit afraid? -- -- Actually, where things like that were concerned, the captain wasn't like I am -- not skeptical the way I am about my predictions (the ones I make for other people, that is). Compared to me, the captain, you know he believed in my "fortune telling predictions" more than I did, you see like. He had stepped onto this boat shouldering what was like I mean the "cross of fate," and set out for the vast ocean realm where seas raged and sent billows of foaming froth soaring into heaven like you see, I mean all in search of a meal like you know. That, well like something like that wasn't how I was living in this place: I may be searching for my livelihood in this remote, desolate harbor looking for a living, but I don't have anything at all like this like "cross of fate" to carry on my shoulders weighing me down like that. And as for his, the captain's, his predicted fate -- Would some proof emerge to confirm and corroborate this, would it? **Heaven** only knows!

Just the very moment of like it it it was it was the second you know when the boat you see was leaving like a burly guy with a big frame I mean as tall and strapping as he could be like strode down to the very veri farthest edge of the dock right doun next to the water and assumed a "solemn manner" to bid them farewell by gesturing with his hands toward the boat as it left the harbor with sarcastic sarcastic ridiculing taunts. After that this burly, the big, this big burly fellow like raised his left hand and gave like three or four exaggerated salutes you see like one right after the other, ænd then to follow this up he kicked up his legs and pranced around on the dock goose-stepping back and forth several times back and forth these big goosesteps. But the thing that amazed me was how not a single person like see nobody on the dock even so much as looked up you know so much as I mean like batted an eye. He went on for some time hanging around all alone out there by the water's edge hanging around going back and forth amusing himself down and back and back and forth whatever, and then he like walked over to where I'd got myself settled you see, where I was like. The dumb **bozo** was getting ready to **clown** around again! This slugo, he was a giant porker the kind they set up as an offering for the salvation festival,* I recognized who he was, Chang Fa-wu, from the day before when he'd done the same thing under the same circumstances in just about the same the same situation. Chang Fa-wu, I saw the jerk that day by himself at a spot just next to the water like see tangential to the mooring dock where I saw him with his klouthz stripped off down to like you know that white underwear they have on underneath, just as he was taking this rusty fuel drum filled with a load of gasoline and like lifting it up you see with just with just one arm see like. I mean it it it was it was was a sight to see what power the like muscles in those forearms it took to have the strength to do a thing I mean something like that, and just then during that moment there wasn't a single person either who like paid who paid any attention whatever see to him you know like at all. At that point see like curiosity kinda got the best of me and I got you know like **so curious** -- that I walked over up next to him like, I mean you know where did he get strength like that? He, he kept on and on pumping this thing up and down something like you know over three times, and gave me this dumb, silly grin, really silly looking, and then before I'd said anything like before I'd greeted him or I mean you know asked him anything, whatever, all on his own he himself gave me this cheerful kind of welcome, he sed:

"This here gasoline drum here it's like empty see, not one drop you see of fuel left in it, that's how come it's so easy see to lift it up, up over my head like like that see."

"<u>Damn</u>! So what the hell do you think you're trying to prove?" I asked him that way, I don't suffer fools gladly, not at all.

"It's fun!"

--------- He wanted to attract attention.

Second question:

"Then what do you here for a living --"

"Oh! Over at the Bureau," He pointed over past the temple, the Matsu Temple, at the hills, evidently.

Good grief! So there was another whole world over there all along
holy, holy shit.

"What about you?" It was his turn to ask questions.

This Chang Fa-wu, Burly Chang, a big gasping, panting wheezer of a guy, he was, this dark slick oily black hair all kinked up into coils, coils of coils of tight little, tight kinked up kinky curls (there was a lock of it that swung down dangling in front of the front of his forehead like a question mark sort of you know like), and a pair of a couple of eyes as round as a goldfish's. He looked, this burly guy, at the very most no more than around about 23 or 24 it it it's it's it's more or less I'd say like that sort of sɔːrtəlaik ("Actually, I'm already 37 years old man, see, you know like," he said -- later on he told me that once I mean see, like you know like.) After these past three days in a row, he'd had no idea I was here in this in this place like, see, for the past few days, because their Bureau, I mean, it was being given like an inspection see, because the last time when they'd been inspected not long before that I mean there were too many you see far too many personnel absent without leave, the old gentleman who's the Director of this Bureau you see he got marked down or something for a slight demerit like by the old gentlemen who are his bosses higher up: -----Therefore, this time for the past few days when they came back to reinspect the Bureau all over again you see their Bureau Director strictly forbade the Bureau personnel from leaving their posts at all, even for a little while, and that even included forbidding them to leave the Bureau to come down the hill down here in the evening after dark, --- Only just on this day, today, Sunday (this guy he had already come down here I mean like, on Saturday morning he'd walked down you see like, whereas he, the old gentleman director, wouldn't even let his subordinate personnel in his Bureau come down), had he gotten approval to come down the hill, I mean, see, like. He was like the first person in his Bureau whatever to find out you know that I was here see. That's the reason why it was only after this happened that I went on over up to the Bureau like then I mean. ----- The cock's crowing ----- It's just this like one chicken you know who's doing the crowing and whatnot like, the big rooster that that the boss woman raises I mean like there's only this one big old rooster that's the only one she keeps. I have no idea why she keeps you know an old rooster like that one around the place here, it's enough to make you think it couldn't be anybody else but nʌn ʌthər thæn their family's grandfather, really couldn't tell for sure but.

Right now it's just now getting on towards midnight -- the roosters around here are used to sounding off like this just about now in the middle of the night -- no matter what you say. Roosters who crow along about midnight are definitely not a portent or an omen of any of any luck or prosperity --- the most appropriate thing to do would be to slaughter it cut its head off I mean you know. ------ Get her, you say, to take the like you know this family grandfather, "the Venerable gentleman," take him out and hack off its old bean bag like that, right, eh? No way for sure -- that's patricide. I wonder whether I want to decapitate this rooster, the old rooster, like that whether it's really because I what I've wanted what I'd like to do is to **eat chicken** --? **Freudian** "p s y c h o a n a l y s i s." Maybe the first person like to think that up was like I mean it -- ah, a shaman -- could have, that could have been what was going on in his like I mean psyche, that's what, he could have made this I mean used this as an excuse, a pretext. Probably, if you look at it I mean this way it lŏŏks like like then in that case then all these sacrifices these sacrificial rituals very likely were most probably all so that they could put on like I mean you know put on a big **feast** ---- and would that include in it I mean, you see would that also contain **human** **sacrifices** ? -----------

What's weird, what's really weird: I've realized that around here, in the Matsu Temple around here I mean, I've never once the whole time like seen any of the sacrificial offerings used for "feasts," see. Most likely what it is itititit is is that they're so poor that when it comes to offerings they don't have any way to to to make to to make make an offering, you know, see like that's what it it it is most likely. Still, as a building the construction of Ma Tsu Temple here makes it the fanciest building by far in like the whole the entire harbor town. A poor harbortown   a wealthy temple; ------- poor people   wealthy deities. That's exactly the way it is, ----- down in the countryside ----- every last single piece of property down like like to like to to the shirt on your back all see comes under the possession of the upscale venerable deities above itit's theirs, see, like you know, ---- I can sum it up for you, reduce all the talk all the verbiage and bring it down to one short, simple way of putting it, everything all belongs in its entirety under the possession of the highest supreme Venerable Heaven the Heavenly Venerable himself, itit's his that's what I mean like you know. - a - where was it I got to just now, like I mean, just before the rooster crowed you know?   **I can't remember, I clean forgot, pure clean, pure and simple, simply completely clean and pure forgot.**

Since I'm on the topic of the temple, the Ma Tsu Temple here, from a distance it looks, well, from far off itititit's sort of sort of something like I mean it's like you know simply like a seashell, a giant spiral conch that's painted all sorts all sorts of colors, garish colors, garish, every kind every garish kind of color run riot like perched up like this prominence along the edge of the seashore, at the edge of the shore sticking out like some stiff hard bony horn. By the time you come up on it, that is, like once you know you get a closer look at it from close up: You discover how practically all the entire mass of the whole temple itself has been nearly nearly almost completely dug out by people who carried out the excavation of it until they'd carved it into an empty hollow, empty, empty so it's just as if it had been chewed clean clear through by worms until it was eaten out by them sorta. Anywhere you look all over everything that's visible people have left their family names and their given names inscribed everywhere squeezing in just as many as they possibly could carving flying dragons, phoenixes, unicorns, strange strange creatures of every description likelike like that whatever like engraved deeply into every square inch of space all over in little little squares tiny little squares on the stone walls and pillars, the wood partitions and and the wood pillars too   (somebody else of course was asked to do the ghostwriting.) It's as if you know you could like say the entire temple looks like some one of these colorfully engraved jars they make to keep your brushes in, one of those containers. Every square inch of the place, each tiny little <u>nook</u> inside this temple is something created through the crystallization of <u>how</u> determined and devoted they were, it's a manifestation of

their own "faith," each and every one of them -- **Even metal and stone yield to sincere devotion**   ! -- Truer words than these were never spoken, none truer than these classic lines, is that not so? On it goes, faith, faith,
     carving away and carving away,   there's faith for you why it's simply like all these bugs, these bugs like see chewing away like chewing away you know until like they've nearly chewed it away clean gleaming colorful empty cavernous hollow. Faith, yes indeed, it's   drops   of   water   boring
     through   stone,   it's   iron   cudgels   ground   down   into   needles,   FAITH,   it's   terrifying!

There's something sort of ridiculous kind of about the gods on display inside the temple. Local -- Taiwan -- temples all have pretty much the same arrangement inside them. "Buddhism" and "Taoism" are both located in one room, that's for both Buddha and people. This room is always the same with this or that Buddha, a bunch of them, and humans, too, -- except for Ma Tsu -- so there's Sakyamuni, Venerable Kuan the Kuan Ti, Kuan Yin, the Sun Deity, a Moon Deity, a Wind Deity, a Horse Spirit, Ox Spirit, and Lü Tung-pin. . . . and and Jesus just about almost like he almost like he almost made it in there too, not quite, you know. Now this assorted grab bag of rakish creatures, the game they're up to like see isn't Buddhism and neither is it Taoist. It deserves a label more like: Greek polytheism.

There's one other statue, this one's named for Li T'ai-pai. And the amazing thing is that he's a General,* like, you know, like. The way things are going at this rate there's a possibility that maybe some day I -- Lone Star -- will get the chance to sit in this shrine to enjoy eternal life eating my way through the sacrificial meat from one age to the next, how about how about that, like, you know like. There are characters from the thethethethe novel *Investiture of the Gods* living in the temple, too, like also like. That way, like, that way the day I write myself a novel too like that see then it won't just be me, but even all those "imaginary characters" cooked up in my brain like see they'll also be able to get a a seat in the temple and help themselves to all the "sacrificial meat" they want too, like, how about that, see. On top of that there are "visiting" deities, deities checking the place out who've come over from Hua-lien together, in a group, to stay at this "inn" like, I mean, itit's like, "The Number 1 Tourist Hotel in Deep Pit Harbor."

In this temple it's the concept people have of what constitutes "substance" and "spirit" that's what's totally different from what people hold to in other places. Like the pious men and devout women here clasp their hands in front of them holding on to incense sticks and start in bowing away to the clay idols of deities and bodhisattvas; Now if you walk in front of them (once they start that) they just go on bowing away at you, -- they know they can bow right through you   pass through you   penetrate through you to that deity that bodhisattva behind you. The "substance" that's originally you instantly turns into   "spirit": the "spirit" that originally was the bodhisattva's, the deity's whatever, now <u>that</u> gets transformed into like I mean this substance which positively must be worshipped standing rigidly resolutely in that spot, any other way won't do, won't do at all, see.   I mean, see, it's like it's like X-rays or something, the way they worship with their incense and their bowing, it it it goes it goes goes **right through** you   clean through   straight through   ,   so you look like like look like something "transparent" I mean, that's what it looks like.

And when they kneel down they get very **animated, animated** to the point they look like incredibly agile monkeys, or chimpanzees or something. Once I saw this old woman, so old she'd lost her teeth and all you know, she was eighty if she was a day for sure like and you'd see her go prostrate flat down on the ground, then spring straight up on her feet see, and then slip down flat out on the ground again like before like, and then hunch up and stand back tall as before again over and over, so graceful and practiced it was as smooth as watching a ballet or something. If this was taking place during her ordinary daily activities instead, then with all this popping down on the ground, hopping back up again, and so forth, she'd have already strained her back good that's for sure. Getting down and back up like that was about as physically demanding as something like the movements in a full squat-thrust exercise. Once when I kept count on her, altogether she did her morning warm-up squat thrust calisthenics going down and up, down and up altogether sixteen times in a row without stopping.

How much do I know after all about something as ridiculous as Buddhism?   (Or Taoism? Forget it, since the only thing they care about here is the screwball stuff they call Buddhism, so that's what I'll pay attention to also: The line I care about you can call Buddhism; the line I don't care about we'll call Taoism.) How much does whatever I know of regarding the Buddhist creed amount to? Or, if there's anything I know about it, I mean like, I've read one of the Buddhist sutras: *The Platform Sutra of the Sixth Patriarch*. My biggest discovery in *The Platform Sutra of the Sixth Patriarch*: every sentence in the sutra means more or less the same thing. The only thing that needs to be put in as an introductory preface to a complete edition of this book would be the verse:

> Bodhi originally has no tree
> The mirror also has no stand
> From the beginning not a thing is
> Where is there room for dust?[*]

This verse sums up the meaning of every sentence in that book already. Since

that's the case, why'd he write so much - what's that they used to say about a whore's footbindings? so long and so stinky, what's the point? It was a waste of the Sixth Patriarch's precious time, precious as gold and silver, precious as precious could be, and it's a waste of ours -- not, of course that ours is precious, not in the same class as gems or gold or silver when it comes to preciousness, but still at the least, at the very least it's time that's as valuable as, say, like a pile of cow dung, or pig shit, or horse droppings, or dog poop, meadow muffins, -- whathaveyou.   That just about includes the whole sum total of the total understanding I've got of the whole sum of this total doodaedal about Buddhism (and that goes as well for Zen and all that other stuff whatever they call it) that personally I'm squarely opposed to.   That's all there is to it, just like <u>that</u>!
Such as this I have heard. . . . .*

Let's have a swig, wet my whistle   .   Eeee, after this one last drop it'll be dry as a bone.   That'll I mean "evaporate" off evaporate like won't it?   I'd be sunk if I didn't still have some of that <u>insecticide</u>. There's still probably a little bit of some water left over in the thermos bottle, ---, oh no, no, I used it all up this morning with incredible extravagance to wash my stingkən feet off (it had been over twenty days since I'd washed my feet last), so because of that I used up all the water in the thermos bottle 'till it was almost completely gone, see, like. Now here I am out of ammo and no help in sight.
Strange. What I wanted just now was to get a sip of something good and wet from the liquor bottle to soothe my throat there like but instead I actually wound up with my hand on a cigarette getting one of them out you know, like, like. . . what I wanted in the first place was to get rid of this itching in my throat, and what I've ended up doing is dry roasting it. Never thought that would happen. Never mind. I'm damn well gonna <u>smoke</u> one **eniwei**.

Now   as I was saying   about the Sixth Patriarch, actually this is what I think: his stature as a "religious figure," if you want to call him that, doesn't even begin to compare with how astonishing he was, amazingly astonishing he was, as a poet, extraordinary, a super poet.   That poem "Bodhi originally has no tree" that really should be considered hands down the finest, the very finest, and the most enduring, simple little verse ever written in the history of Chinese literature. In my view the Sixth Patriarch deserves a place alongside the most brilliant poets in history based on just that verse alone. That little poem of his can stand up to all those so-called poems, the hordes of them that have been used like so much "cannon-fodder," so many of them they surge up over and over again, wave upon wave so it seems as if it were "<u>human wave tactics</u>" the way they never end.

Now, the poems poets like to write today are even worse failures!   What was wrong with poets back then in the old days was that they wrote too many poems, but now the problem isn't that poets write too many poems, no, like, see, see in a place like Taiwan it's got to be just too easy to get something of a name as a "poet," ---- for one of these kinds of poems just three lines, or maybe five or six, are good enough. It's the same as publishing one of those tiny notices in the classified ads section of the newspapers -- if the readers who subscribe to the newspaper all decided they'd like to like write a poem I mean, you know, it would only take three days to publish them all -- and if they published the whole lot of them probably nobody'd complain about overcrowding.

-- -- Still, I'm a poet, myself, too!   In all modesty, I am a "**renowned poet**" with a reputation that's not bad, not bad at all. In fact my illustrious name has appeared in five volumes of poetry; ---- and besides that, my distinguished name has appeared listed on the roster of the founders of six poetry associations. (I have a pretty well known pen-name "The One-eyed Recluse.") But then see like I mean what's the use of a reputation? What the hell's the use of having a name but no money, um, ah, see? If you could get rich writing poetry I can guarantee you it wouldn't be nearly so easy to get a name in this business: the reason it's so easy to become **renowned** writing poetry is all because no one will envy you the least little bit if you become famous, not one bit, not a bit. You want to be famous, fine, you go ahead and be famous!

Herein I hereby solemnly declare with all solemnity that I announce to the nation, to Asia, and to the world: I've already laid down my pen and shelved my manuscripts . . . . oh like, sometime ago, as long ago already as nearly half a year that long kind of. **Indeed, why should I go on writing?** I mean like why? I am perfectly well aware well aware that there's absolutely no way I can write up to a state that really really matches the top rank of the very best poetry: --- such as "Bodhi originally has no tree" --- and frankly I really really don't want to be like ranked I mean with you know with some like incompetent, hackneyed poets see, see itititit's like it's just for <u>this</u> reason just this like, because I feel itititit's so it's so humiliating to be ranked shamelessly with some stale, some mediocre non-entities who pretend to be poets, it's on account of this that I went ahead on my own and like I mean "<u>**voluntarily ceased production**</u>." And, to tell the truth, apart from the fact that the reason I quit was because I was unwilling to be classed among a bætch of inferior poets like these, like besides that I mean, well, why shouldn't I unload all the misery that goes with writing stuff that you could say doesn't have any style worth what you could call anything but nondescript. I'm not saying that it hurts so much to produce during the creative process itself -- you never have any feeling that it hurts at the moment of creation -- I'm talking about how bad it feels after you've failed in your creation. When I discover failures in my own personal creativity it's never right away -- no, it's actually quite a while after I've finished creating a bætʃ of poems, a long time after, a good long time -- say maybe even like well as long a time as as say three or four years -- and what's more it's always when you'd never, never in a million years ever expect it. Like, for example, you're riding on a bus, on your way somewhere or other whatever like see, and just then you happen to overhear somebody talking about something or other and they say something -- why, I don't know -- I really don't have a clue why it is -- but what they say gets me all stirred up about some sentence, or just one single word, I'd put down in some poem I'd done that I'd written maybe three years, or it could actually be as much as four years, before. All of a sudden I feel like like this it's so flawed. I'm provoked into this huge, growing, towering, immense sense of dissatisfaction with it -------- when I've just discovered one of these like flaws you know I mean for the first time I feel at first like itititit's just this like searing wave of scalding heat surge over my face, then I get this shiver along where my spine is ------- to the point that I start to realize that I'm, well, I'm like I mean the sort of person when you get down to it who is never going to write anything decent you know no matter what he does no matter no matter what. From that moment on, really, there's no way to describe how lousy, how depressed I feel. All day I'll feel so lost and empty it seems when it comes to eating there's almost no way I can get it down, and at night even when it comes to sleeping I can't even get to sleep at all you know I mean ---- it itit even gets to the point that I finally end up where I've wondered like whether or not to commit **suicide.** I'll go on this way in this despondent, depressed condition for as long a period of time like well as long as maybe two or three weeks in a row kind of kinda like you see. Something like this it'll happen like say once pretty much every three or four months or so more or less. Since like the moment it happens it it it it just appears I mean like out of nowhere it it it's so it's so so quick the way see, you know like it there's not the least hint or forewarning that takes place up front so it it it it just seems that **"fate has decreed"** already that it ought to descend at just that moment already like. Suicidal urges, and all on account of a piece of poetry like that, on account of like a tiny little "classified ad" ------- Have you ever heard anything like it, already? Thank heaven, thank heaven, really and truly, I've put an end **put an end** once and for all to such a such such a stupid, meaningless misery ------- I don't need to suffer through self-torture like that anymore, already like, not anymore, like, like I was saying on the other hand if we were to to to to, see, I mean carry out a careful examination then what we might find is that my motives for all that writing I did they were never all that honorable enough, you see. Each time I read some piece of poetry written by someone else (-- an ancient --) that was really striking, then what I'd do myself is that I'd like you know I'd like imitate one just the same just like it ---- hoping I'd produce something like something I'd like, imitate it. There's no **honor** or glory to speak of in something you know like that I mean. That's just exactly like looking at a pornographic picture of some sort and then wanting to go out and get laid the same way. Reading a good poem and then wanting to try to learn from it; looking at porn paintings, photos, whatever and then afterwards wanting to go get laid, you know, sorta like ---- what use like I mean what glory is there to speak of in something like that, you know, I mean, see?

I do not write poetry myself -- and I don't think any of these poets in Taiwan should, or can, write poetry either: In any case with all the poems they have written already they haven't been able to do a decent job on one yet, so like, -- why not ---- like I have ---- give it up and quit wriwriwriwriting writing anymore like, huh? The poets in Taiwan, the ones that are "famous" (of course I am one of the ones who ought to be included in this group -- as One-Eyed Recluse!), the poems these weasels write they're awful! ---- Shan-shang "Grassy Knoll" Ch'ing, dogshit, "Lightning" Lei T'ien, dogshit, Lü Fei-"Floating Frost"-shuang, dogshit, dogshit, "Riverman" Chiang Ho-jen, dogshit, "Lily" Ho Hui-hsüan "The Orchid," dogshit, dogshit, Teng Hsin-ts'ao "The Wick," double dogshit, a pile of dogshit, stinking dogshit! ------ Something like writing poetry you know it's got to come from out of need like sort of, you see like, it ought to be like **sexual desire** like that sorta that way like I mean it oughta happen when it oughta happen sorta like, see, ---- the poems they write in Taiwan are either so impotent they can't get it up or if they can get it up they can't keep it up. Someone in the process of composing poetry should like should enjoy it to the fullest ---- again like just like "sexual intercourse" that way like ---- (both exhilarating and fatiguing) ------ I'm prepared to say this, I mean like: When these people who write poetry are in the process of writing poems they don't get the least bit of any pleasure to speak of like you know. Oh, these people, they have   sex   all right,   they have   sex   but it's as if they looked over those erotic photo, painting illustrations and then went home and got their old ladies to go through it with them puzzling it out play-by-play, but all they get out of it is fatigue without any pleasure to speak of. I'm no different, either, in any respect, ------ however, **no one** should write anymore, ------ and everyone should follow my example and **quit writing.** I'd like to take a piss. ------ Ooh, really chilly outside! It it it it's stopped raining it it seems like.   In fact it is still raining just a bit,   so where will it be tonight?   Over under the banana tree.   Keep things spread out, the banana tree one night, the base at the corner of the wall the next night, the road the night after that -- that way it won't smell. (Twelve Thousand Miles of Outhouses)* sort of like you know.   Even to find a place to pee it's so twisty and full of loops you have to go around this way and turn back around that way to get there. The banana tree's already started to wither these past few days ---- don't know whether it's because I pee on it all the time. There's the lamp shining dimly over at the inspection station over there, tucked away behind the ridge line of the hill. I keep on mistaking it for sunrise coming up from concealment behind the hills. That beats all for absurdity, a sunrise coming up from the north.　　　　False light!　　　Fɔ:ls messiah! --

Hallelujah! Hallelujah! ------ I've got it! Chang Fa-wu! (I brought him to my room a few days ago). That was the day after I learned about his "single-handed skill," when this big fatso came over to hang around my stand again, ---- it was evening then. When it came time to close up the stand he helped me fold up, and he carried the soapbox back on his shoulder (I hadn't yet at that time started putting it away in the Religious Articles Store　　　to receive spiritual power). This super-heavy-weight gargantuan fatso made it his own proposal to come over to where I live to have a look at the place. When we went in to my place it was so totally dark that you really **couldn't see your hand in front of your face**, so as soon as he stepped in he slipped and fell down with a boom, ---- I don't know whether he tripped over some vermin or slipped on some sorta dogshit ----- anyway you couldn't see a thing. After I got you know the candle lit he looked the whole place over up and down one end to the other and then he said it's a nice place, he wanted to move in with me. (He had no idea at all how much I value my own solitary **"private life."** I may live like a dog all right, but I still put great value on my solitary, independent "<u>individual</u> life"). Then in the next breath he completely surprised me by undressing down to his underwear and announcing he wanted to get some sleep. He said he hadn't slept well for days, and in a flash he'd burrowed himself into my quilt like. Then he spun around upright and said, "Wow, bed's too short!" Next he confided in me. He said he was preparing to report for the Junior Grade Civil Service Examination. He said he was the only person the only one in the Bureau he knew who was advancing. He said he'd been pessimistic to begin with, but after his friends had given him some encouragement he no longer felt pessimistic anymore --- now he was **optimistic**. He wanted me to teach him proper "composition," since the Junior Exam would test composition and he wanted to know how he could get like the very highest grade in composition, ------ "You fortune tellers are definitely good at writing compositions -------- and I'm good at sizing people up. One look at you and I could see you're educated　　real good　　you are." Then he made a proposal he'd like thought up for me sort of, to have me go over to his Bureau the next day to buy a meal in their mess hall. You could have filled a ten-pound basket with all the inane things he had to say, but this was something worth listening to.　　　　Actually pretty practical. A meal for four dollars only ---- any place else a meal cost five dollars! And what's more they have a meal plan so you can sign up for the next day's meal the day before -------- shows real respect for the **freedom** of the **individual**. The next day I went on over to check it out once and give it a try. Even the aroma was pretty good, too. After that I decided to make myself a regular at their mess hall there.

And what an impressive organization it is, what a marvel, what a wonder, what a grand, stunning thing, situated at a somewhat elevated location on one of the mountains by the harbor right along its circumference, quite difficult to discern screened behind a deep, dense thicket of trees, and for that reason commensurate with the grandeur of its title, an **Evacuation Organization** set-up. The way the Evacuation Organization works here -- -- exactly as the Evacuation Organization works everywhere -- -- is to flush all the non-essential personnel -- -- no, let's just go ahead and say the like all the **unwanted** personnel -- -- flush them all down here to this Deep-est damn Pit-hole Harbor port. At a glance you'd never imagine that the Evacuation Organization's been here for over three years already. From what I hear people back in the headquarters organization in Taipei have just about clean forgotten about this place entirely, like, you know. And it doesn't have any relation at all to anything in its surroundings in the least; the way this organization ranks in this port -- -- the two have less in common with each other than a horse and a cow in heat. They say everybody in this setup is trying to seize any chance they can get to move back to headquarters in Taipei, any chance. Why? -- -- Because they're afraid the branch office here will be cut back or closed down. Truly awesome, this august office, awesome as it is, carries the full title of: "Bureau of Compilation, Research, Investigation, Editing, Filing, Classification, and Management of Materials on Regional Speech and Popular Local Customs During the Past Century, Deep Pit Harbor Branch Office. Its acronym works out to BOCRIEFCMMRSPLCDPC, DPHBO. The abbreviated acronym is BOCDO. Since BOCDO's been worried they'll be shut down they've been working their tails off stuffing themselves with every possible assignment they can cook up. They've even scoured as far down as Kaohsiung County where they hauled off a township's budget to bring them back and work on them, give them a good like working over like. Apart from all that, they've got another thing going they've dreamed up compiling a volume called *A History of the Founding of BOCDO* to give themselves some way to maintain their official function. And they've been editing this *A History of the Founding of BOCDO*, they've been at it now for three damn years already! Truth is they've been taking their time editing it on purpose -- -- since the sooner they finish it the sooner they face the threat of being **closed up**. Honestly there isn't another organization which in the length of its lifespan has had anything that can come even like close I mean like anywhere near like to matching the length of time this one has taken to write the history of its founding, you know. Besides that, they have one other task to perform, sending and receiving official correspondence, like the regular report documents and whatnot they like send out to their superiors every week -- -- the various and sundry directives which they receive issued from from higher up in the Bureau every week. All the buildings currently used by BOCDO are the leftovers of buildings left behind by previously assigned organizations, entirely built out of wood frame wood planks nailed together, board after board like you know, uniformly painted a dark forest green shade of color, accented here and there with some bright, flashing red fire extinguishers spotted about within the dark forest green shade of color tone, tone. The principal building in the BOCDO compound is divided mainly into the two large long rooms which are of the greatest, the utmost importance. Apart from these several more rooms are attached, including the dining hall, kitchen, and bathrooms. The two principal rooms include one used as an office, and the other used as a dormitory to house male bachelor personnel.   There's a square squared off opening open to the aperture that's the aperture of the window inside the bathroom over at the place you see where you can look out and see that reef promontory jutting out down there along the surface of the ocean the one that looks like it's an arm with its fist raised, stretched out like one that's so thin, so thin thin thin slim delicate jagjagged. I can see it there, see it everytime it's like my turn to stand up there and undo the buttons to open up my fly and take a turn to take it out and take a good long leak, I can see it.

The first time I went into their Bureau office with Chang Fa-wu there was one of them in there I heard as he was talking to another:

"Did you know that Ch'iu Ta-p'eng is dead?"

"Ch'iu Ta-peng's dead?"

"That's right, he's dead. -- -- He was like poisoned, poisoned to death you know."

"Who did it?"

"T'ung Ma-tzu's old lady." That's what it sounded like he said <u>T'ung Ma-tzu</u>.

"**Well, well** -- --" said someone half laughing, half sighing, -- -- I think it was Lin An-pang; -- -- another one of them was Sung Hsi: "Now there was a guy I really, really liked, Ch'iu Ta-peng, -- -- of all people he really didn't deserve to get done in like that so young, get knocked off by somebody like that, -- -- Where is it? Come on, let me see. "

"Not yet, I haven't finished reading it yet."

The two of them wrangled with each other to grab the page of the supplement in the newspaper. **So,   that's   how   it   is.**

Right there just in the opening of window space there in the office I saw a different sort of person, altogether different entirely unlike the others as he could be I mean like. There was this extremely small, I mean tiny, person sitting in a vast, capacious broken down old chair made out of now grungy rattan weave all leaning over precariously. His torso was wrapped in an outer jacket a deep thick wind resistant one, coffee colored brown, with overlength tubes for his arms that had been kneaded and squeezed all over into furling hoops, nubs and loops.

The collar of his coffee colored jacket outerwear was turned out into this turned out ring collar of imitation protective fur so thick and full it bulged and puffed spewed out in billows. The full furry pile of this ring collar was topped by a deep dark fiftyish somber hued face so extremely thin it looked like a glistening slick skull carved out of ebony. When I first saw him, his tiny, delicate body, his thick, heavy coffee-colored clothing, and the heavy fur that poured out of his collar all made me think this guy looked like you know like a monkey I mean like the way he was all coiled up huddled inside that round rattan chair. Honestly, that's just what he looked like, a monkey, especially when he also put on a pair of these like thick furry gloves furry you see like.

On the wall in the vicinity of the window near where he was sitting, it was astonishing -- -- there was a notice on a sheet of white paper pinned up there, and along the top of it were some large bold square characters that looked like some black pigs:

> Correspondence Office, Access Restricted.
> Secrecy Comes First.
> Official Directives, Access Prohibited.
> Not To Be Disturbed or Removed.

Later on I heard him say, "I asked the Dean of the Literature School at National Taiwan University to fix up these lines for me." It was only later that I learned the point of these lines was like solely to get in the way of Sung Hsi like I mean that's what they were for, see like Sung Hsi and he didn't get along at all, they'd lost it once and blown their tops at each other, so now they weren't on speaking terms with each other like between the two of them. (So Sung Hsi, since he and this other guy, the little midget, weren't talking to each other, sometimes when he's in a rush to go fetch some official correspondence like see then then just then at the moment he's not around Sung Hsi will steal over quietly, sneak over stealthily, shuffle through the pile of documents grab a bundle of them and walk off with them, just take them and take take off.)

Now this fellow -- -- T'ang Lin --- -- he's no more, standing up, than a little over four feet tall. Not a dwarf then exactly -- -- just a runt -- -- a runt that's a hair or so taller than a dwarf. He's got a personality that goes with his height pretty much -- -- he loves to hear the sound of his own voice, that empty, hypocritical prattle prattle, it's like nothing so much as the most spoiled obnoxious brat although he's so old now he's got this worn-out wizzened mummified face. Besides that outerwear jacket of his with the turned out imitation fur collar covering his shoulders, he's got one other thing that's his registered trademark, this guy. He goes around all the time incessantly with some like cigarette holder always stuck in his mouth that's been made out of bamboo like, so it looks like he's got this I mean pipe or something like in his mouth sorta you know. And there's one other thing he's got that amounts to the "Registered number of his certification of rights to exclusive use": Everyday he'll like everyday take well a square box of chess pieces and bring it over to the office you know, take it right on in like, and once he gets a break he'll go off looking for someone to come over and play a round with him, go a round see like you know, so he carries this chess set back and forth, brings it in and takes it back out with him I mean it's just as if it was the sole asset he possessed apart from his own body.

T'ang Lin is a clown -- for sure; -- For the most part the cause of the reason why he's played the clown is because he himself he knows himself how low his own his position and his stature are both, so if he didn't go on allowing his colleagues to make fun of him and ridicule him just as they please, if he didn't go on making such a complete fool such a clown of himself, then probably well hardly anyone in the Bureau would like talk to him anymore that's that's sort of why y'know. Still, even now while he goes to such lengths the way he does now to like demean himself see, T'ang Lin being the way he is he has this self-congratulating, self-aggrandizing way about him that he lets slip out as a way of making up for things: -- -- he'll point out some news story about corruption or something so backward it's totally humiliating and say -- -- other events that go on don't leave him room enough to speak of for a foothold where there's an opening for him to be able to slip in one of his smart mouth remarks -- -- "Thear ju hæv it -- -- these Chinese -- -- no matter what they do they never get it right!" Besides this, he's like got another way that you know serves to show off his own "exalted position" like I mean he'll say, for example, something like -- -- : "That's right, right,   the year-end committee report on the activities of the general affairs section we made for BOCDO in 1961, why, I participated in it!" Or else he'll say: -- -- "The New Year Celebration activities we held in the Bureau in 1960 -- -- the banquet -- -- I participated in that, too. " Precisely because he's like this he enjoys you know announcing his "views" see all the time: -- -- Here's what I mean: You'll see him all the time with that tube that cigarette holder made out of bamboo that thing, his noggin that old beanbag of a head just wagging and bobbing away see like while he talks on in this this pretentious front of his this air of importance he gives himself: "Right, sure, well now . . . . **the way I look at it**. . . . : . . . ." Otherwise, you hear him saying things like this: "If I were you I wouldn't do that! . . . ." But, even so, he still totally lacks   "self-confidence,"   Despite the way that he starts off with his that lead-in saying "The way I look at it" you know whatever way he you know see looks at it if if someone with any doubts about it just asks him the least little question, just asks even, I mean you know right away he'll immediately like start to give in doing some real backing and filling: "-- -- Oh?!"

he'll say.

Beyond the way T'ang Lin pretends to be so happy, beyond the way he throws himself into a fake clown act the way he does, he'll also let slip remarks that show he's a total misanthrope with a deep, deep layer of pent-up resentment that's built up pretty deep. For example, when he heard the news from Taipei about a colleague he'd worked with before for a long time who suddenly drowned himself in a river,   he   said: "He jumped into the river and drowned himself -- -- now <u>that's</u> the way to go!!" One day the newspaper brought up the subject that the stockpiles of atom bombs in the present day world were now "plentiful," enough to blow the entire world away, and he said: "Let 'em drop dead, the whole world, everybody, that would be the best thing -- -- let 'em all drop dead on me, every last single solitary one of 'em all of them all drop dead on me -- -- even if I was the only one left I could still get along I would see you know I mean see like."

"If everyone in the whole world died like all of them wiped out like well you know then, -- -- if you were like well the only person to survive, how could you go on living?" Someone put that sort of question to him.

"Don't you worry about that -- -- it just shows what a pack of wimps the whole lot of you are -- -- just goes to prove I'm the only one with balls around here -- --"

"Balls, eh, all you've got's the pubic hair, balls my ass -- --"

This runt does something else that just makes you sick it's so nauseating, and that's the way he goes around with this sort of self pitying, self commiserating manner he has with his head tilted over to one side talking away in this affected mincing cutie cute cutesy tone. I saw him once when he was holding a cake of brownish rice crust in his hands, coming out of the kitchen there like you know like toddling along swaying back and forth swaying this way and that see and well his head that melon head tipped tilting over leaning to one side, nibbling these oh these like tiny bits of mouthfuls that way like see and talking in this mincing tone that's so precious like the way a little girl will act that cutie cute cutesy way: "Umm -- -- I just <u>love</u> to eat -- -- rice crust -- -- umm -- !"

T'ang Lin the little runt that he is the squirt, he and fatso the hulk Chang Fa-wu the two of them together they make quite "a pair" they do indeed, one tall enough to set him apart from any person of average height, the other short enough to come in well under the run of most folks, one of them a vast, colossal blimp, big as they come, the other thin, withered skinny, skinny as skinny gets, frequently the two of them often arm in arm with the arms of each wound around the other's hugging each other in an embrace, exclaiming: "Brothers -- -- you and I, that's us!   "

T'ang Lin bends over the top of his desk there like you know like his concentration totally absorbed with all his might working on his like you know his "official documents" one official document after another working away on them see like so like -- -- and in fact his job is nothing more than to just stamp official documents and give them a serial number. When he's doing this, though, if anyone comes around to tease him and ridicule him,   he'll completely like I mean ignore them kind of he will see.

Take Chang Fa-wu, he walked on in over to T'ang Lin to pull some nonsense on him and stir things up, so he came up behind T'ang Lin's back and covered over T'ang Lin's eyes up so, -- -- but T'ang Lin's arms, hanging there so stiff and rigid they wouldn't budge, they didn't move a muscle, he didn't move them didn't flinch one tiny bit, just sat there you know, just like he was in rigor mortis like, like right there. "ǎ? What's this, no response?" So then Chang Fa-wu went and grabbed that bamboo thing T'ang Lin uses for a cigarette holder, the tubular tube thing T'ang Lin had out on his desk top, got hold of it and stuck it in the corner of his own mouth hanging, hanging out kind of hanging out kindalike like and said: "Hmm -- -- mm, mm, hmm -- mm, mm, mmmmmm, mmmm." Chang Fa-wu with this thin bamboo tube of a cigarette holder doodadad clenched in his mouth he stuck his face right up in front of T'ang Lin's and gave him this studied look, looked him over very closely, very carefully, looked him up and down see like, and then, he took that bamboo doohickey out of his mouth, and stepped back to one side bowing and scraping and saying over and over again: "Yes, sir. Yes, sir, Your Excellency, sir, Chairman T'ang, Director T'ang; my apologies, I'm very sorry -- -- my respects, sir." Chang Fa-wu put that bamboo doohickdoohickey of a cigarette holder back up in the corncorner of his mouth there like you know, then walked around to the back of T'ang Lin's head, and rapped him on that old bean bag skull of his: "You see -- --" His cigarette holder holder doodad tube fell out and while it fell he just caught it with his hand when he stuck it out just at the right moment. "You see -- -- there's no problem, no problem at all; -- -- you can play around with him anyway you like he can take it anything's okay; Look! He's fun to play with!   -- --   It's all because last Monday at the weekly commemorative meeting for Dr. Sun Yatsen our superior, our Director, lectured everyone, criticized him for one or two things, so now, look, now look at how at what a nice guy like you know see how good he is -- --"

After that, I mean like after Chang Fa-wu came in then after him there was this cook, Lao Ch'iu's the name they call him, he came running up too, over next to T'ang Lin see like and started in rubbing his bean pate head and I mean he shouted at him, he called him: "Midget, aw, little midget man, little midget." T'ang Lin didn't answer him.   So then Lao Ch'iu rapped T'ang Lin on his noggin, his skull, with the knuckle of the middle finger on his right hand, he used that. Getting rapped on like that by him must have hurt T'ang Lin, he must have been in pain actually extreme pain, it must have been so painful for him he simply must have been on the verge of like I mean bursting into a rage like you know like right on the edge like. In a little while after a short time had passed, Lao Ch'iu gave him a pat, slapped him on the back, and shouted once: "Son." Then he yelled at him again: "Turtle boy! Cuckold's son!" All of a sudden T'ang Lin came alive, reached around to give his back a feel, and peeled off a sheet of white paper that had like you know like a turtle see drawn on it to show he was a bastard. Then T'ang Lin said: "-- -- Hey -- -- now just wait, hold off a while and I'll mess around with you later, -- -- last time when the Director like talked with us you know what he said was that his orders were to forbid people messing around during work hours, -- -- you hold off, hold off a while till we get off work, I'll mess around with you all you want then I will   then."

It wasn't too long before this resonant bell rang in these resounding reverberations signalling the end of work hours. T'ang Lin calmly and deliberately straightened up the official documents and so forth on his desk into rows of neat stacks, then he brushed his pants off shook them back and forth back and forth like two or three times see, pulled out the old round rattan chair he sits in you know like, and then he pushed it, that rattan chair, he pushed it back in with a shove and slowly walked calmly out of the office.

Not five minutes later more or less, -- -- T'ang Lin came racing back in charging around screaming and bellowing -- like some sort of whirling cyclone, with one hand holding up a little old lead type of water bucket covering up the top of his head, and he went to grab a broom. Then with one leap he jumped straight up on top of his desk where he had all that stuff he had just before taken such care to sort out and straighten up, that stuff he'd arranged so neatly like I mean the way he'd stacked it it it up all in order see that stuff: he stood straight up high on top of the surface of that desk of his see like up there you know, waving that long handled broom around with the handle in his hands, shrieking at the top of his voice "yayayaya" like some demon you know I mean it it it was this freakish freakish howl like see. Just then that cook Lao Ch'iu came flying into the office holding a pair of iron fire tongs the kind you use for lifting coal lumps, and he rushed blindly at T'ang Lin and recklessly bæŋd away clobbering wildly on the helmet T'ang Lin had on his head. T'ang Lin took such a pounding he sat on his office desk top, that old tin bucket of a helmet completely jammed down covering his head so that with his head hidden inside that old lead tin water bucket you couldn't tell whether he'd been knocked senseless or whether he hadn't been knocked senseless.   That lead-lined water bucket had been beaten up until it had caved into such a bumpy mass of pits there were pitted dents inside pitted dents. "Hey, hey, hey, how can you destroy government property   like that?" -- -- People standing all around them shouted at them see. Right away Chang Fa-wu ran up to pull them apart and get them separated like you know so then he said he urged them: "Okay, okay,   now let's not hold it against him, okay   he's a little guy." T'ang

Lin sat there dazed in a daze with his legs stretched out on that office desk top and his head peered out from underneath that old lead lined water bucket he had on, looking kind of dizzy, disoriented, kind of.

"Give it back -- --, give it back -- --, damn you you stinking bastard!" That cook Lao Ch'iu like screamed see as he swore at him.

Little as he is, T'ang Lin took advantage of this chance to get his second wind, and he came too fast, but real fast, so quick as a wink he'd slipped off his desk slid down it and took off like a puff of smoke running to make it outside the office. In one stroke Lao Ch'iu grabbed him by that turned-out fluffy jacket collar fluff of his, hauled him back, and shoved him gave him a shove and pushed him down into the place Sung Hsi was assigned to sit. "Ah, I feel like a fool, ah what can I say, **I feel like such a fool!**" T'ang Lin yelled out -- -- struggling as hard as he could straining against Lao Ch'iu with all his strength. "It's okay -- --, it's okay!" Chang Fa-wu next to him patted his hand and called out: "He's here, he's here with you now   , your buddy's here.   " Wham, the window opened suddenly and a face with this chilling look poked right in and said: "Nobody like nobody see sits in my place like you know." "You can have my place, please, by all means, I'm asking you." T'ang Lin said. "I want mine back. If you don't give it back I'm gonna pull your pants off -- --" While he was saying this he reached out to undo the belt to T'ang Lin's trousers. "Yea -- -- yea -- --" The shouts went up, and everybody was hollering at the top of their lungs. Sung Hsi, being civilized, very civil, very polite and well mannered, looked away. "I give it back, I give it back -- -- ah, aw, I feel like such a fool -- -- my place, I feel like such a fool -- -- my place." "It's all right now, just forget it, forget it,

He's just a little guy, don't bug him like this I mean a little midget like this who doesn't stand more than three inches tall when you add him all up total -- -- I apologize to you for him   there -- -- I salute you, here, I give you a salute of respect." Lao Ch'iu didn't even so much as look Chang Fa-wu in the eye didn't look at him, but yelled at T'ang Lin: "Hand it over!" So T'ang Lin dug around down in his pocket and pulled out something that when he brought it out looked like a mahjong tile from some mahjong set, that was a piece of like see "Pineapple shortbread" you know that's a famous product they make around T'ai-chung there. In one vicious sweep Lao Ch'iu grabbed it away from him savagely. "I tell you, -- -- I'd just only just, gone out to take a leak when I heard Lao Kuo say you'd gone in and walked off with it, -- -- of all the cuntstinking stunts -- -- do you know how much a piece of "Pineapple shortbread" costs? Thirty cents a piece, that's what, and so-and-so (--I can't remember the name--) sent me this so I could have a piece to eat, and I've been dying to eat it for days just waiting,   and now you've crushed it all to bits so it isn't even a piece anymore, -- -- just look at that! And the paper's all torn up too!" He peeled open the paper wrapping off the piece of Pineapple shortbread like see, I mean see like taking himself with the utmost seriousness of like total self-concern he went ahead and stuck this piece of "Pineapple Shortbread" into his mouth and see chewed it up like you know.

T'ang Lin quickly rose out of that chair, stood right straight up and fastened the leather belt tightly wrapped around his waist.

"From now on no one is allowed to sit at my place just because they feel like it, no one sits in my place anymore no matter what the reason, no matter, it's off limits, stay out of my place like you know," Sung Hsi said as he walked in and gave his chair a push to shove it back, "If anyone else if he comes around and sits down in my place again, I'll write up like a 'document' I mean you know I'll send it up to report them to the Director, turn it over to him. I'm asking you now, I want to know whether I ought to, everybody sits at his own place I mean like you know -- -- right now go ahead and write and write up a report on this   "

Chang Fa-wu was making fun of T'ang Lin, telling him like, "You, you ought to be I mean thanking me like well see -- if I hadn't saved you, your little hide -- -- you'd be, Little T'ang Lin, you'd be duck soup by now, yeah, one dead little duck -- -- that makes me your own "Holy Jesus Blessed Lord Patron Savior In Heaven Above" while he was talking he pressed the palms of his hands together and waved them up and down a couple of times like that I mean praying like this worshipping motion see you know, "In that case the only right thing for you to do is for you to thank me, that's what you ought to do, so come on, come on, and give me three kowtows!"

"Kowtow to you, you big fatso!!" T'ang Lin's eyes lit up suddenly as they landed on a newly discovered target like this which just happened to be exactly what he needed, that came to him like I mean suddenly struck him as he hit on it like you know. Chang Fa-wu he like ran full speed ahead you know right out of the office with his hands up in the air like so like. T'ang Lin was right behind him racing to catch up when he crashed into Li Yü-chen, the woman they call Foxy the Vamp, got knocked so silly he was seeing stars.

"You've gotta be blind you   you're gonna kill yourself chasing and racing around like that aren't you? Tired of living is that it or **what** like!?"

By now T'ang Lin was completely turned right around so that he was turned around facing exactly opposite the direction he was originally in trying to get outside and facing around behind her looking like some well-to-do pillar of the community about to leap on top of her. But then, T'ang Lin took that broom he had in his hands turned it around and used the tip of the handle on the broomstick to lift up the hem a little down at the bottom of the ch'i-p'ao Li Yü-chen was wearing and expose the like white panties there you know like up there above her knees there see.

"Drop dead, you, you, pig. Mama's gonna chop you off you wait and see when I catch up with you you'll see you lowlife." Li Yü-chen took off after T'ang Lin she went after him like in hot pursuit see -- -- T'ang Lin had already dropped that you know that broom he'd thrown it away and was making a run for the door to get out.

Chang Fa-wu came running in through another door yelling at her:

"Foxy, hey, vamp, Foxy the Vamp."

"Foxy, you old vamp, hey, I saw your thigh, the whole thing all of it, no white meat there!" Lao Ch'iu the cook was shouting in this loud voice toward the door, from behind her there.

Li Yü-chen caught up with T'ang Lin outside, and T'ang Lin he was making those arms of his making those arms dance in a spin like a Ta-tung brand electric fan. That way the two of them were at a stand-off see like they just stood there you know like stood each other off in a deadlock there like. So then pretty soon T'ang Lin took off like you know he ran back into his office there I mean like see.

"Hey, midget, you little midget you just wait and see, one day Mama's gonna pinch you good pinch you to death just like pinching a bug   !   " Li Yü-chen came in and said to him.

"Foxy you old Vamp -- -- if you come around here again like a man-hungry flirt swaggering around, pushing people around, I won't just flip up the bottom of that ch'i-p'ao of yours like the way I just flipped it just now I'll do more than that."

"What are you gonna do -- midget -- -- ? I bet midget here I bet he's gonna get inside our own Foxy vamp's panties that's what he's gonna do like you know, see."

Li Yü-chen's face blushed it went red all over, and she I mean came after the cook Lao Ch'iu to give him a beating, and Lao Ch'iu he pretended to run away like I mean get away like from her hide I mean see, like.

"Not at all, not at all," Chang Fa-wu said, "It's Ch'iu Tsu-chiun himself, he's the one who wants so bad to get into our old Foxy Vamp's panties there, get inside them to smell around our old Foxy Vamp's ass give it a good whiff," Chang Fa-wu said while he wiggled the tip of his nose wiggled it around with his hand.

"Up your mother's twat, stick it up your mother's cunt, -- -- you stupid jerk, dumb swine -- -- " Lao Ch'iu threw a punch that caught Chang Fa-wu in the chest, whack! it sounded, and Chang Fa-wu shuddered, he staggered back he staggered and right away then Lao Ch'iu shoved him back toward on the desk table, -- -- then socked him again, socked him right onto the floor I mean right onto it see

"Good shot -- -- well done, really well done   " T'ang Lin also like joined in see I mean came over to you know give Fat Chang the Pig a punch. Li

Yü-chen she wasn't slow to come on over like to step up and you know get even you know with Chang Fa-wu too see.

Lao Ch'iu sat himself down planted his rump on Chang Fa-wu's stomach sitting tall there like you know facing with his back towards you know Chang Fa-wu's face I mean see so like his head jutting forward at sort of an angle raised way high up jutting out and his arms folded up around across his chest there. At that point T'ang Lin stuck out his hands and dug them see down into Chang Fa-wu's throat like his wind pipe you know, so Chang Fa-wu started beating like on T'ang Lin's back; and then Li Yü-chen started in pulling on like Chang Fa-wu's ears sorta with her hands like, yanked them so hard they were stretched out like a stick of chewing gum or something, and Chang Fa-wu was screaming really like in this shriek you know and like reached out with his other hand to hit Li Yü-chen. Whenever Lu Yü-chen had the chance she'd pound on T'ang Lin's head, so T'ang Lin was thinking up all kinds of ways to grab Li Yü-chen's throat there.

All of a sudden somebody standing close by where they were, raised his voice to yell out: "The District Director's coming!"

The tangled snarl of people piled up on the floor in a heap of bodies immediately broke up everybody in a different like direction, as they got to their feet to stand up and got straight up on their feet there sort of like. But then somebody else came walking past the aperture of the window where they were, slow as molasses so slow it was exasperating how slow, not the District Director, but a colleague who goes around like he's sleepwalking so slow he's like some mental case, a goffer named P'an Chung-liang.

"Ho, ho, ha ha, hee, hee!" Everybody else standing around started you know laughing see.

Lao Ch'iu said: "   It's time for me to get dinner started. I'll be looking for you tonight to settle the score!"

T'ang Lin stood at the head of the office his head held high stuck up defiantly crying out: "**The District Director,** -- -- wouldn't scare me even if Chiang the Bureau Director came down from Taipei himself."

Dinner was served in the dining room. Altogether there were two tables, round ones, both of them, with these small little round shaped rounded wooden bench like stools for chairs like sort of arranged all around them ththere. The tables were set each place arranged with an enamelware bowl that was turned upside down, a pair of chopsticks, and a lightweight aluminum spoon with a point sharp enough to slice the skin off your lips. There were two platters of cooked dishes and a bowl of soup placed at the center of each table, the servings were pretty small and skimpy. The dishes were diced turnips fried in hot peppers, and the other one was a howler with some pig skin mixed in sort of like you know. The soup was a bowl of like this simmered like soup of something marinated in hydrochloric acid with some water added. The director of their Bureau and the secretary didn't quit work that day until it was a little past time to finish up, so when they came by the dining room they were invited in and sat at our table. To listen to him, this director of theirs', made you think of a proprietor of a drugstore set up in one of these wooden mobile trailers (the kind with the like the four revolving wheels underneath it that turn around that kind) that's what he was like. But still he had to pretend to some sort of refinement, with those eyeglasses he wore. I couldn't tell from what people said just what connections he'd relied on to get posted down here in this region. Some people in the Bureau said he was "the best," and some said he was   "crooked."

There was an official announcement posted in the Bureau, the characters sort of scratched out by him with a brush in his own hand in this awkward scrawl: "Recently a colleague or colleagues of this Bureau has (have) been defecating outdoors in the vicinity of the Bureau. Take full caution." Just what caution was he talking about? Did he mean after all that he wanted his colleagues in "this Bureau" to take caution not to step in the shit outside? Or did he mean he wanted to caution these colleagues who were shitting outdoors to be careful not to like I mean let people see them you know like when they were taking a shit outside see? And he has another habit, -- -- he likes to play around with idioms, and the way he plays around with them he finds just exactly the most "inappropriate" misuse of them. Like he'll say, "The accomplishments displayed by our own Bureau this year past do not match those of the previous; we can say indeed '**public   morality   is   declining   daily**'." He saw the goffer P'an Chung-liang would never stay put at his place in the office but always enjoyed wandering and stumbling around aimlessly in the open space outside the office, and called him to come back inside where he gave him a lecture: "Settle down. Like they say, don't be 'restless within quarters!'" As if he didn't know that was meant for wives fooling around with other men.

This Official Bureau Director came over and he sat down atatat the table see like you know; -- -- right away Lin An-pang came up and like I mean with this deferential oh so deferential manner he served the dinner to his honor the Bureau Director and his secretary, see. T'ang Lin well he'd already helped himself to his dinner and he'd already gone through the: "ah, what a splendid meal today, how do they do it?" and like then gone right ahead and started in on his own dinner without paying attention to anybody else, just focussed on himself you know see.

"Sir, I can report to the Director, sir, that today we have a guest with us, -- -- a leading fortune teller, a major theorist famous all over Taipei, a household name in Taipei there isn't any one old or young who hasn't heard of him, Lone Star, -- -- we're especially honored that he has agreed to be with us here in a great harbor, rightly considered as everyone knows as everyone is aware is celebrated like all over Asia, -- --what?"

"Sit down! I said, sit down!" Ts'ui Li-ch'ün called out,   "just eat your dinner!"

"Sit down, now, sit down!" The Deputy Director said.

Chang Fa-wu dropped back down.

The Director leaped to his feet I mean he jumped right up, and held out the palm of his like his big hand you know to me see: "A pleasure, a pleasure, really a shame to have missed an opportunity to meet before, really sorry not to have had such a pleasure."

"Sit down! Give me a break and sit down!" Ts'ui Li-ch'ün yelled: Chang Fa-wu -- -- just a moment before -- -- had decided sorta that he wanted to like stand up again so that he was standing up looming over everything like you know.

"May I know your name, sir?" The director asked.

"Get out of the way!" Ts'ui Li-ch'ün was fuming.

"Great food, just look, -- -- there's plenty of it too. Now this is what I call 'A land of plenty with wealth for all' -- -- 'A wealthy state and prosperous folk'; will you look at how much pig skin there is at this table,   there's enough here like it's simply so much you know to like enough to make a leather shoe big enough for my foot here you know. -- --"

One after another everybody one after the other burst out broke out laughing like you know I mean ravenous like see. And it was Chang Fa-wu he was the one who laughed louder and harder than anybody, and longer, longer, too.

"Nobody tells jokes better, better than you, Director, sir, I just love them love to hear you tell them," Lin An-pang put in right away.

"That's, that's his one special pleasure in life, the Director, he just loves to tell to tell jokes!" The Director was laughing so hard his face was like it was squeezed so tight it was compressed into a fistful, and red, so red it looked like Kuan Kung's* just like his as red as that you know that face of his.

"Excellent, excellent -- -- well, since we're so well supplied with dishes we can go easy on the rice and eat our fill of the platters; -- -- you know what they say, 'when there's meat and vegetables, skip the rice; when you're short on meat and vegetables, fill up first on soup.'" The Deputy Director said.

"Director, sir, you can see we eat pretty well here, the dishes here aren't too far below the quality you find at the Yuan-t'ung Hotel in Taipei, isn't that so?" Chang Fa-wu's hand had an arm lock on the only piece of real, lean pork in the pile of pig skin that he'd fished through and picked out, and it was a relatively good sized one too, all of the size of like a coin sort of as big as that, and what's more, he held this piece of meat straight up resting in mid air right in the middle of everyone, caught the eye of all the people sitting at that table so that every eye was fixed on that piece of meat slice he gripped in his chopsticks, -- --

holding it up there the whole time he was talking, -- -- until finally they watched him as he brought the meat back over to his own bowl and put it down in there.

"What Yuan-t'ung Hotel -- it's **Yuan-shan!**"* Ts'ui Li-ch'ün yelled he was so like I mean so furious.

"It's Yuan-t'ung! It sure is the Yuan-t'ung Hotel! When was there ever a hotel named the Yuan-shan Hotel already? You really are one completely ignorant, immature out-and-out 'hick' of an ignoramus if there ever was one!" Chang Fa-wu swore at him.

Ts'ui Li-ch'ün, -- -- you could see if it wasn't for the Director and the Deputy Director sitting there at the table, he would have responded to Chang Fa-wu's cursing him like that I mean he wanted to jump up, go over and ram his fist down his throat, give him a taste of that. Ts'ui Li-ch'ün's eyes just fastened onto Chang Fa-wu glaring with his eyes, and at the same time he fed the soup ingredients he'd scooped up in his spoon between his lips down into his mouth.

"Well, well, I'd say, ah, -- -- if you compare your food here to the dishes at the 'Yuan-shan Hotel,' I don't know how many times, how many times better yours is," the Director set his chopsticks back down on the table, and said like I mean like: "Just look at what you have here, you've got **exotic gourmet fare from land and sea**'" Chang Fa-wu listened to him blinking his eyes with this stupid dumbfounded look, and the Director went on talking: "I don't know what's so great about the western-style food they serve at the Yuan-shan Hotel, it's so expensive it's incredible. The things those Yankees eat, oh, -- -- hɔŋmm -- -- hɔŋmm -- --" and he acted like Chang Fa-wu just had, just like him, those gestures; -- -- waved his big, bumpy, bulbous, big nose around, -- -- "mm -- -- like some stinking poop   , hwu:, the Chinese food we have is better by a long shot -- -- Chinese food! -- --   Okay! Okay!" Then he started in laughing himself haw haw haw he burst out laughing at the top of his voice; of course the others laughed one after the other doubled up and falling down bent over and sprawling "Chinese food -- -- best in the world!" He stuck up that fat, unbelievably filthy, black smudged thumb of his and crooked it back. "Chinese food -- -- that's the stuff!! Chinese food,   **One hundred percent pure Chinese,   loyal and true through and through!**" He was so pleased with himself when he said that he picked up a little piece of diced turnip and ate it down see like. -- -- All of a sudden Ts'ui Li-ch'ün called out to T'ang Lin: "a! Come on, T'ang Lin, let's have a contest, I'll match you eating   hot peppers   " "You're on, you're on" T'ang Lin's eyes those eyes of his gleamed; he was from Szechuan! Up to that point since he'd been tired out up to that moment, T'ang Lin's face had this yellowy yellowish jaundiced color, and there was like this bluish, throbbing blood vessel see I mean protruding out where it flowed through down the crater of the middle of his forehead. Right away T'ang Lin, just as enthusiastic as he could be, grabbed up his chopsticks

84

you know and like picked up one of those red peppers see, opened up that mouth of his good and plenty, and put this red pepper right in his mouth see like you know. Then, all of a sudden, T'ang Lin flung his chopsticks down, half covered his mouth with one hand, and screeched at the top of his voice like some pig getting slaughtered like this" "Yee -- ah, ah! Damn!" Then after a minute, he picked up another one of those red peppers and put it inside his mouth there. "Yee -- ah, ah -- -- ah, ah!" And again he brought his hand up and you know he cupped it over his mouth sorta like see. Now, Ts'ui Li-ch'ün, well -- his eyes were brimming I mean full up with like tears you know -- -- and he had the old noodle noggin had it, his head, see, bent down low, chewing away on that mean, I mean the meanest, red pepper down inside his mouth there, and he was smiling to himself like in this you know secretlike secretive way like sort of see.

At the dining table there, Lin An-pang had some sort of guilty feelings something he was ashamed of, the way like he was eating his food that way like -- just the way he looked all hunched up bent over at the waist and the way he looked holding his that aluminum soup spoon, it was as if he was stealing a drop of Immortal Essence or something, ladling out just a little bit into his rice bowl where he'd like he'd stir it around some to mix it in with his rice see you know like that. Another one -- -- I forget his name,   his name,   what is it -- I just know his surname is "Yang" -- -- sat leaning, leaning back leaning way, way back out away from where the table is, gripping his enamelware bowl in his hand the whole time without a break, so that I never did seen him see him lean over up close and bend over next to the tip edge the edge the edge of the rim of the outer rim of the table, nor did I ever see him once let that bowl out of his hands, I mean he never parted with it, so much as set it back, set it back down down on top of that table ever you know. another one -- -- named Liu, it seems, that's what I remember -- with this face, a squared-off square shaped big boney jagged face with this naturally deep dark swarthy deep complexion, who never spoke a word I mean the whole time like you know like, so it seemed that the whole time he had his mind someplace else on something else, on the one hand he was right like there sort of eating his dinner like I mean, and then again it was like he was silently reciting to himself, reciting "The Faults of Ch'in."*

The secretary -- Fu Shao-k'ang -- had his hair cut in a little crewcut flatop like up there, with a small patch of whitish furry hair sort of growing right in the middle where a tuft of the hair along the front of his little crewcut sloped down, and a good long black whisker sticking out of a dark mole down under his right jaw was growing out. He asked me, he asked:

"How did you happen to come here where we are to tell fortunes?"

"ä," the Director said, -- -- right away he put down the bowl and the chopsticks he'd been holding, "How about giving my face a reading,   hey, how about it?" That said, he took off the eyeglasses he was wearing and set them down like you know and then then he showed me a face with I mean like these swollen, puffed out, bloated eyelids see like.

"Your face is   quite, quite presentable   " -- -- I answered him sorta you know like that's how I put it.

"Will you have a look, please, -- please, have a look," he said, with his two hands clasped together into a big ball of fists like holding them up the whole time in this gesture of respect, of supplication over and over again.

"How about another day, try it another day, we'll pick a time and a place, go over you with a good close reading, give you a careful reading."

"Ah, please, please, oh please do a reading for me, do a reading," he went on non-stop gesturing in supplication, and after that he raised his hands up over his eyebrows, high up like you know I mean, -- -- imploring me, begging me with this gesture of deference. He didn't even realize at all that what I'd just said to him like it was you know like an expression of respect for him -- -- he actually thought what I'd said to him just now all that was some kind of refusal!

"Ai, ai,   go on and give our Director a reading, let him have one, -- -- there's nothing the Director likes better than having someone read his face for him like lilililike you know," -- -- even other people had the same idea he did, the very same idea.

And on he went gesturing away over and over again continuously non-stop without pause.

"If I were you, -- -- **I'd give him a reading right now**   !" T'ang Lin started in saying that see you know -- -- he'd just finished eating his supper, and he'd gotten out that bamboo thing like he uses as a "cigarette holder," so he was in the middle of puffing away "swallowing clouds and spewing vapor."

So of course there wasn't anything I could do but give him a reading you know. Actually reading his face turned out to be one of the rarest of life's weird experiences! The whole time I was talking to him about like his face, he was busy keeping his expression straight giving himself a well-formed, a "well proportioned" countenance see, and it just simply looked like he was making this freakish looking grimace at me   ;   Well, the only thing I could do was drivel on some drivel like for a while like see like, and naturally the most crucial thing was to say something about how any time now he was soon due at any moment for a big promotion up to like you know Central Bureau Director see, you know like. Right away His Honor the Director he looked around all around, waving his palms waving his palms constantly, and like you know like holding back this smile he had and saying like he said you know sort of: "I couldn't, no, I really couldn't, it's not for me. I don't have any interest in a job like Central Bureau Director -- --; -- -- ʃʌks -- -- "

"If I were you -- -- **I'd take it!**" T'ang Lin was quick to follow up with that comment -- -- -- --

86

His Honor the Director, His Excellency -- -- had a face you could say was I mean like this dark leaden heavy heavy mess! What I saw when I got down to reading, -- -- what I saw was the "**face of a nitwit,**" and to add to that besides, an "**unlucky face**"!

Then, after something like about three minutes, about four minutes, about five minutes -- -- Chang Fa-wu all of a sudden shot over see fast as an arrow he was so fast, ran over like up in front of this Director of ours see I mean you know and stood there with his arms and back rigidly braced at attention like see you know and he called out in this loud, excited, this ardent voice, he called out:

"Your Excellency!   I shall serve you rice, sir! -- --"

"Very good,   just make it about three-quarters of a bowl   that'll be fine" The Director said this when he spoke, when he replied.

Chang Fa-wu instantly picked up the Director's round bowl, and flew off running over to where the big pot they serve rice in is see like.

"Sir, I must report," he ran back over in this crestfallen dejected way to say, " -- -- there's no more rice   ."

Then with both hands, rigid and straight, absolutely rigidly straightened out straight and rigid, he returned the bowl he had taken back over to this Director of his, -- -- and surrendered his "rice bowl"!   Next see like what happened next he started calling out one after the other:

"Send out -- -- send out P'an Chung-liang! He is to procure and deliver **Hsiaolung dumplings**, procure and deliver **sliced meat dumplings**, procure **meat ravioli**, -- -- and **steamed meatpies**! -- --"

"What are you talking about -- -- Hsiaolung dumplings, sliced meat dumplings, ravioli, steamed meatpie -- --" Ts'ui Li-ch'ün yelled out he was I mean so indignant he was sort of swearing you know like

"Please, please, -- -- don't trouble yourselves on my account -- -- as for me, I've already got a "swelled head and stuffed shirt to match" as they say, I'm quite full, yes, quite full, quite full -- -- please, why   don't   you   sit down   , please, have a seat, have a seat."

"Your Excellency, I must decline, with all respect, sir, it would be better for me to stand here, I feel: Your Excellency, I was unable to serve you food just now, sir, and I really ought to stand up right here for a while, sir, -- -- I can bring my bowl over and eat standing up here."

"Of all the mother xxxxxxxxxxxx ---! -- you, I'm telling you, sit down!" Ts'ui Li-ch'ün was yelling I mean he was so angry he couldn't like stop you know he like lost it he yelled: "Sit down, you! When the Director tells you to sit down then you sit down!"

"That's right, that's right, sit back down!" The Director said like you know see like.

"Yes, Your Excellency. Yes, yes, sir," Chang Fa-wu's face it blushed red you know, and he sat down, -- -- after that he just hung his head you know like, blushing red all over red red all over -- --

"We do have a couple of mentally ill persons here -- -- Among them there's one called P'an Chung-liang -- --"

Chang Fa-wu suddenly interrupted Ts'ui Li-ch'ün by getting to his feet kaplop and starting to sing a song in a good loud voice:

"Charge! Charge! Fearing neither wind nor rain, chests out, striding forward, Charge! -- -- now that the dining ceremony is concluded, I'll sing a song to lift my superior's spirits, -- -- ambition soaring high high as mountain peaks, indignation -- --"

At this point the lights in the dining hall suddenly went out I mean off like, and all you could hear was the sound of people calling out over and over again like shouting you know like:

"P'an Chung-liang! It's   P'an Chung-liang !   "

Somebody rushed out, I could sort of sense it from like the squared off square glowing pearl colored space of the doorframe frame.

After a second just a moment later, I could hear outside whack the sound of a heavy blow, a punch.

Then there was silence.

And after that well then the lights like came back came back on you know see.

By that time Chang Fa-wu was no longer in the room anymore already; he had like I mean he'd just like burst his way outside already outdoors I mean like you know like see. The guy from the other table -- -- the one who'd just before rushed outside and punched out Chang Fa-wu -- -- his name's Sheng Ch'i-chih -- -- came running back into the the office. You could see Chang Fa-wu see him outside the office still hanging around out there running back and forth back and forth over and over facing toward us inside the office singing away right at the top of his voice:

"Determination solid as brass and hard as iron; Our aim lofty and eternal as the heavens."

"We have two mentally disturbed persons here," the Deputy Director continued to say.

"If I were you, **I wouldn't sing!**" T'ang Lin said.

"I imagine you all have eaten enough to have **swelled shirts and stuffed heads** too just about, so now why don't we, let's everybody call it an evening, let's, as they say, see how all the monkeys run off when the big tree falls, how about it now I mean like let's see let's see," the Director stood up to say this and burst out laughing to his heart's content.

Just then all of a sudden a strong, chilling, creepy gust of air as cold as ice blew down, it like blew down sort of from overhead up about directly above high, high up like; -- -- the electric fan with these like long, long leafed blades that was installed hanging from the ceiling overhead switched itself on and started churning around grinding sort of. At that moment I heard Chang Fa-wu outside the window let out this big laughing roar of a laugh.

"Chang Fa-wu! Chang Fa-wu! It's Fat Chang messing around!"

In a flash Ts'ui Li-ch'ün had bent over forward at the waist, and it was like it looked like an arrow sort of released from a bow string see, and the sound that went with it it was a low, rumbling sort of long growl that came from down inside his throat, I mean, the way he shot forward there toward the door you know I mean it was so fast. Chang Fa-wu by this time was long gone see like gone without even so much as the trace of a shadow even you know like.

When I went to the Bureau this time, from the look of it it seemed like my luck was taking a change for the better. My astrological dates and Fu Shao-k'ang's were compatible, on the whole, -- -- believe it or not, a good match. The day before yesterday Chang Fa-wu drew me into writing some characters in brush for him so he could you know stick them up hang them up sort of I mean, and the characters that I wrote out for him read: "Close Door When Entering or Leaving," got posted up high overhead over the door to the bathroom there. I wrote those damn characters out wrote them so they'd like look you know bold and imposing, in the style of "the stele of the Yen Family Temple,"* and they really turned out to have awesome forcefulness. The way Fu Shao-k'ang acted when he saw them was something like this, I believe, he stood right in front of the door that door to the bathroom, he had his pants pulled down still, he'd totally forgotten to pull them back up, and simply stood there in place with his mouth open hollering on and on you know about how great they looked: "Those characters are great! Those characters are great, that's the Yen style!" And, to my complete surprise, Fu Shao-k'ang began speaking to me on his own accord, telling me a vacancy in the Bureau might open up here: Somebody, maybe named Ch'ü, was now requesting leave, probably he'd found a better job already, in sum, he very likely wasn't coming back -- he, Fu Shao-k'ang, wanted to help me seriously look into the possibility of a way of arranging a position for me here, and he told me to wait about a week or so more or less to see what the possibilities might be like, if any. What Fu Shao-k'ang did wasn't only an act of showing "concern for persons of ability" but he also did this as well out of a sympathy he felt for what my life had been like and the situation I'm in. The next day when I went to their Bureau for a meal, he asked me again you know he asked I mean, well, (-- the same question he'd asked me already twenty-four hours before) -- -- he asked me like well why you know like like why I mean I'd come here see like sort of. So I started in piling it on saying anything I could think of, pouring it on non-stop: "I started out in business in Taipei, -- -- the export business. Unfortunately, the partner I had, who was from my home town (hey -- -- well, well,　　he was named Fu, too) that I set up the business with   to start with,   drove me bankrupt. This old neighbor of mine, I could see, well, -- -- he was in pretty poor health, and his family was a tremendous burden for him, so I , well, -- -- forget it -- -- I won't go into all that you know -- -- what it came down to in the end was that I just took off myself to look around try and see if I could do some fishing like you know, see whether I could see carve out a realm for myself. . . see what I could do to find another place for myself. . . ." and so on and so on and so on and so forth. He didn't just feel concern for my "**ability**," he even "**worshipped**" me, pure and simple. He couldn't praise me enough, he said I was "a true gentleman of the old school," the way I'd acted; he said, I was a model of probity, and he said I was "Yen Hui reincarnated." Check it out, check it out -- -- all right -- -- anyway I wouldn't be any the worse off for waiting a while,

Chang Fa-wu told me you can pull down over seven hundred a month working here. According to him, that's a lot more than you can get fishing, you know, like nearly one hundred dollars or so more, somewhere in that range more or less. Chang Fa-wu himself makes only five hundred a month. Still, he didn't show a trace of envy, not a trace -- -- he was so "respectful" of me simply to a point that I didn't know how a person's psyche could bear it you know. I mean -- -- he was saying things like: "After all you made captain in the army* -- -- You ought to be worth as much money as that."

But how could something as good as this be true, and this had to be too good to be true, so, on the contrary, I couldn't believe it would truly be brought off successfully, you know what I mean like. I've had far, far too many of this sort of experience of this kind in the past like this, -- -- I know this one couldn't come through.   It had no more chance of coming true than a tale from *The Arabian Nights*. And just so, I took it as something "modestly proposed -- -- and skeptically received," and let it take its own course by itself.

After a few days in the Department here I discovered that everybody in the place was actually an invalid suffering from some malady or other. The entire Evacuation Organization was in fact a sanatorium -- -- the central organization in Taipei had organized all their injured and lame, all the old, or weak, or crippled soldiers, into a corps and sent the whole lot sent them all down to this region. Whenever you're in the Department no matter what time it is, you don't have to listen to them talk away for more than ten minutes before you'll hear the topic of their conversation wander back to one thing, "illness."

For instance, to cite an example, the day before yesterday when I went over to their office to wait for lunch there was a whole bunch of them "shootin' the breeze" about one thing and another and while they were going on like that see, like, I could hear Lao Ch'iu making himself heard braying away about -- I swear I couldn't hear anything more than **snatches** of whatever damned thing he was saying -- -- but it seemed it was that his illness had been acting up suddenly a couple of nights before: ". . . and then my right leg went numb -- --

and then, right after that, my right hand went numb too. After a while, I slowly started to get some feeling sort of back like in my left leg again, but at that point my left arm went numb again so I couldn't feel anything at all, -- -- fuck it, I'm sick all over -- -- can't die and I can't get well, either!"

That got everybody listening to him starting to laugh "hah hah hah hah" like chortling away.

A fellow who looked younger than him, I think his name was something like Pi as I recall it seems, this guy asks the cook asks him: "How old are you ? -- --"

"How old? Forty two!"

"I'll never live to 42," the guy said in all seriousness. And everybody standing around started in laughing over him, too, with a hearty "hah hah hah hah hah hah hah hah" like.

"That illness you've got -- --" Lao Ch'iu the cook said, "it's not serious. I've seen people with it who're 45."

Later that same day, in the afternoon, I saw something else at the Bureau:

Lin An-pang went over next to Sung Hsi's desk and said to him, "ǎ, Lao Sung, -- -- I want to tell you something -- -- last night before I went to bed, not long before that, I suddenly discovered one of my eyes -- -- my left one, that eye -- -- couldn't see! I closed my eyes good for a minute and then opened them again. It was a little better then, but my vision was still blurry! so then I closed my eyes again, -- -- and then this time I saw this strange thing, something really weird, weird really odd, -- -- just at the top of my left eye, just above it a little -- -- there was this roundish thing, round and red, red red like red all over, shaped like an egg, -- -- and it's still there suspended up there still now -- -- ǎ, Old Sung -- -- I was wondering, so, could I put in for a two-day -- -- just a two-day -- -- 'sick leave,' I mean, -- -- that way I could catch the train to Taipei to see a physician, so is that all right?"

"-- -- Huh? You say you see an   egg?"

"Yes, I see this   chicken's egg."

"Huh? The egg's red, -- -- that's what you say?"

"Yes, red."

"The egg's red, strange, -- -- is it a real deep reddish red?"

"That's it, right, a deep, reddish red."

"Have you seen a jouk in this egg?"

"A yolk? -- -- No, I haven't."

"Isn't that curious? -- -- Just the same size as a chicken egg? -- -- Is it bigger on top, smaller at the bottom, or small at the top, bigger at the botəm?"

Lin An-pang raised his head back and covered up his left eye, the one that he had lost sight in, with his hand, and looked over up into where there was light.

"It's getting to be bigger than it was before. Right now it looks pretty much like the size of a rubber ball sorta like about as big as, -- -- hey, wait a minute   , there it is,   it looks like right in the middle there's something like an egg yolk, -- -- can I request leave tomorrow to go to see a doctor in Taipei do you think do you?"

Sung Hsi just answered, he answered him like this, he said:

"Aw, I can't help you there, -- -- you can't arrange a request for leave to go to Taipei unless the Director himself gives his approval you know, -- -- there's no way I have the authority to give you a decision for something like that." -- -- He picked up the knight-errant novel he was in the middle of reading when he'd put it down on the desk and went back to reading the novel without giving Lin An-pang so much as another thought. So then Lin An-pang slowly walked away, very slowly, off in the direction toward where it was light you know like with one hand covering up that eye of his, the left one that had the problem that one.

It wasn't as if Lin An-pang just suddenly had this eye problem of his and that's all see, like I mean he was already like a TB case too. But you've never before ever seen a such a patient like he is with a case of TB like that that kind kind of who's got so much optimism as he does. He'll say things like he'll tell you: "This TB of mine's no big deal, nothing to it, it's nothing," and wave it off with a wave of his hands, "Altogether there's two kinds of TB: My kind's no big deal." -- -- It's as if he were like comforting you or something, -- -- almost as though you were the person with tuberculosis instead of him, -- -- he'll go on and say: "There's a lot of neighbors from my hometown, -- -- they're all running pharmacies and such, -- -- and I went and asked them all about it. And I still go to see them all the time and ask for something effective to cure TB -- -- and they give me free all the stuff I take without charge, everything -- -- so when I have time I go see them and get myself some medicine to take, get some medicine to take," he mimes it with his hands, makes some gestures to show how he puts the medicine in his mouth, "-- -- I'll be doing fine before long -- -- it's nothing, I'll have this licked in no time."   Lin An-pang's pate's as bald as a billiard ball up top there, so he combs his hair across you know like from one side to the other kind of kindalike like it's a sheet of black silk or something the way it looks. His skin is pure white and fair all over; and he's got a big, big, long, broad, wide, wide mouth, really wide -- -- Yesterday I was also at the banquet the Department gives as a sort of group celebration like of birthdays during the first three months of this year, the first quarter see, (-- -- actually I don't have any idea what month or day or even hour I was born really not a clue like so I'd just written whatever came to mind when I was filling out my ID form and took that as my birthday kind of sorta like,) so everybody put up two yuan each to get together after the supper and pay the kitchen to get them to cook up some extra small dishes to go with a drinking party we were going to have to celebrate the occasion sort of. And Lin An-pang sat down next to my place, he sat up real close next to me there, (there was still an egg there -- -- according to him -- -- he could see in that eye, and what's more there still was a yellow yolk core in the middle of it), and he asked me, he put it to me like this, he said: "I want to ask your advice about sᴧmethiŋ -- -- do you mind? I wanted to ask you this, whether a person with TB -- -- somebody like that -- -- whether they shouldn't be allowed to drink alcohol at all, no matter what their condition, if that's so?"

"Should be -- -- I've never heard of anybody with a case of TB who was allowed to drink as they pleased." (Actually this was the first time I'd ever heard anything about a matter like this, like this one, at all.)

"No, no, no. I don't drink at all," he kept on waving his hands while he talked: "even though I have TB -- -- let me ask you again -- -- alright? Do you mind? -- -- Say, ah, say there was this person, say he had TB, now if -- -- just occasionally -- -- he had a sip, just had just a little sip, -- -- he couldn't have that, either -- -- could he?"

"Of course not -- -- if he's not allowed to drink then naturally that means he shouldn't drink any, not even a drop."

"I don't, I don't at all," his hands waved.

Then after a while had gone by sort of, why he started asking me questions all over again he well he said like:

"Let me ask you another question -- -- do you mind? -- -- I wanted to ask you whether someone with TB should also shouldn't be allowed to gamble (he made stirring motions with his hands as though shuffling mahjong tiles around,) or go whoring (this time he was stumped for gestures that he could act this out with,) right?   "

"Absolutely not! He shouldn't!" I uttered this prohibition as if I were scolding a child.

"I don't at all, not at all, -- -- I'm the sort of person who really behaves extremely well, extremely proper, never gamble, nothing to do with prostitutes" (this time he actually did make a gesture, -- -- just like a gesture like waving his hands like.)

Still, though, Lin An-pang, well he couldn't resist a temptation like sipping a little of what he liked so much, and he watched some of the others play the "guess fingers" drinking game with the keenest interest, the most intense interest, the strongest interest. Then you know he well he couldn't hold out any longer against his own temptation sort of so well I mean so like he he joined right in too, cocked his fist up back over behind his ear to one side and the next thing out came his fingers like he stuck them out you know see like. And each time he stuck out his fingers almost he'd lose, so then to his great delight it was sheer pleasure for him to down the penalty drink each time one cup after another on and on like that you know.

Somebody like that, -- -- don't I know it -- -- could be at death's door, I mean they could be laying him out inside his own coffin like you know, and he'd still have this totally optimistic slap happy smile on his face I mean like he'd be grinning from ear to ear, he would.

Around noontime the same day T'ang Lin had gotten so completely carried away with excitement when he got his hands on one of those those big large kraft paper envelopes, those sheath things, pouches, pouches sort of that they use to mail official documents in one of those things -- -- with a tiny little "Fight TB" postage stamp on it so small, you know -- -- he'd gotten so carried away that he'd yelled over to like Lin An-pang shouted across to him you know I mean he'd **screamed** like that sort of see, he'd said: "Hey, get a look at this, people donated their money to you, see, for this postage stamp, like you see that, eh?"

"Wha? Ah,   hah hah hah hah -- -- but how come I didn't get even a dime out of it, eh?" He said this pointing towards his own the tip of his own nose like.

There's another case in the Bureau, another sick person -- -- goes by the name Yü Shih-liang, that's what he's called -- -- who is about as "interesting" a case as Lin An-pang. The thing about Yü Shih-liang is that he's such a gentle, gentle person you know I mean like -- -- you could scream at him the worst insults all you want and he'd, why he'd, he'd like I mean express his agreement with you and he'd say so to you in the mildest way like see. He has this long, long, narrow, thin, thin facial face sort of like, a short, close cropped crew cut that sits up on his head the top of his head there, and something like the thinnest of thin wrinkles for a mouth, so small it's like two pieces of thread, thread it's that minute, and then there are those teeth of his, a row of the tiniest little thin grains of rice, itsy bitsy little thin grains one after the other one by one that you can see the way they look like that each time he wrinkles up his nostrils and laughs in that amiable gentle way of his, that soft meek way. Yü Shih-liang was also sick with pulmonary tuberculosis you know like, "It was summer the year before last," was what he said, "I tired myself out moving one of those big banyan trees that was blown down in a typhoon and then sawed up into pieces, lots of them like, you know, so in the middle of the night I started spitting up blood, one mouthful after another." His body now is as frail as slender and delicate as a as a thin wisp of a willow branch one of those threadlike things; but then he showed me a photo of what he used to look like, taken about ten years ago, and he looked completely different from what he looked like now, not at all the same. In the photo he looked at least about twice as big as that slight puny body he has now, just about that much bigger. You simply couldn't believe your very own eyes -- -- if he looked any more different you'd, well, you'd begin to wonder whether or not he was, after all, -- -- neurotic? But still those beady little grains of rice kernels he has for teeth that showed up in that photo of him (it was a shot from the waist up) were entirely identical to that row of teeth he has now, (-- -- except that his smile back then was like the kind of smile that revealed this like row of teeth all lined up like sorta glistening with this dazzling gleam the way they sparkled like you know, like that.) They say that there's no way that teeth can ever be altered in appearance so to speak, -- -- some friends of mine in police circles once told me something like that I mean see like: even supposing there was a situation like this where a person -- -- just by a chance in ten thousand even if something like this happened to him -- -- where there wasn't a scrap left of him so much as a shred of him left except just a single tooth see like, that wouldn't create any problem at all, you could still identify him as so-and-so and such-and-such. The reason he's gotten to like like he's in such an "emaciated" state of appearance like you know umm it's not solely on account of his TB that he's gotten like this way see, but also it's because it's well it's got something to do with his wife's mental abnormality. Altogether over the span of the past eight years his wife's illness has acted up a number of taimz -- -- so far these past eight years, -- -- during these eight years everything that's needed doing in the home no matter how important or how how trivial, needless to say things like washing clothes and cooking, all of it he's had to do like by himself alone you know see. The day before yesterday, -- -- in the evening -- -- not too long before we eat supper, about then like, he sat in the office, and without thinking about it he just fell into talking to me about all this you know well sorta talking like: "The very first time, -- -- there wasn't any special reason: -- -- one day I was going to go into Taipei: at that time we hadn't yet moved to Taipei, and we were still living in Chung-li it was um, so the day before she told me she wanted me to buy her a pair of leather shoes, and so what I said to her was um you know I said lilililike you know sort of: "Fine. If you'll draw what they look like for me then when I go to Taipei tomorrow I can pick up a pair for you and bring them back." So right away she traced the outline of her foot, okay, but then when she drew a picture of the shoe it was really pretty awful looking: so then I said to her "Why don't you draw it so that it looks a little better, all right? -- -- What you've drawn there   looks   pretty ugly!" As it happened, just at that moment, there was this Mrs. K'ung who lived not far away, close by just a couple doors down from us, standing at at that moment next to my wife. Mrs. K'ung's husband had been transferred to work down in Tainan. So at that moment Mrs. K'ung was standing there next to her and what she said um, it was you know, um like um see: "-- -- Gosh -- -- you're really a case! How come you can't even draw a decent picture of a shoe?" As soon as my wife heard that well did she did she like ever get angry I mean, boy, like that instant she took off and ran into her bedroom and closed the door behind her you know see well. Then later that night in the dead of night along around about the middle of the night, midnight more or less, she started in like you know started um acting strange you know, I mean, she said: "Why was it that   you said my drawing was bad, -- -- she also said my drawing wasn't good enough, -- -- just what's going on between the two of you that's such a secret you can't talk about it to anyone openly?" That's how it was, that's like how she started to lose it, really lose control. So after that I had to put her into the hospital, and there I was with not a cent to my name, and no choice but to rely on some colleagues I worked with and a few of the people I was close to from my home town, to contribute a little money to commit her to the hospital, where she stayed for just about close to two months or so before she came out again like got out I mean. After she got out of the hospital I had her rest as much as possible, let her get a good rest, and took on everything that needed doing at home myself -- -- but even so even with this arrangement she's had these sudden relapses constantly, where like her old symptoms will recur at any time I mean you know   like,   that time in 1957," it sounded like he said '57 pretty much, "that was the most serious. That episode, what took place then, was really and truly awful, just awful, awful -- -- the way she looked she looked absolutely **terrifying**!   She coiled her hair up and piled it coiled up high on top of her head then cinched it up tight like tied up with a piece of hemp string sort of. This hemp string the length of it just hung there dangling down suspended where it swung around. There was half a piece of bamboo chopstick stick that had been snapped in two stuck through into that pile of hair she'd tied up in a bunch like there sort of. She was wearing a **different kind** of stocking on each foot. On one foot she had a long ramie stocking, rolled down over and over layer on layer until it was all piled up like, and on the other foot she had on a tiny little short sock, a deep dark green color. Really that time it was really **awful** -- -- that time she had a fit that went on nonstop for three or four nights or more straight without sleeping, refusing to go to sleep, that's how bad that's how scary it was, and it went on for so long I was dead tired, it was like I'd been through something like a marathon race, that kind kind of experience, you know um I mean it it it well you know, it was a bad situation   , I didn't have any way to go out and raise more money again to send her to the hospital, --- -- all of my colleagues at the office who were willing to contribute had already 'contributed' long ago already -- -- by that time we'd already moved to Taipei and were living there see like -- -- no one would be willing to donate a second time -- -- so the only thing I could do was to keep her like at home there you know, and so then on account of that, the longer I kept her at home the worse she got. And every day I left her at home during the day I was so nervous so extremely upset I couldn't calm down -- -- it wasn't just her alone, there was also the problem of fire safety for the home itself, and the two little ones who needed to be with her, whether that was safe or not. So, later I told my number one and number two sons to drop school and stay home to look after their mother and two little brothers, but even so I still felt uneasy.   She was always walking in and out of the place holding a big vegetable chopper from the kitchen. She'd keep holding that cleaver up saying: "   Why don't we have any sausage? Even at New Year's we don't make any, -- -- so I'm going to make some now, a few pounds of it ! " As she was saying this she'd reach out and grab one of the smaller boys, the child she'd always grab was always Lao San,   since um in those days the son we called Lao San was actually on the plump side then sort of you know," At that point, when I heard that, I burst out laughing, this guffaw of a laugh -- -- and the bridge of Yü Shih-liang's nose, at the same time, it wrinkled up around there and he joined in laughing with me too see like and, and then, then right after that I mean like his voice changed I mean it got absolutely somber the way he said it: "   But compared to a few years ago Lao San these days looks a lot thinner, a whole lot thinner by far. "-- -- As he said this he shook his head slightly, just a little, back and forth. I couldn't help laughing again in that guffawing sound. After that Yü Shih-liang went on talking: "Lao Da, my first son, he was a good boy, only ten years old then   and already each time this happened he'd always he'd get in between his little brother and his mom to protect him with his own body, block her, and he'd say: "Mama," he'd say, "If you're going to kill someone then kill me, don't kill my little brother!"   And the strange thing is, so strange, it's really so strange, once my wife heard him say that whenever she like heard those words you know, right away she'd put down that vegetable chopper and set it aside like and at the same time she was putting it away she'd suddenly burst out laughing for joy, chortling and chortling away out of sheer pleasure like see. But then just as quickly she'd start in weeping, tears coming down like rain they'd flow, and she'd sit there wanting to be able to catch hold of the little one, pick him up in her arms and hold him in her embrace, just hug him in her arms like like see, but all the kids everyone of them was scared of her and they kept away from her as much as possible did all they could to keep away   from her,   that illness, what a pity it is too,   such a shame it is. Sometimes you'll see her sitting by herself staring straight ahead with this idiotic look she's so lost in some thought,   nothing to say, not a word, just tear drops, running down covering her face all over the way they roll down like rounded round pearls off a broken string.   If you saw what she looks like when she eats you'd feel for her too, really, how sad, how pathetic she is like I mean you know, I'd always take her a bowl of rice, fill it up over half way sort of with like white rice -- -- with some soy sauce on top and add some beancurd whathaveyou mixed in like sorta, and leave it on top of the table -- -- then when I'd come back home in the evening I'd always take a look you know like, and most of the time the food in her bowl hadn't even been touched by a chopstick at all, not even touched, like. Sometimes I'd find her bowl had been moved and set down on the ground like see, and there were times when all these ashes left over from the burnt coal were dumped in.   Not too long after that I started thinking again of every way I could to raise like enough funds you know to put her in the hospital see um totototo have her committed I mean.   There like there wasn't any other um special reason in particular why things got into the you know the state they were in except um well just plain   **poverty**, the kind of poverty that like itititit just kept on and on and on accumulating and mounting up over these past several years sort of like you see like.   We overdid it a little on children.   When she had Lao San and Lao Ssu, our third and fourth, I tried to persuade her to get an abortion, but she well no matter what you said to her she wouldn't do it, even said she wanted to go ask a priest to see if she could, see like.   Each time she talked with the priest he told her it was against Church rules to do that and was forbidden, so she -- -- " Suddenly just at that moment Chang Fa-wu and T'ang Lin came running in, one like behind the other chasing him, -- -- the one doing the chasing was T'ang Lin, the other was in full flight ahead of him, both of them ran circles twice all around in a circumference around us like frenzied lunatics the both of them, and then it was like in you know the blink of an eye sorta like, -- -- like a puff of smoke -- -- the two of them ran off and disappeared without a trace, without even a sign of where they'd gone you know that you could find not even not even that even like see.

He, that's Yü Shih-liang, he lowered his eyes slightly, just a little bit, and picked at the crevice under the finger nail of one finger with the finger nail of another finger, something you could see him do all the time, a way of acting, a gesture, a look he had you could see all the time whenever he was talking.   Then he started to go on talking: "Later, it was   last year, she had another attack where she went totally deranged, -- -- that was after she gave birth, -- -- and compared with the terrible episode she'd had in '57," -- -- good -- -- good -- -- so it was '57 after all, that takes care of that! -- -- "   it was just as bad!   I still couldn't think up any way to raise the money for her to be admitted to the hospital to totototo get to get some treatment you know like I mean like.   But this time that church she went to all the time helped her a lot, a whole lot like you know they did a lot for her see like um you know um so well, now that priest she'd gone to see at that church, he's been a big help to her, arranged for her to stay in this therapeutic treatment nursing home medical hospital that's run completely as a charity by these Roman Catholics where you don't even have to pay them so much as a cent not a thing nothing at all for all the medicine, the therapy, and the nursing care she needs.   And now,   since I'm not living in Taipei and I don't have someone at home to look after them, I've placed all four of my children each in a different orphanage like ah well um see." When he got to this point, Yü Shih-liang, he raised his eyes, looked up with such an amiable, gentle smile of utter warmth and gentleness and like said you know like: "I don't know whether this last episode she went through was linked in some way that was related to her giving birth; all together she had an extremely difficult time   giving birth; extremely dangerous; in the end it it it it was you know um like stillborn, so I mean she well miscarried you know sort of sortalike. I don't know whether giving birth this last time was bad for her like ruined her health, and that set off a recurrence of her her illness see you know like. Giving birth this time was really risky, it was a big risk -- -- she just about lost her pulse twice -- -- so then the attending physician gave her a shot right away   -- -- and then later on he gave her a blood transfusion, -- -- the doctor ended up giving her   three transfusions altogether,   that many.   By the third time he transfused her I didn't have any money left on me to pay the fees for any more of these expenses. I still needed to come up with another thousand. To pay for the blood plasma, -- -- I had to pay cash on the spot. The money I'd borrowed and brought with me to pay the medical expenses for the birth, well, they were all already spent on the first and second blood transfusions, see, -- -- so all I had left over on me at that point was altogether only just a little over three hundred. That doctor saw I looked like I was having a hard time, so then he asked me, he said: 'Just what do you want,   **your money**   **or her life?**' He had a short temper, that doctor. Actually, the way I see it personally, it's no,   you know, it's no big deal, no big, enormous deal, if you know somebody dies. It's just that he kept on pushing me that way, pushing me to give him some definite sorta answer, so the only thing I could do was go along with him, to do whatever there was, no matter what, to have him get someone to do anything there was to do to save her.

Then he told me: go out and raise the money right now this instant -- --- meanwhile he could bring her out of it and save her, -- -- he could telephone a place that sells blood plasma and tell them the purchaser was temporarily short of cash at the moment, but he'd be over in a little while right away to pay for it see like. But, that doctor told me, he wanted me definitely to bring the money back that day to the hospital there, -- -- he said, because, if he didn't you know like get the money to that place I mean that sells blood plasma well then you know like you know like I mean he'd you know then in that case like he'd lose his credibility, -- -- he'd never be able to buy blood plasma again after that you know like see, so well -- -- I don't know either why every time there was a blood transfusion he had to like have cash to pay for the blood plasma, I mean you know,   why we couldn't wait to pay for ət along with the rest of the total bill when she got out of the hospital like you know. Probably it was a situation where that doctor just didn't much like to see me owing him too much money,   and since he could demand payment in advance he went ahead and had me pay him in advance.   Actually he didn't have any reason at all to ask for it in advance, -- -- most likely he **got carried away by excitement** for a moment, suddenly for just a moment, and probably even he himself had no idea when he came up with the idea that things you know had to like be done like that way see, um, well. I was about to go out and get together some money to pay him back just as he wanted me to do, when he asked me: What did I have to give him that he could hold on to as his <u>collateral</u> while he took care of the emergency blood transfusion for me? That had to be another new legal condition that he'd thought up on the spur of the moment for him to impose on me. You know I like I didn't have a thing I mean not a thing on me that was valuable enough you know like to give him as some sort of collateral see. So then the doctor said in that case he said I could just leave my ID card with him there for him to hold on to as the collateral like ju nou. So I gave him my ID card and left it there with him. I went out, without a clue where I could go to borrow the money. And I don't know why, all of a sudden I had this unbelievable urge to go out and splurge on something -- -- and I actually did go for a ride in a pedicab like see, you know," I couldn't resist heh-heh-heh laughing heh-heh, heh-heh again, "I'd hardly ever taken those pedicabs before, --- -- just when there was a need to in an emergency, like for example when when my wife needed to go to the hospital to give birth, that's the only sort of time I'd you know like hire something I mean like a pedicab. Actually the reason I like took a pedicab this time see was probably well most likely it was because I was like so tired you know -- -- and just at the same moment this three wheeled pedicab was like going along right beside me following along next to me step by step like. After I got in the pedicab, well, then like I started wondering whether I should look up that priest there that my wife always went to listen to for advice um like that one I mean like, so I went to look up the priest -- -- and as it happened by chance he wasn't at the church. So then I went on riding around like in the pedicab you know see and I didn't get out until I'd taken it all the way see like to the front door of my home. Fortunately there's still someone around like Mrs. Min," -- -- it sounded like, -- -- "who lived in my neighborhood, an outgoing, generous person, -- -- after she listened to me tell her what the situation was, on her own she took out the money she'd just then drawn out in her loan association's lottery, (it came to exactly one thousand by sheer coincidence) -- -- and turned the whole sum over to me.   So then I went on back over you know to the hospital to see. I'd just thrown away too much money on the pedicab ride, so when I headed back onto the street to the hospital this time, well, I didn't even so much as ride the bus back over there you know --- -- I walked it back on foot like that I mean like on the way back you know. But I didn't get very far before I started feeling like I regretted that sort of, -- -- it was one long stretch of road, a long way to go. Now it just so happened that it was the Midautumn Festival that day, -- -- and every household along the street had you know had brought out a few small stools and benches like that sorta thing outside like see to get ready to get set like to enjoy the moon I mean, well, then, you know, you know, um lelelelet's see, um when I walked back in through the front entrance of the hospital (by that time it had taken such a good long while a lot of time had gone by, I mean, believe you me, it had well it had like see by then,) this nurse rushed up in front of me and loudly questioned me, she said: 'Well, it's about time. What did you take so long to get back here for?' Instantly I asked her: 'What is it? -- -- Did something happen to her?' 'Why did you take so long,' she said: '-- -- Why I was beginning to think well most likely see you wouldn't be able to like make it back here not by this evening anyway sorta, you know like, that's what, that's what I was thinking, see.' 'Well, -- -- is she still here or not?' The nurse, this young woman, gave me this look of disdain: 'Now where   else   would   she   be   if she's not here?' I handed over all the money I had raised, the entire sum, I turned over to this young nurse, -- -- I'd taken out a square piece of handkerchief to wipe off my sweat when this young nurse presented yet another new question to me, which was, um, well see like um, what she said to me was about how I ought to think about what to do to dispose of that you know like that little child they'd like they'd just delivered. She said this wasn't the sort of thing the hospital had dealt with before, -- -- still, if I could say offer like a hundred NT see sorta, then the errand boy they had there at the hospital could take the stillborn fetus out for me and give it a burial sort of like, sososort of, see. Now I couldn't pay out a sum like a hundred NT, -- -- altogether I only had a little bit more than three hundred on me, that is aside and apart from what I'd just spent on the pedicab ride, I still had a little over three hundred left over, -- -- and I didn't know whether or not this little bit of cash was going to be enough to get our whole family through the month. So then that nurse said, in that case, I could just take it myself over to the cemetery grounds on the hill at Liu-chang-li and dig out a, a pit to bury it in there someplace. But she definitely wanted me to take care of it tonight, this very evening, -- -- she said she could not permit this, -- -- this thing -- -- to remain there overnight until the morning. With that I then received from her that 'thing,' -- -- the thing had been wrapped in newspaper and tied up, then wrapped up in another layer on top of that one. Then,   I borrowed a small spade for shoveling earth, from the hospital. Next, then so once again -- -- for the third time that day -- -- I got into a pedicab and took off. It didn't take long, and I was too embarrassed to get out right next to where the hill was, so I got out out at a place that was about three bus stops away from it. After I got out I kind of regretted getting out a bit too soon. The further I walked the more people I found, -- -- until by the time I'd climbed up the hill, I discovered that the whole place was teeming with swarms of people all over the hill and the valley, -- -- because it was the Mid-autumn Festival that night -- -- so lots and lots of people had come to the cemetery to enjoy the moon there, -- -- and now the cemetery well I mean it was almost more packed with people there than Hsimenting in downtown Taipei you know just about you know see like," -- -- I couldn't keep myself from laughing again, hah hah hah, hah hah hah, like you know: -- -- And Yü Shih-liang's nose started to wrinkle up just a bit, just a little bit there right in the middle of the ridge there, -- -- he went on talking: "And so I just blended in and mingled with these folks, and raised my eyes too, looked up just the way they were doing, as though I was admiring the moon up above too. And I waited that way, waited just like that until nearly one o'clock in the morning, until those folks who'd come out to enjoy the moon there had all gone, until every last single solitary one of them had all cleared out, before I started in digging out you know like the pit with the shovel. By the time everything was buried and all covered up over and I'd come back down off the hill, -- -- it was already two in the morning you know so," right, two a.m., "so it was lucky that it was that night and you could still get a pedicab at that hour -- -- because it was Mid-autumn Festival!" So then, for the fourth time in one day, I took a pedicab again. And this time I rode it straight home again. While I was sitting in the pedicab on the way back the whole way I kept thinking thinking to myself you know like you know you know I mean what the kids at home had been up to there what was going on sort of you know,   but when I got home I only saw Lao Ta and Lao Er -- -- sprawled out -- -- just stretched out sleeping on this worn out old sofa in the living room. As for the other two young ones, though, I didn't know where they'd gone. I went out to look for them right away then. I found the two of them outside under a streetlamp next to a trash bin playing with cards, having a card game. Brought them back home.   Went into the place and suddenly I smelled this rank odor that was there, -- -- I looked around -- -- it was a pound of pork liver I'd bought that morning to cook to celebrate the festival, and half a duck on top of that, too, all of it now one spoiled rotten, stinking, rotten mess.   I myself hadn't had so much as a bite to eat the whole like, you know, day and I didn't know about the kids, whether they'd had anything to eat or not either. I wasn't about to ask them, either, didn't have the nerve to find out, just coaxed them to get to bed like and go to sleep, and leave it at that see, you know. During these past two years," -- -- two years, -- -- I think it was -- -- "my oldest, Lao Da, had been able to help out around the house cooking, -- -- and he'd (that is, sometimes) he'd cook a meal all by himself see like so -- -- the reason things were in such a state that day was because I hadn't talked with him that morning about cooking lunch, and dinner, for the you know the younger ones I mean well you know well like sort of sorta. I hadn't been home very long at all when our next door neighbor, a fellow named Hsü," -- -- I think that was the name, Hsü, -- -- "walked over, over like to, to my place, um he, well he you know he stood outside my door and he called out: 'Hey, Yü, old buddy, still awake?

102

Good,   perfect, -- -- Wang just took off and we need another player, -- -- why don't you come on over and take his place for a while, how about it?'" -- -- Wang, -- -- I think that's what it was -- -- Wang, "   I thought that was pretty good timing. I could take the opportunity to earn a little cash, -- -- so then I went out and I took a seat and joined them at the card table you see like like there see. But, I never thought that after I'd played just a few hands, why, then I lost it all, cleaned out clean every cent -- -- and on top of that I lost over two hundred more even than I had on me to boot even. The good part was that everybody there they all knew how much I needed money at that game then there so they were all willing to give me a break until later on, until I could return them the money, oh, a little later after a little while. By the time I got home it was already about" -- -- four o'clock -- -- "itititit was so late by then you know like well by then well so, so I I hit the sack to grab a little bit of some some rest for a while, -- -- but I tossed this way and turned that, -- --- couldn't sleep, -- -- and after about five a.m. I got up out of bed, -- -- and I washed a good tubful of her clothes I'd just brought back from the hospital to give her a change of clothes, -- -- well, I tell you,   it's really hard work trying to clean the clothes of a woman who's just delivered. By the time that was all taken care of, the leave I'd requested from the Bureau was used up already by then you know see, so well, so soso then I returned here to Deep Pit Harbor I mean like see. What was so unexpected was that before long, -- -- she had a relapse of her old illness and started having these bad fits again see again like you know really bad fits I mean like. So then, it was so hard you wouldn't believe, you wouldn't believe

how   hard   it   was,   to get permission for an extended, I mean extended, leave to go to go back to Taipei, see, you know, -- -- I mean the director didn't seem too happy with me at all over this, you know this situation like not at all you know. My luck's been lousy from the start.   In the beginning they had three girls available in the first place to give me to pick one from at the start to start with that's that's the way I could go. Why, I don't know, -- -- my fate's no good, -- -- I just had to pick her of all people, I mean you know her you know," at that point Yü Shih-liang started to smile in that warm, gentle way way of his the way he smiled like you know sorta like, "
As things stand now, I hope this time she can get this illness of hers good and cured once and for all, I hope it it it it'll it'll be thorough, this time like you know like see I mean like really cured for good you see, sure, well, so   we'll see this time   whether they can't cure her completely. I'm hoping that after another, say, six months maybe,   she'll be able to leave the hospital right away, -- -- and the kids, I'm hoping they can come home, too, -- -- dinner time -- -- time for us to go eat now -- -- I hear the kitchen's boiling some dumplings with pork filling especially for us tonight, how about that, you know."

There's another person in the Bureau, it's Chang Fa-wu, -- -- now to look at him, just judging from the outside, he probably should rank as the very you know the healthiest looking person of all in like the entire Bureau. Actually, though, it's not that way at all. Chang Fa-wu's really all for show not for go, behind that appearance there's nothing, not a thing, totally empty -- --, a pure, unadultered dolt of an airhead if ever there was one. In fact, when it comes to strength, if you compared Chang Fa-wu to a lot of people here a lot of them you know like a whole lot you know then well, say, well then he's why he's much like I mean he's much weaker see. The cook, Lao Ch'iu, said, -- -- Fat Chang's getting beaten up all the time by the others, and he's punched him out -- -- Lao Ch'iu has -- -- a lot too.   If you can still believe anything Chang Fa-wu has to say has any credibility then most of the time he usually still suffers at night from insomnia a lot (that day when he first came over to my room,   the bath house, -- -- you know he'd said then you know that he hadn't like slept for like several days kind kind of kinda like.) So if he really if he can't sleep nights the way he says, well -- -- it's really weird -- -- how could he get as fat as he has if that's what's going on -- -- I mean like that way the less he sleeps like see then the ruddier his face gets, all florid like, and the more he goes around like huffing and puffing the way he breathes like heavily sort of. "Of course you can't sleep at night -- --! You don't do a single damn thing all day long, -- -- just sit around the whole day contemplating your navel and relaxing, -- -- of course you have insomnia at night and can't get to sleep," -- -- that's the way Sheng Ch'i-chih spoke to him you know like as scornful as he could be like see. Actually, Sheng Ch'i-chih doesn't get much more done during the day than Chang Fa-wu does really. You see, Chang Fa-wu well he's really and truly really really truly just like that, let a whole day go by without doing so much as a single solitary iota of anything, won't do squat. About the only thing Chang's good for the whole day is combing his hair (it was only later that I learned why it is that he always combs his hair you know that way so it's got a lock of hair that curls down his forehead so it looks like a hook in the shape of a question mark, -- -- it's because he's like trying to like hide this shiny scar he's got sort of on his head there like, or making a cup of tea to drink (-- -- naturally the only thing he uses is government issue <u>tea leaves</u>, -- -- but all the same you know he just puts in just a few, just so much like -- -- not enough to steep in any color at all into it even   ), and he drinks this until he's bloated like a drum so bloated bloated he's ready to like burst you know see, so like once he's tanked up on this   then he goes off

and takes a <u>leak</u>. That way it's like there's this water always circulating constantly through his body. I just can't stand him, this guy guy Chang Fa-wu! He still likes to make the dumbest the most immature jokes that   even a fifth grader   in elementary school wouldn't stoop to, you know. I mean like, for example, he's always, he's always saying things like he'll say to you: "ah -- -- . . . ah. . . How're you doing, sir, everything okay, your health, feeling in a good mood, business going well? Everything fine? So if you say everything's fine, just fine. Then let's, let's **shake hands**, one more time with **feeling.** " Or else he like he you know he comes up behind you and shouts, I mean he yells at you you know see like and then races off, fast as he can, he hides, so when you turn around he's nowhere to be seen -- -- then he'll run out at you laughing away like ha ha ha ha, -- -- hold his stomach while he   laughs -- -- laughs so hard he just keeps on you know keeps on going see like without stopping you know. Now then, at times like those like those see, if you don't want to pay any attention   to him   , if you go on with what you're doing and pretend not to hear anything, just go on walking along sorta like see sorta, -- -- why then he'll stick to you right up close following right behind you, hiding here and there over and over sorta like hiding you know see, he'll start in doing that, -- -- and keep on yelling out your name, **surname and given name** both.

This evening he almost almost came close to getting himself punched out by the cook, Lao Ch'iu. -- -- what he did was he ran over you know to Lao Ch'iu you know and he said like he said you know something like this, it went: since he'd had indigestion really bad for the last two or three weeks -- -- he probably had a "stomach condition" see -- -- therefore he couldn't eat rice at present, -- -- he could only eat -- -- **noodles** -- --

There's another person too who looks like you know like like very healthy like. At least he doesn't look as though he's ill. Ts'ui Li-ch'ün -- -- he's always angry, always looks like he's ready to fly off the handle like -- -- those big eyes of his always blinking, batting away constantly, -- -- his hands stuck down deep in his pants pockets. What he looks like is   energetic, -- -- as if he were ready for a good fight with absolutely anybody anytime anywhere,   that's why I say he's probably not ill. Altogether he seems, well, seems like an extraordinarily you know lonely sort of person kind of like I mean see, -- -- it seems like he doesn't get along with anybody in the Bureau here, -- -- it seems as though there may only be one -- -- T'ang Lin -- -- who's the only person he has any kind of relationship with -- -- everybody in this Bureau, but everyone, has a relationship with T'ang Lin -- -- and he's the one and only person in the bureau who's got no choice -- -- if you want to have a relationship with him he has to have one with you. I'd never imagine a **runt** like him could be such a "master of diplomacy" as he is like -- -- I mean he can actually carry it off you know so that nobody can believe he doesn't really want to have a relationship with that fellow that's what I mean sort of you know.

So, well, -- -- that's the way you can see him all time -- -- the one -- -- the one named Ts'ui Li-ch'ün, standing there sorta you know sorta seething away he huffs and puffs like, hand down inside the pockets of his, his western style trousers, -- -- his eyes maybe looking like like way way way out out ahead sort of into like the distance kind of kind kind of you know like, -- -- and maybe his mouth working away mumbling see talking to himself in some mumble that he repeats to himself like nnnmmm uh uh uh like sort of like see. One time I heard him he was going on nn mm the whole time reciting from a *tz'u* poem sort of saying like it went: "Waters falling, flowers flowing, Spring has gone away -- --!" (-- -- not flowing water, falling flowers) No one knew what that stuff he was saying he was saying was supposed to mean after all. Once, -- -- I recall it, -- -- he sat down in front of T'ang Lin, looking for him to talk to I mean see, -- -- and while he was talking he just slipped it in: "Waters falling, flowers flowing, spring has gone away -- --"* I have no idea what that was supposed to mean. I saw him off to one side, his head bent down, scribbling and doodling on a newspaper scribble doodle doodle, and what he was writing down was that sentence he kept on saying aloud constantly over and over again like. One time he charged in and started yelling away calling out to T'ang Lin: "-- -- T'ang Lin, damn, tonight I'm going to teach you the four-corner character indexing system, this is the book, -- -- If you haven't learned how to look up characters after just half an hour, -- -- you can have my head!"   Another thing he likes to say: You can have my head!   "Good, eh, great, -- -- the four corner system, -- -- let's you and me go over it, study it for a while, it's good to learn more about the same things, eh!" And I've heard Ts'ui Li-ch'ün heard him say the same sort of thing to T'ang Lin, say: "Damn, T'ang Lin, -- -- Tomorrow I'll put up the money myself, -- -- get someone to go into Liu-ho and bring back a catty of pork, then wait'll I cook up a special dish for you, -- -- If it's not just right you can have my head! -- -- waters falling, flowers flowing; spring has gone away -- --."

"Fine, fine. You go right ahead and cook something up, -- -- of course it'll be fine, just fine, just fine the way you cook it -- -- and when it's ready, sure, -- -- **I'll have some."**

There really isn't any **freedom** in being someone like T'ang Lin.   For example,   yesterday,   around midday after lunch was over, I hung out around that bureau of theirs for just a little while longer, watching T'ang Lin while he crawled up on top of his desk to knock off a few z's snoozing up there sorta like for his noon siesta nap, -- -- when all of a sudden Ts'ui Li-ch'ün charged into the office and ran up to T'ang Lin's desk and shook him awake. He said: "-- -- T'ang Lin, come on, come on and play some chess, -- -- get your chess set out, -- -- it's time you let me grind you into a pulp, make it two games." So T'ang Lin didn't have much choice but to get out that chess set of his, -- -- and, at the same time, he had to shout for joy that he was going to let him butcher him.

Actually, there's someone else in the Bureau as lonely as Ts'ui Li-ch'ün. Then again, not the sort of person who needs people as friends the way that someone like Ts'ui Li-chün needs   friends   .   Yellowish sallowy

106

yellow complexion, sharp pointed nose, face showered in pockmark pockmark pits. When Sheng Ch'i-chih's talking with somebody, if it's not someone else he's mocking behind their back then it's somebody standing right in front of him he's mocking to their face but if it's someone else who's talking with him he doesn't take the least interest in him at all, just looks off   in some other direction. He's the one and only person up to now in their department who still hasn't talked to me! Fuck him! What's he think he is! So let him act stuck up -- -- I'm more stuck up than he is! One time it seemed he was walking on over up toward me in my direction with a document or something in his hand, and it seemed like a rare sight to me, the way he smiled, smiled just a bit, that was unusual, the way it looked like he wanted to ask me a question to help him out or else to help him polish up some unfinished or some rough spots in his writing. I gave him a cold look. Instantly he looked as if he hadn't seen me -- -- turned around and stalked off.

I may not have talked with him, but I've heard a lot, a whole lot of what he's said to other people. They're things, the sort of things, that only he -- and nobody else, -- -- would say.   Once he said to someone, somebody -- -- I don't know what his name is -- -- he said this: " -- -- Hey, got any cigarettes? Let me bum one off you. I know what a **skinflint** you've always been, -- -- all I wanted to know now is whether you're really as **stingy** as people say you are. -- -- don't have any? -- -- Is this for real, or are you faking it? How about letting me frisk you, check you out, see whether you've got any or not? If I find you've got any on you, any cigarettes, -- -- see it's going to look baaad bad for you, you know! That proves it, -- -- they were right all along, -- -- **tightwad!!**" I may not have talked with Sheng Ch'i-chih yet, but already I've got this guy marked down as the worst, the very **worst enemy** I've ever had in my life, it it it it's he's it he's it.

Just this evening even (yesterday evening?) I even saw him again -- -- made me hate him all the more after I saw him, hate his guts through and through -- -- saw him just as he was walking out walking out just then out the back door of a place called called something like "Moonlight Mansions"* or something, just in the that alley back of that row of freshly painted, bright colored row of bungalows. Look at that -- -- that placid expression of satisfaction he wore -- -- that face of his, that mug; his head wrapped up in a little deep tea-green turban thing of a ski cap made out of woolen yarn. The jerk, he was even coming out just then out of the house I'd been to the first time I came here. My eyes were ready to explode in flame while I watched, my eyes fixed in close attention on him, -- -- well, okay, -- -- at least the slut who walked him to the back door and saw him out wasn't the one who'd taken care of me the time before, when I'd first come here. That   jerk,   so unpredictable, the way he walked out of the bungalow -- -- he didn't walk off, see, he kept hanging around poking his head out this way and that until finally he didn't even go away but walked on into another place, another one of these low bungalow-type buildings.

As for me, -- -- well by the second night after I'd hidden out here in the harbor telling fortunes and reading faces, by that time I couldn't wait any longer to go look up the place where I'd find a girl to party party party heartyheartyhearty. And it was just at dusk on that day I saw that woman with a face like the Goddess of Mercy herself, Bodhisattva Kuan Yin, -- -- I was seeing her for the second time. I thought, -- -- I wonder whether such a female, a woman with that Kuan Yin look, whether she could help me purge myself clean to wash away the raging lust that burns inside me -- -- I was thinking constantly about that woman how she looked so much like Kuan Yin, until when I approached the vicinity of the partyheartys party heartyhearty partyparty, partyheartys prettypretty fullfresh partyheartys. By then, of course, I'd forgotten all about the girl who resembled Kuan Yin -- -- and I made my way into a place, -- -- the one Sheng Ch'i-chih -- -- had just before then come out of.

I was led into a pigeonhole of a tiny, little cubicle like, partitioned off with slats of sugarcane and nothing at all but I mean not one thing in it except bare tatami mat and that was it. There wasn't even so much as a single cotton bedsheet on the tatami even, see. You know, now that's what I call economizing. Probably it's to get you into action fast, get it over with quick, and keep you from wanting to hang around, just get up and go as soon as you've finished. That way they can speed up the turnover rate to turn over faster. Not a thing -- -- not a thing -- -- except for just a stack a stack of white toilet paper on the tatami.

That broad, -- -- that whore -- -- a grotesquely **ugly** one, -- -- had a huge, gigantic huge huge head, -- -- and a skinny little body thin as a twig just exactly like a kid's. She should have been named: "Yuck" -- -- because she'd stay perfectly still and then always roll her eyes till they were white, -- -- purse up her lips and say: "Yuck!" All she wore was a thin sheer, simple cotton shirt, and over that a thin, lightweight pale green light sweater, -- -- and a pair of short white socks touched with yellow the kind worn when it's summer. I went to hold her hands, -- -- the hands were so cold they were like ice, ice cold, cold as ice. She said she didn't want to take off her clothes,   since the weather was so cold.   I didn't have any patience for this, I shouted: "Strip -- -- strip -- --" and at the same time gave that thin, pale green lightweight sweater a strong yank to pull it off, and she got pissed off: "Stop pulling it -- -- don't pull it -- --! You're tearing up my sweater -- -- yuck!" Then she took it off herself. I got undressed too. In just a few moves I was peeled down bare, not a stitch left on. Damn, it was so cold I couldn't help shudder and start shivering. At that point, standing there stripped naked, I started to get really embarrassed about everything that was wrong with my body, -- -- I have a black mole on the left side of my chest that's got the shape of a little baby infant's palm, and there's this long black hair growing out of it too -- -- the mole -- -- see like. So I rubbed my arms and watched her undress. My hostess undressed slowly and quietly -- -- as if lost in thought, and then looked down and scanned her own body. She then proceeded to pass the bras she had taken off under the tip of her nose and sneak a whiff. After that she scratched her ribs a couple of times where it itched. When she took off the skirt she had on she -- -- especially -- -- paid the closest attention to carefully examining a purplish red clot of blood on her knee, and then moistened the tip of her finger with saliva and rubbed it around on the clot there where there where it was. At that point I reached over and pressed that patch of purplish red. "Hey -- -- ouch -- --," she yelled -- -- screeched -- -- "That hurts! Don't touch it -- -- !" I smiled, baring my teeth see. We hung up our clothes, -- -- on some thick large nails covered in blood red rust that had been stuck on the sugar cane partitions. Some bits of stray wispy threads already hung from these nails, guaranteeing a nice sized hole in your clothes once you'd hung them up. All of a sudden she raced over to the partition on one side and, with the fingers of one hand curled into a round tube, peeped through it peeking and peering through it. The sugar cane partition was punctured everywhere with peepholes you could see through.

"Anyone next to us? -- -- Let's change rooms."

She went on looking around.

"No one," she said listlessly with frustration, " -- -- they've gone already - - -- "

"Is there anyone? Is there? -- -- If there is I want a different room. -- -- "
(I have an amazingly powerful sense of shame, very strong.)

"No, there's no one there!" Her eyes bulged up, -- -- ferociously, she rasped: "You talk too much! -- -- **what a pain!**" She rolled up the whites of her eyes, -- -- " **Hurry up** !"

So then the two of us shivering all over you know it was so cold like we slowly came together gradually step by step. -- -- As I went to lay down on her I couldn't, really, I couldn't stop from sneezing right on her smooth, flat stomach. Instantly I reached out to wipe it up, wipe off that slick smooth skin on her stomach.

After that I suddenly scrambled back up again: -- -- because I'd discovered to my surprise that she hadn't stripped off her socks and taken them off -- -- and if her socks weren't off it was just as if she hadn't taken off anything at all. I couldn't be satisfied with that at all. That's what a **picky** person I am. But, no matter how much I tried to persuade her to, no matter how I tried to think of a way, I couldn't get her to take those socks of hers off for me.

Before proceeding on to begin with a routine of "calisthenic hand exercises," there were still at present several things to be done. -- -- First, I planned to give her a kiss, you know. Truly I have no idea what could be harder to do than give her a kiss, I mean it like it was as hard as if it was a **rape**. She'd just twist back and forth, left and right, to avoid it, punch me with her fists, kick me with her feet, see, that's what it came to see. "Stay below the waist, -- -- nothing doing above my waist," she said.   Now that's a weird idea.   Is that supposed to mean that chastity is located at the lips of her mouth? -- -- They all seem to say the same thing, so maybe it's some religious commandment. And if it is a commandment imposed by some religion, then you ought to show respect for her **religion**. My lips, -- -- shifted course, and landed on her hair.

Next, I made yet another request of her, and that was: I wanted to look. "What are you looking at? What is there to look at?" I looked. There was nothing to look at. If you're gong to say you know that there's something good looking about snatch well but you know **hell** gate just absolutely can't compare for looks with a person's face. It's such a lump of folds and wrinkles every which way it's just such a mess, sort of, you can't make any like sense you know can't make anything out of it at all. Well, still, all the same, plenty of ordinary folks like it, they like it **a lot**. So much that they'll even **lick** it. Does that mean I should go ahead and lick on it lick it up like that too you know, is that it? Absolutely not. I can give it a rub with my hand and that's as far as I go. Even so, even if I rub it I don't get any pleasure to speak of from it, doing that, I mean, you know sorta. Then again, the way she'd trimmed herself there showed a lot of skill, not bad at all, the way she'd trimmed it into a nice, tidy little beard like.   Each person has their own distinctive, individual "style."

That just about did it. I was ready to begin. -- -- I still had another question: "How about, eh, how about -- --"

"How about what?"

"How about -- -- you know."

"Just how about what? -- -- Come on, tell me, just tell me."

"A blowjob"

Needless to say, that naturally got a flat rejection from her on the spot then and there. Truth is, I don't like it all that much myself either, that stuff. It was just that since I was spending my damn money for this, -- -- so it only seemed worth the price if I could say whatever could be said. After that I started to go lie down you know again see when I suddenly realized, -- -- I'd forgotten completely to fondle her breasts. -- roll them around awhile. -- -- So I slid my arms around that skinny little torso as flat as a board and I embraced her like and so then you know then it was like in a flash. I got this instant hard-on hard as a bone the way it came up. And I went to put on a condom -- -- a condom is a must for me -- -- I don't want any social diseases. "What're you doing, -- -- what are you **doing**? Why didn't you get it out beforehand?" "Because you

110

kept on pestering me: Hurry up, hurry up, hurry up, -- -- so I hurried up so much I forgot all about taking one out." I got one out, got it on, -- -- Manfred the Monk drooped over and curled up to sleep. All anybody could do then was just find the patience to wait it out a little while you know. "What are you doing! -- -- You, to hell with you, forget it." She got up and lost no time going to get dressed. Mutiny! Revolt! Quickly, there wasn't much else I could say but that I'd give her more; without waiting I pulled out a bill from the pocket part of my suit pants where I reached into the legs hung up hanging on the sugar cane board wall, -- -- it was a five dollar bill I mean that I had there, see, you know. She grabbed it -- -- snatched it up -- -- but since she didn't have any pockets on her -- -- all she'd had on from head to foot was nothing more than a complete set of her own bare bare birthday suit, -- -- and on account of this she set this bill with a face value of five dollars paper currency set it down next to where our bodies were locked together in an embrace. But then she couldn't feel at ease with that so she picked up the note again and held on to it down inside the palm of her hand, and then while we finally got down to the process of exercising our way through a set of "barehanded calisthenics," she kept that note squeezed tight down deep <u>inside</u> the palm of her hand

And so we waited, sat there on the tatami and waited there -- -- she with her back to me, lay there on her side curled up like a worm, just lay there curled up like a little worm, -- each thinking their own thoughts about what was on their own minds: -- -- it was the same as when you're waiting on a platform for a train, -- -- one person waiting for a train that's passed by, and one for a train that's going to come. I don't know how many times I said to her: "-- --Here it is!" (just as if what I was talking about was **a train,**) then she'd rush back over on an express train back from where ever it was far, far away she'd gone to, probably it was her hometown she'd gone back to. She'd raise her legs way up high, way up there so they formed a "V" for victory, to welcome me, an Arc de Triomphe. But right away I'd say, "Oh, it's quit on me again!" To get me to shoot my wad sooner I said there was a new position that was was almost sure to help, really incredible and all, you know, how it ititit could help us out. I told her to get down on all fours and assume the posture of the human race before it had learned to stand up erect at "attention" -- -- and then let me kneel behind her. "No way! -- -- Not from behind!" How she yelled and screeched and carried on the way she did you know it it it it was it was amazing you know. "What are you so upset about, -- -- I didn't say I was going to do it in your rear end, I just said that I'd do it from behind you, -- -- don't get so jumpy, -- -- you'll understand what I mean once you do it," -- -- she did understand, and **still she refused me.** I started in again, to persuade her to try yet another new position, -- -- this was one I'd seen before when I was leafing through a book on "secrets of love making," -- -- this time it was purely a new direction in "experimental creativity," -- -- the posture which had been worked out and exhibited was altogether novel, and the form it took displayed considerable beauty and extreme complexity. -- -- Unfortunately, though, what the results proved was: -- -- **the form is far superior to the content.** Probably when I was going through you know it was sorta like a lotus position there were a bunch of moves during it I couldn't remember well enough, so as a result of that the two of us ended up locked together see so like there was no way for us to get ourselves untangled, and as a result of that we spent fully more than two minutes time -- -- I twisted my neck in two places -- -- until we managed with a lot of effort to dismantle and untangle ourselves. And while I was in the middle of concentrating all my energy and effort on carrying out this "experimental innovation," right in the middle of this she -- -- suddenly asked out of nowhere, -- --: "Say, how about telling my fortune now, okay?" -- -- I felt like I'd been **ambushed.** -- -- After all, I'd never imagined that, -- -- she recognized me. "I'll tell you in a minute, hold on," I was just then in the middle of innovating.

She started getting listless again -- -- and weary -- -- so then she started to ride that train home again. I thought to myself that all these fancy moves, the mystical motions and whatnot, -- -- it looked like they didn't seem to have any use whatsoever, -- -- so I'd do better to try something more down to earth, something really really ordinary, -- -- only thing was, so then I told her we'd try it with the woman on top man on the bottom, yang for yin, yin for yang, the world turned upside down. "Whew, it's no use. The only thing that would do you any good is to see a doctor." "What do you mean 'no use'?" I seethed with anger, -- -- eyes fixed on her full of fight -- -- Manfred the Monk instantly rose to the occasion, standing tall and proud. Right away, she -- -- was all cooperation -- -- dipping her head she lowered herself down on me, but with one hand I quickly blocked her hot (-- -- and still a bit moistened moist)   snatch, and cried out urgently: "Slow down -- --!" Probably because I'd played with myself when I was young and previously suffered wet dreams, -- -- I constantly have a problem with premature ejaculation. And just then I was ready to ejaculate. "What are you up to -- -- -- -- -- --?" She squatted down. My body in a coil rolled up from below her triumphal arch. "What are you doing? What are you doing? What are you doing? -- --" She must have said twenty "what are you doing's" in a row. I cried out suddenly, face flushed and ears burning red, I shouted: **"I'm coming!"** It was like a starved tiger, a hungry wolf, -- -- the way I lunged forward, -- -- not out of some sort of primeval lust the way they talk about the place of food, drink, and sex in the Five Cardinal Relationships that sort of thing, -- -- but out of fear of missing an opportunity, now that I was cocked to shoot, -- -- I couldn't hold off see waiting for it even a moment longer you know like. "Slow down, slow down," it was the sound of her pleading that came from beneath me as she was trampled under the iron hooves of my invading force. Swiftly I drove forward and like in one thrust see broke in and brought down her city you know so, well, -- -- right then and there I ejaculated thoroughly thoroughlylyly. I thought I could hear this "puff" sound, a weak little soft sound like. "-- -- Eh? Is that it? -- -- so soon?" I pushed it around another four or five times, -- -- prolong the time it took a little, -- -- the time I spent afterwards probably pretty much matched the time I took **during the process** itself, I'm certain. "That's the way I'm used to doing it, -- -- when I start out at first I can be pretty quick on the draw, even faster maybe a little, -- -- but then after that I last a long time, a good long time, -- -- I can last as long as over an hour, I've gone as long as that." She acted as if she simply hadn't heard. "After a while you want to do it again one more time?" "Sure, but if you want to do it some more you'll have to pay some more." "How much?" "The same." "Can you offer a special rate, -- -- say, a forty percent discount, -- -- how's that, -- -- what do you think?" "Can't do it, -- --" "

Can't?" "Well, what's it going to be? You want to do it again or not?" -- -- " In that case just forget it." I was still on top of her. "Get up! Get up!" She said loudly. So then I crawled off her and stood, stood all the way up. That's when my voice suddenly broke and I completely panicked, and I started yelling: "Oh -- -- no! Damn! Damn!" "What is it?" Instantly she sat straight up and bent her head down to check out her snatch, inspecting the hellgate and asking "What is it?" "Oh, no -- -- the condom broke -- -- it's broken!" I was fit to be tied I was so upset you know, I mean, -- -- I was so upset, -- -- because I didn't know, I didn't know whether I might have picked up something -- -- a "sexually transmitted disease." She got up, and while she was going over to put on her clothes at the same time she -- -- rolled her eyes, rolled them up so they were totally, completely white, big big like <u>big</u>, and: "Yuck -- --!"

Ever since that night, for days now, I've been worried constantly, right up to today, about you know about like sexually, contagious, sexually transmitted diseases. Really, you know like I don't know even like the first thing when it comes to something like you know like a social, a sexual type dididisease like, I mean. Everything I know about sexual diseases has come from what I learned from the ads for treatment of social diseases in the newspapers see:

syphilis,　　　gonorrhea,　　　hardened soft chancres,　　　cloudy urine,
split stream urination,　　　inflamed urethra,　　　red sores on penis,
 . . . . But no two ads ever use the same words, -- -- I've put in a lot of time studying this carefully at great length, and I've found that never is the content of what one ad says the same as that of what any other ad says, that's right. Especially, -- -- when it comes to something like the way they write "soft hardened chancres," what're they? Even now I don't have the most elementary, the most basic, the simplest idea. I only know the two characters for "chancre" are 下疳 , the 疳 reads like the 柑 of 椪柑 .* I've made up my mind no

matter what I'm going to look that up in a dictionary and check it out once and for all; -- -- I'm not going to go on pronouncing them the way I always used to like 剾 . Whenever I've had the time these past few days now -- -- I take out Manfred the Monk to inspect him, looking him over anxiously to see whether there's anything like red sores or something on him. Sometimes, even, when I'm with other people, you know, like I'll get this urge I'll want so much to toto take out Manfred, let him out so I can take a look at him. Truly, I don't know why it is that I have to get laid, -- -- there really isn't anything so enjoyable about it to speak of, you can say. All I'm left with when I'm done all I'm left with is just this powerful, this overwhelming sense of regret, that's all: For example, I regret spending so much money that way (how much cash I actually have on hand still, actually, -- -- oh, no point bringing that up), regret also that I didn't exactly achieve complete and totally perfect success;   and I also regret regretting whether I've caught a sexual disease (-- -- syphilis -- --) and on top of that dizziness, eye strain, listlessness and fatigue and all that see like. It's beyond understanding, really inexplicable, inexplicable and beyond comprehension: I know perfectly well that every broad is actually alike, just the same, -- --below the waist they've all got the same totally uninteresting "hellgate" looks just like an anus; the feeling each time I ejaculate isn't that much, just doesn't amount to more than nothing very much, -- -- but still, still, if I see one I want one; if I see ten I want ten; see a hundred I want a hundred. I know a parable that presents an analogy for this sort of stupidity. It goes something like this, that there was this guy, who spent all night long beside a pool of smelly water trying to think of a way to snatch the moon inside this pool; when he saw the moon was in the water he jumped in, "splash," and dove into the water, -- -- but the result was that he didn't snatch one blessed thing, and he climbed out, stinking all over, and got up on the bank next to the pool. He stood there on the bank, and after a while, he saw that the moon in the pool of water was coming together and forming into a moon again, so he jumped in once more, -- -- so for a whole night a whole night all night long you know the whole night see, he just kept on like jumping in and then climbing back out onto the bank and then jumping in, ...

We've all been, all of us, swindled. All of us, -- -- not just me, -- -- but everyone! It's those people like Freud, whoever, who've hoodwinked us into worshipping a new kind of religion, called "**sexual freedom.**"   What **sexual freedom**? I, for my part, I've heard only one thing that contained genuine wisdom, and the person who said it, frankly I think is greater than any philosopher of the twentieth century: -- -- He was a former colleague of mine where I worked in Taipei: Lao Lu. Lao Lu said, "Why do you have to have a crew to fire a cannon when you can shoot your own pistol by yourself and have as much fun? -- --" **Great!** Now someone like that is somebody who's achieved genuine, true **"sexual freedom."** Two's a crowd, -- -- doesn't amount to sexual freedom, -- -- only Lao Lu's way really amounts to sexual freedom.

Yet, I, however, I do not have this freedom -- -- I remain hidebound and inhibited. Even as far sunk into poverty as I am at this point in time, I'm still so bent on "firing artillery" that I try to think up ways to "amass armaments" and "stock munitions," no matter what there isn't a day that goes by that I'm not thinking about how to get enough cash together to enjoy at least one hen's egg. And then, once I've got a little money in hand you know then, well, -- -- I need to "map out strategy," -- -- and allocate "entertainment expenses" see, you know, (: -- -- overnight: seventy yuan, -- -- relaxation: thirty yuan, -- -- tea: fifty yuan, -- --) actually the overnight allowance is an unnecessary expenditure; -- -- eliminate that one, that item, there, yeah, that's it. It was yesterday evening then when I went out in "pursuit of pleasure" for the second time here in this deepest of deep pits deep down in deep harbor town. That was, really, it was an **experience!** I was so concerned about "sexually transmitted diseases," that I'd already made up my mind not to go in **"pursuit of pleasure,"** so it wasn't a "pursuit of pleasure," -- -- actually, it was just, just a "search for suffering," that's all -- -- I figured that after a while in the not-so-distant future, at some point, I'd have an opportunity of some sort to go to Jui-ho, or maybe I could ask someone else, -- -- if it was possible -- -- to buy a box of condoms that were truly safe, we'd see when the time comes, we'd see. So, these past few days, I relied on hand rubs to resolve the problem. But last night, yesterday evening, -- -- I broke my vow -- -- broke the vow of abstinence, that is, see.   Absolutely no one could have guessed, that yesterday evening, when I went roving out on a stroll cruising through the crooked winding little lanes back behind the bungalows among the supple fresh hebetic budding of the party heartys where they partyparty heartyhearty, ---- that's where I saw the woman who looked so much like Kuan Yin herself, standing in a doorway there, -- -- to welcome in any passerby who passed by passing through. I was planted there, planted upright, like a telephone pole a pole. Then, all of a sudden, I let out this laugh like, you know, heh-heh-heh like; -- -- I went with her inside into her wooden bungalow there you know inside there.

She took me far into how many places far, I mean far far far deep, I mean into the courtyard deep deep who knows how deep inside the depths far inside the building.* On the way we went through all these thin, narrow winding corridors, turning back and forth and around and about until we entered what seemed to be another apartment, and after that we went up a little bit to what seemed, a little bit, like it was **upstairs**, that was the feel of it. Good! I liked it upstairs!

The room, -- -- this was even a genuine room -- -- not one of those pigeonholes; -- -- this was a **chance encounter** in a million it was so miraculous, and, obviously, with still more fun to come; -- -- I thought she probably was attracted to me, she had to be, -- -- otherwise it would hardly be worth her while to be treating me as handsomely, as splendidly as she was. It all happened faster than I can tell it -- -- she stripped off her clothes from top to bottom, head to foot, underwear, outerwear and all, clean down bare to her lovely, swelling, full, fair, snow white flesh, like a ripe, succulent luscious white grape, -- -- the goods were so good, so good, my eyes could hardly take it all in, they were so, so good, -- -- how'd I ever run into this much good luck! Probably it was the moment Mom and Dad brought me into the world to begin with, the constellation was right on dead perfect, not a minute too soon or too late, right on the zodiac; over and over again and again I silently gave unceasing thanks, -- -- thanks to Buddha, I prayed in my heart. But, I also began to worry whether I might not um you know let her down sort of, sorta like?

I was startled nearly out of my wits, -- -- so startled I let go of the condoms in my hand and they fell from my hand I was so startled, (I also carry condoms with me, you know just like cigarettes sorta kinda like, -- -- even despite the way that one failed the last time, -- -- I couldn't bring myself to just throw 'em out, -- -- this time I was prepared to wear two of 'em, it doesn't hurt if you're looking for protection to have a little "added security"), so the thing that startled me was: suddenly, there she was, stark buck bare naked, lunging on top of me like a wild beast on the attack, and she plastered herself on me, plastered herself on me in a tight grip, stuck herself on top of my body; -- -- her hand, -- -- at the same time -- -- she thrust her hand down toward Manfred the Monk, -- -- and stroked him wantonly aggressively, like utterly lascivious, wild and reckless.   Talk about failure, I came on the spot. "Oh -- --" Disappointment showed itself on her face. But then, the surprises kept coming, -- -- suddenly she, -- -- took a breath, -- -- knelt down, -- -- and started to **suck** me off. I was one **lucky** guy,   also   one very **unlucky** guy, -- -- too bad the timing wasn't right, my time had just run out, -- -- it would have been fine a little earlier (just before I ejaculated), -- -- or if it were a little later, that would be fine too (after I was ready to come the second time.)   She was like a hungry ghost, draped in hair, small, weak, moaning sounds coming from inside her mouth, -- -- such a woman with a face like the Great Kuan Yin, -- -- a revelation of human nature, -- -- my tongue clicked with amazement.

Desperately she tapped it, slapped it, squeezed it, pulled it, -- -- working as fast as if she were in a rush to put out a fire, -- -- but it was all so useless none of it made any difference. She was a bit heavy handed the way she went about it at times, -- -- I was getting to where I'd had enough of that, you know, -- -- it was getting all red and everything from the way she was handling it, it was turning red. I said -- -- I forgot there's something I have to do, -- -- right now, that's right -- -- I have to go, -- -- when it's already dark as pitch black on a night like this, now of all times, -- -- I have to go, to, to look into someone's fate tomorrow for him, anticipate whether it's going to be lucky, or, or whether it's going to be unlucky,   "I'm a fortune teller, you know."

She didn't seem to have heard me at all, -- -- the only thing on her mind was rubbing it, and she still rubbed, flogged it, pounded and kneaded it and yanked on it. Suddenly she stood up, -- -- because she saw, she could see for herself that -- -- not only wasn't I cooperating, -- -- I was even getting a little shorter kind of even. Her leg flew out, and she kicked me way down there in my groin down there below my navel (with her toes, full, plump, fleshy, full ones all painted in red nail polish,) -- -- I rolled a long way, a good long way all across the tatami. She let out a yell and raced over to the door, bent down over there and pulled a knife out from under the tatami, a long, glistening, gleaming sharp thing, the kind fruit vendors use to cut open watermelons. She blocked the the doorway there to the room. That's when I became a prisoner in the secluded brocade boudoir of this powder puff woman warrior.

She ordered me -- -- to play with myself. She wanted me to demonstrate for her all sorts of weird looking bizarre poses -- -- to show her all kinds of stuff like that. At the same time she was standing off to one side, -- -- and with one finger crooked, -- -- while she was constantly working away there furiously all the time, -- -- her, one hand working away like that, -- -- and one hand rigidly grasping onto to that long, sharp fruit knife, face going red all over, deep blood red all over. After that she came over, her eyes filled with a vindictive, malicious look, and pulled my little critter, -- -- Manfred the Monk -- --, all around the room in circles, -- -- we kept on circling around the room three or four times; the whole time I was groaning in this weak pathetic sounding whimper. After that, -- -- eyeing it, eyeing it, she lunged forward, and whack smack whack smack one blow after another until I crumpled and saw stars. "You cunt! Fuckyamutha fuckyamutha yamutha's cunt, ..." My voice rose as I cursed her, -- -- she responded with a punch, (this time the punch landed landed above my stomach, -- -- at the midline -- -- or I should say, to give it its proper academic name, my "diaphragm,") She said to me as she laughed: "

Curse me again   !   " Just like the time before, I rolled away over and over a long way, a good, good long way a long way away. She leaped forward in a single bound, and grasping her knife, held it up against the side of my neck, and she wanted me, she ordered me: Kneel! Kneel down! Kneel! Sonufabitch, this was sex at the point of a knife, literally, that's what it's called. There wasn't anything I could do but kneel obediently. So then, then, she put a big, huge fat breast, the whole thing, into my mouth. "Suck it! Suck, suck,

suck it!" She said, forcing me to do it. I rolled it around in my mouth -- --- pushing it back out.   But then though, this full, huge, thick, soft breast blocked my nose tightly -- -- I practically choked, asphyxiated on it.

After that she suddenly spread her thighs apart like two big columns and that big big big black snatch, the **"Gates of Hell"** big and black came right straight down toward me (sure, it was dripping wet all right, soaking wet, -- -- but I could hardly breathe,) -- -- she wanted me to french it, -- -- this time that's what it was all about. I raised my head, -- -- looked up at her, -- -- think we could let it go this time? -- -- **No you can't!** -- -- I started, I started to cry, you know, -- -- there was nothing I could do, I had no choice but to lick it, I mean, see.

If I didn't do a good enough job licking it she lit into me with her hands and feet and gave me a good beating, -- -- "just like a dog," -- -- I thought -- -- if you took all the blows I'd gotten in a lifetime, -- -- and <u>added</u> them all <u>up</u>, -- -- I figure they still wouldn't come to as many as what I got from her that one time. -- -- Can't find a cigarette, -- -- I can't believe they're all gone, -- -- and no booze, either, -- -- or water, either, so then she wanted me to get up on all fours and wave my fanny up high, get it way, way up there high as the sky. What's going on? What are you doing?   In one leap she vaulted up onto my rear end and sat up there, then she pressed her snatch (she couldn't bring that off, -- -- she didn't have the equipment) pressed it up against my rear end there, going back and forth, -- -- that way, I suppose, she figured she could get off that way, -- -- and maybe that way go through the motions messing around so she could think she'd "done it" just the way any ordinary guy could, too. Then she yelled something, hopped forward onto my back at the waist (came close to practically breaking me in half), and shouted: "Crawl! Crawl!   " At the same time she struck me with her fist like hailstones all over my buttocks, and then I crawled, fast, crawled fast around all over the place as fast as I could go I lumbered around blindly until finally I collapsed from exhaustion, -- -- no, it wasn't that I collapsed so much as that I <u>fell</u> face forward like a dog eating shit, my nose and mouth pressed flat down onto the tatami you know like on top of it. "Now I want you to get out of here! -- -- Get out! -- --" but I laid out flat on the floor and couldn't make a move. "I'll get you out of here, -- -- you still won't go?" She went around to my rear end, grabbed the knife, and proceeded to jab me a couple of times, -- -- I came alive, but quick, -- -- there were two red streamers running down my rear, -- -- I crawled frantically, frantically I crawled toward the doorway of the room which she opened, crying out forcefully a couple of times, and stumbled through outside. She threw my clothes out then, -- -- I tucked them under my arm, -- -- and took off headed downstairs, -- -- when I looked back, -- -- there she was, her towering body, white as white as jade, jade and glistening wet with sweat, fists balled up at her waist, arms akimbo (I don't know what she did with the watermelon knife, where it got to,), her legs were spread apart, -- -- standing high up, way up high, at the top of the stairs there up there. That cunt, that fuckin' cunt! -- -- I won't forget this! I'll

118

get even with her no matter how long it takes! A true man gets revenge if it takes three years to get it! (or is it ten years?) -- -- Anyway, I'll get revenge or I'm not a true man! So this time I got suckered, all right, -- -- like a woman falls for the wrong guy, -- -- it was that face of hers, the way it looks so sublime so much like Kuan Yin, just like her! -- -- It's like they say: **Wisdom grows out of experience: You can't have the one without the other.** Next time I'll know better, next time I'll be a lot smarter than I was this time, by a long shot, a long, long, long ʃɔt!

My ass is so sore! Now that I think of it, -- -- does my ass feel sore because of what I was thinking about, -- -- or was my ass sore to begin with itself, see like? Yeeeow, ow, ow! It's brighter than a Peking Opera actor's face, redder than Chang Fei's.

Yeeeow -- --ow -- -- ow -- -- ow -- --

There are vicious ones, -- -- and mild ones. And some seem like young brides. There was one like that, -- -- a teahouse girl, -- -- who got a pretty hard time from me. That's right, -- -- I gave her a hard time. That was the day after I was scared of STDs, -- -- all the same, at this point, there's no way I can explain it, but my need for female companionship was at an even higher pitch, more intense than before I'd shot my wad; more than ever I seemed like a witless fly searching for a way out in blind desperation; (each time after I finish up my business, it's all the more as if I never finished. ; 1 minus 1 does not equal 0, but 2,) -- -- I couldn't think of anything to do but, um well, go on over to a teahouse like um you know sorta.

The place I went to was very quiet, -- -- extremely quiet, (-- -- it was upstairs, too; this time too I was already upstairs, -- -- and the chairs were still in such good order it seemed there wasn't a soul in this "upstairs,"), -- -- no music to be heard, -- -- just a rustling sound like ocean waves, *huahuahuahua*, actually wasn't ocean waves, but the sound of the rain, the way it saundz when it's raining out here. She was the sort who didn't want to talk, and even if you asked her a question wouldn't give you an answer practically, -- -- although she wasn't at all nasty in the least. She always looked like there was always something on her mind, constantly thinking about something like kind of kinda like. Her face was paper white, even if you were in the dark you'd sense that her face is as wan, pale, pale and white as white paper, and her hair was tied up and bunched together in a bun in the back of her head. You could smell she had halitosis when you got near her. "What's your name?" As soon as I sat down I discovered that expression, that look, she had as if she was memorizing "The Faults of Ch'in," -- -- so it seemed like whether or not this was a good way, -- -- I asked. She's not answering. Most likely she's probably named Mei-chu, I thought, "Beautiful Pearl." They all seem to be named Mei-chu. If you don't believe me, then try it on any of them you meet, all you have to do is call her:

119

"Hey, Mei-chu." -- -- and she's sure to answer you. "Mei-chu," I said. No answer, -- -- I'm not getting any answer from her at all.   Sleeping Beauty, that's probably what she is, sunk way down deep in her dreams. So then, (I was just like her! -- -- short on talk, long on action -- -- completely like her!) I went into action, strictly according to the book, item by item. She still didn't wake up. She was fast, deep, dark, sound asleep, -- -- probably taken a dose of some anesthetic. !   No, not really after all, -- -- Sleeping Beauty did wake up once in the middle of something. It was when I was, -- -- I was in the middle of undoing the buttons down her front. I have no other regrets about life than these three: the first regret is the number of spines on *shih* fish, the second is the middle hundred pages of novels, and the third is that there are just too damn many, too many buttons down the front of girls' clothes. "Wait a moment, hold it, just a moment, . . . I'll get you someone else, how's that, . . . just take it easy a little . . . ." she said, and then, having said it, went back to sleep all over again, see, like you know.

Right while I was in the middle of hearing a sound like ocean waves in the sound of the falling rain, I suddenly remembered a voice, a sentence: "What did you just do that to me for?"

"Are you angry?"

"-- no."

"You **don't** like that, -- --?"

"It's scary, when you do that.   Do you have a girlfriend?"

"What do you think, do you think I have a **girlfriend**?" I was agitated, the way I asked her, really annoyed.

"Well if you did have a girlfriend, and you treated her that way, -- -- she'd be pretty scared, too," she stroked my hair gently, -- -- it was one of those evenings early in spring when it rains a misty, fine mist like fine drizzle of a mist, -- -- years and years ago. She'd just finished saying: -- -- "My father, -- -- used to be a construction worker, -- -- one time, when he was working, he got careless, he fell, and injured himself. After that he couldn't work anymore, ... Because my mother had always been sickly, she also had no way to help people with their laundry and make a living that way, ... My little brothers and sisters were also too young, and there were too many of them, six altogether, ... ah, ..." Her voice broke and she began to sob kind of, "Don't ask me anymore!" She stood up, dabbing her eyes with a handkerchief. ". . . Sorry, I'll be back in a minute." "-- Where're you going?" "I'm going out to get a breath of fresh air, -- -- calm myself down." "No, don't go. Sit down, sit, sit down."

"I used to love school, ... My teachers all said I ought to go on to junior middle school and continue studying, ... If I had the time now, I'd get out my textbooks and go over them again, ... Why don't I leave this place and go find another job? I can't find any, you need a college degree to get a decent job, ... I don't think about anything else, now, -- -- marriage? Who'd be willing ? -- -- I can say now that I don't think about anything else, I think about nothing else except how to raise my oldest younger brother, to keep him in school, and support him through university, ... After that? -- -- After that I'll die, ... I don't think I'll live very long."

She was rather pretty, but with a dark ring under her eyes.

Down my head went as I viciously drove home my assault on her. She still didn't say a word, -- -- although beneath my unrelenting assault she let out quiet moaning sounds she uttered softly in painful groans. After I assaulted her each time, while we rested, I faced her with a sense of understanding and intimacy, like Sleeping Beauty and the Prince on the White Horse, and I said not a word, made not a sound. . . . I didn't care to ask about her past.

"What do you feel about your life now, is it hard to take or not?"

"It's okay.   It's not much of anything. Every day I just go to work and then get off work," She said go to work and get off work, "Once you get used to it, it's not much of anything."

"Well, do you go out much, then, for fun, when you have the time?"

"Not much."

"Why not? You ought to go out and enjoy yourself, go out often to relax, forget your worries. -- --"

She nodded her head sadly and smiled wanly.

"As much as I can I try when I've got some money saved to send it back home send it to my mother."

"Aw, you ought to think about yourself more, you ought to do more to look after yourself, take care of your health, you should go out for a walk when you have time, let your body and your feelings loosen up more."

Once again she smiled slightly and nodded her head that sorrowful way.

I'd never been so moved. Inside that dark, tiny, confined little booth, I began to think of great questions I had never thought of before in my whole life: What, for example, is life, is being, all about after all? Why does a good girl like her have to suffer like this? -- -- When faced with another's pain, what can you **do**? Can you like do something to **help** them out a little kind of kinda? With countless girls like her, -- -- Mei-chu -- -- probably she was called Mei-chu, too -- -- like her in this world -- -- what is there that would enable each of them, each and every one of them, to free themselves from a life as miserable as this? I thought about this as hard as I could, as hard as I could, -- -- but I couldn't think of anything, -- -- in the end, I thought, maybe, the only thing you could do is, when you have sexual relations with them, do a better job screwing them, -- -- at least then they'd get a little something out of out of it sort of sorta like. Actually, there's no better place, none better whatsoever, than a teahouse for an education: -- -- in a very short span of time, it can teach you all sorts of things about life and and society as well. -- -- the tea room is a classroom -- -- and every customer in search of pleasure is actually a more thoroughgoing "humanitarian" than anybody else.

When I left, I paid twice as much money more than I was expected to pay. -- -- But I've got to admit, -- -- during those two hours, as much as I sympathized with her, as much as I felt for her and all, I did after all take advantage of her to use her in a big way!

After that, at least three times even, even on evenings when there was a fine, very fine, rainy spring shower, -- -- evening fogs when everywhere in Taipei was enveloped in white hazy white haze, -- -- I went to the teahouse where she worked to see her. I'd never been so happy before. If Mei-chu, -- -- Mei-chu -- -- if she had customers, then I'd wait for her off to one side, tranquil, calm and collected and tranquil. And if sometimes, it happened, somebody was needed to help out, I'd go, on my own, I'd go serve them tea, and melon seeds, and I'd even give them the napkins to wipe their hands, too. So I was in love, right? No, I wasn't, I just felt I respected her, -- -- that's what I said at the time, you know. Then, one night, -- -- believe me, -- -- I sat there from beginning to end like a perfect gentleman, all dressed up and spruced up, sat there next to her, and -- -- I'm not exaggerating one bit, -- -- the whole time I didn't so much as touch one hair on her head nor on her body either. By the last night -- -- the last time, -- -- I couldn't hold back my feelings anymore, and I said: "Mei-chu -- --" Most likely her name was Mei-chu   "Let me help you! You must, -- -- don't say anything, don't say a thing, -- -- you must let me help you! -- -- You're so wonderful, don't you see! You say no! -- -- That only proves how much character you have. I'm going to give you a sum of money, -- -- I'm going to figure out a way to raise it for you, no problem, -- -- I'll give you **thirty-thousand dollars!** That way you can get out of this place and you can you know go back home, home sweet, sweet home, your homiest, sweetest home sweet home, and your mom and dad, you can go back and be with them, -- -- and after that, your brother will have no trouble going on to study -- -- right through junior middle school, middle school, and on to university, ... ah, I'll get you the money! No strings attached, as far as I'm concerned. You don't have to   marry me. Now, it's settled, I'll bring the money to you tomorrow. Seven pm tomorrow evening, seven o'clock sharp, -- -- no, half past six, six-thirty. Here -- -- I'll be here, at this spot. I want to say goodbye now, **don't see me out!** And you're not to say anything more, -- -- that's it, that's my, -- -- that's my, -- -- that's my wonderful Mei-chu, my wonderful, wonderful, my <u>wonderful</u> Mei-chu. Goodbye for now, until tomorrow, -- -- sweet dreams, tonight, Mei-chu, sweet, luscious, beautiful dreams! -- --"

The next evening, -- -- it was raining as always, that fine, thin, hazy drizzle, a haze so hazy, -- -- it was just like fog, and even, it seemed, even thicker and deeper than it usually was, -- -- when the time came, though, -- -- I didn't go, go over to her place as I'd said I would. I spent the whole night, all night, -- -- on the streets and in the lanes, -- -- out in that fog of splashing, beading drizzle, coming and going and going and coming, back and forth, again and again, walking around the city of Taipei. Finally, I walked into a tea house, one of those I'd never been in before. And from then on, I never did go back into that tea house, you know, the one that "Mei-chu" was in, like you know.

She was still silent, wrapped up in herself, her head lowered thinking constantly, constantly, thinking, thinking, strenuously, under stress and strain. So I took out a cigarette, -- -- I thought I'd take a break and rest for a while, -- -- I didn't talk to her.   I could hear a sound, a little bit like the sound of ocean waves. There were several, several times, times when -- -- actually it was because it was too, much, a bit too beyond the limit not to have anything to talk about -- -- I really wanted, to ask her, where she was from, -- -- if she wouldn't tell me her name -- -- what was her age, how old was she, where did she work before she came here? -- -- However, I held back and restrained myself from asking her, see, like you know, see. But that night, I did something I shouldn't have, really. After I'd finished smoking my cigarette, I put my arm around her shoulders, -- -- suddenly, it was as if my fingers had been bitten by a snake all of a sudden, -- -- and I retracted them as if I'd touched an electric current, -- -- I felt something, -- -- it was fastened to her upper arm, a lump of woolen yarn balled up into a lump.*

"-- -- What's that?"

No   answer.

"-- -- I, just now, I, -- -- shouldn't have, really."

Her head slumped even lower, lower daun.

"Is it someone close to you? -- -- Is it someone in your family? Who is -- -- he?"

She raised her head, head up up high, -- -- in an instant her face was turned into, twisted into, a face so ugly that it would be hard to find another face as repulsive as that in the entire world, whereupon she covered this face of hers with both her hands, and started to shriek at the top of her lungs, wailed see I mean wept and wailed you know like.

I didn't know what to say, had no idea what I should say, -- -- I only felt, just had a sense that I was to blame that I hadn't been able to keep from asking her all those questions. I should have taken her in my arms, and hugged her shoulders in my embrace, to comfort her, -- -- but, like you know I mean I didn't like do that. It was already getting late. The way she was going, the way she was carrying on weeping and wailing and sobbing, I was worried that tea this evening would wind up with nothing more than a lot of crying, -- -- so then, I, -- -- it was a completely shameless thing to do, -- -- grabbed onto her hand

and inserted it down there, there in the region of my crotch, -- -- she struggled desperately, she struggled -- -- but I pressed the hand down with all my strength, pressed it straight down, as if it were a small bird being choked to death, like that, until it ceased making the slightest movement. Afterwards, she -- -- it seemed as if she was heart broken, -- -- in fits and starts -- -- she began to wail, I mean, to rend the air and shake the earth even more, letting loose for a minute, then pausing for another. It got pretty cold and clammy, clammy wet and cold as ice down inside my pants, -- -- for a long while, -- -- I thought they'd never dry out, that's the way it felt. I was just as worried someone would come by, -- -- but no one did, -- -- this place was actually too far, actually, too far out of the way, kind of kinda like out of the way sort of sorta like you know, I mean. Next to her I waited, without making so much as a peep or a whisper, for the sound of her weeping to die down, -- -- until I heard that sound that suddenly sounded like the ocean tide!

"I don't know of anything the whole day through worth fretting over!" She, white carter's golf cap cocked to one side, face daubed with a thick, deep layer of rouge and powder, deep red lipstick spread thickly across her lips, she said it exuberantly, then continued with: "Salute!" -- -- She raised her hand to the b-b-brim of her hat. "Salute!" I said. -- -- Don't get the idea that all the girls in the lane are each and every one crybaby sob-sisters, oh no, -- -- there are also some that are so happy they couldn't get any happier you know like, like -- -- it was the night before the night before last, the second time I went out for tea, I bumped into one like this. She wasn't just **happy**, she was **healthy**, I mean, healthy besides, -- -- happiness and health amount to the same thing, one of them amounts to both of them, happiness is the mother of health, just as health is the father of happiness. She had broad shoulders that stretched out amply, wide stretched wide cheekbones, dark cafe-au-lait skin, -- -- and powerfully, powerfully strong **body odor**! As I just said, her face was powdered white and rouged red, her lipstick was pasted on so that it covered an area even larger than her mouth itself, and it was like a thick layer of beard on a foreign razorblade, the way her eyebrows extended out long, long and thick, and thick and heavy. That carter's golf hat, -- -- stayed on her head all the time, -- -- and no matter what, she never took it off, never removed it. She was not just healthy and happy, -- -- she had an appetite that was incredible, -- -- whenever I saw her she was always stuffing herself constantly with melon seeds, always going from hand to mouth. Now, ah, just how, just how I mean you know happy like was she kind of? The sound of her laughter never ceased, -- -- nor did the sound of her singing, either, ever cease. Even if when I was lying on top of her working away on her body, she'd keep right on singing along merrily, singing away cheerfully without interruption, -- -- now that's what you can genuinely call authentic, unadulterated **"workers' songs"**! She was a thoroughly generous, giving sort, as well, -- -- happy people are all generous, completely, they are. When I said: "I was hoping -- -- uh, -- -- to have a look!" then she right then and there on her own, -- -- she pulled up her clothes, raised her dress up high, high up over her high up high. When I'd "looked" her over, she still had her clothes way up high up. I was worried she might catch cold, just a little concerned, -- -- but she was as warm as a cat toasted warm next to a stove. She sings, -- -- probably singing is a good way of staying warm. And she was always smiling and laughing, -- -- that was most likely a way of warming herself, too, could be, I mean, kind of kinda like, too, you know. All of a sudden, out of the corner of my corner of my eye, I saw two round roly-poly rolling things, tumbling away from her body there, spinning over, spinning away, rotating as they rolled spinning across the tatami until they stopped at the, the wall there. What were they? She had a pair of **falsies**! Now of all things the last thing she needed was some fool thing like a pair of something as ridiculous as those idiotic things, and when I say that about her I say it frankly, frankly, candidly and honestly without intending the least flattery or any kind of a show of politeness at all whatsoever. "The bigger the rise the better the prize!" -- -- she said. "They're good enough the way they are already," I said, as my head dove on in there. Laughing, singing, -- -- and then, all of a sudden, right in the middle of everything without a pause there it was loud and clear: a "brrrrt" farting noise. But there wasn't any "Uh-oh! . . . .Uh-oh! . . . . Who just farted? Who was it who just farted just now?" On the contrary, -- -- utterly forthright, -- -- with heroic daring: -- -- "Oh! -- -- ahahhahhahhahhah!"

Really, I couldn't figure out how she could be so **happy** ; that night, when it got to be the very last moment before I was about to leave, I asked her, - - -- why was she, you know like, so, so happy ? "Even I don't know," she, she was batting her clear, ingenuous orbs of eyes, -- -- and laughing aloud at the same time, -- -- she said: "It just seems I was born happy the way I am, just as happy, happy like this. Even if I wanted to be sad, no matter how much I tried to be sad I still couldn't be sad. It's true, every minute, I feel happy, every minute; -- -- anything and everything makes me happy; the whole world, the whole world, makes me feel completely happy, -- -- " She stretched her limbs, both arms, forming a huge, giant arc-shaped full moon in the space over her head. It was then, -- -- as I just said, -- -- that she said to me: "-- -- Salute!"

She had any number of stunts and tricks she liked to play, so many they just kept piling up one after the other. She said to me once: "Open your mouth - - --" "What for?" "Open your mouth! " I opened my mouth, -- -- hoping that maybe a piece of melon or something of the sort, might get tossed into my mouth. Then I hear "ptuuee!" this spitting sound she made at my mouth, gaping open wide, as wide as a cavern, cavernous like, as if it was a spittoon. -- -- Naturally, being the sort of person who loves to make fun of people in a gentle, good-natured way, -- -- she didn't really spit any of the saliva, -- -- "nectar of the gods," -- -- she had in her mouth into my own mouth, see.　　　That's probably the solution to the puzzle of how she could be so happy, you know. -- -- She could be endlessly "**innovative**," "**the more innovative the more surprising**"; she was simply like a magician, the way she could constantly reach into her paper box and pull out all sorts of all kinds of gismos, gadget things and tricks. So now, -- -- I know, -- -- what the secret of happiness must be: -- -- you need to be full of　　　ideas. But then, I don't know whether you have to be happy first to begin with: before you can be "full of ideas." No matter, whatever the story is, she was "**full of ideas**" After she'd made her spitting noise "ptuuee!" instantaneously her expression became gravely serious, -- -- and at the same moment she gestured to me with her hand to indicate: don't make a sound. Her hand delved into the pock-pockets, pockets of her wool dress. She pulled out what looked like a small, glass phial, bottle. She swung it up in space over her eyebrows, -- -- she was putting in eyedrops, she was. She said she wanted to make her eyes, "bright, as bright as two electric lights." And then, too, she was just as generous and giving as always, she was, she offered me some "**drops**." I, only had one eye, even so, -- -- I put some drops in. Cool as ice, felt great.

"I'll tell you a story, -- -- you don't look too happy to me, -- -- I'll tell you a story, give you a few laughs that way, -- -- I'm great at telling stories, you know," she said.

"Good,　　let me hear it, see if I laugh."

"It's about two girls here, where we are, right? -- -- Ah-hua and Mei-hsiang," -- -- that's probably what their names were, Ah-hua and Mei-hsiang, -- -- "So this morning, right, when they got up, Ah-hua put on Mei-hsiang's dress by mistake, -- -- and just then our boss saw her, -- -- Ah-hua -- -- and said to her: "Oh, **Mei-hsiang**! Go out and buy me a pack of cigarettes, -- -- oh, wait a second, -- -- so it's you, Ah-hua!"

-- -- You see, -- -- there's nothing in the world, really, you can't hehe, -- -- nothing you can't turn into something **enjoyable**.

However, I was turning a question over in my mind, -- -- one that wouldn't go away no matter what.

"-- -- Did the two of them, Ah-hua and Mei-hsiang, look a lot alike?"

"Not at all! -- -- One's tall, the other's short."

"One tall, -- -- one short," -- -- something seemed to be gnawing at me.

"I'll tell you another story, and this story, I guarantee, will definitely be funnier!" She took off that cap she wears, then she put the cap back on again. "This time it's about Li-hung and Mei-hsiang." -- -- Probably it was Li-hung and this Mei-hsiang.

"Now this time Li-hung and Mei-hsiang look a lot alike, right?"

"Look alike? -- -- Ah, actually, they do kind of, -- -- they're both quite tall, very tall, tall, tall, tall, and thin, very thin, long and slender, long and slender. But Li-hung is very, very pretty. She's the prettiest young miss we have in this place. Every customer, no matter who he is, always asks for her first, first thing, -- -- if you see her, -- -- you'll know what I mean. If you see her, -- -- None of the rest of us here can compare with her," that's how simple and sincere she was, without any trace of any malice at the bottom of her heart, "-- -- but, she's gone now, -- -- left last week it was already. -- -- Well, so anyway, about Li-hung, so , one day, a customer shows ʌp, right, and he wants Li-hung, -- -- but she didn't happen to be there just that moment, -- -- so, our boss called Mei-hsiang to go with him. -- -- And it was just at that moment, that Li-hung herself came in the backdoor, -- -- and heard someone asking for her, -- -- so she asked, which room? -- -- eh, so right away, she ran to that room too. So there they were, the two of them, Li-hung and Mei-hsiang, both standing there in front of the customer in the same room!" Here again was another one of those marvels that can transform the "unremarkable" into a "joy." She really enjoyed herself telling this story, this new one: -- -- she laughed: -- -- she may not have laughed her head off   exactly, but she did laugh till that hat she wears fell off her head and rolled off her. She, picked up her hat, -- -- fanned herself with it. Then she stuck it back on her head, -- -- and went on talking: "There's more, eh, so after that customer saw them both   he said: ' -- -- Hey, what's going on? -- -- One at a time is enough, okay? -- -- What do you expect me to **do** with the two of you?'"

When I heard that I started to laugh with her, hahaha   out loud.

What a night it was,   we laughed,   we cried (cried tears of laughter,) We sang for sheer joy, and later she asked me to tell a joke, and for a moment then, I couldn't figure out what to do, I couldn't come up with anything, -- -- so then in exchange I performed a couple of "voice imitations." After a while, she ran out of ideas too, -- -- both of us ran out of steam, -- -- but, it didn't matter, didn't matter, -- -- right away the lightbulb went on over her head, -- -- she took off her hat and put it over down on my head, -- -- once again, she'd created a new, yet another, marvel. Next, and this time she was onto something that got her all too charged up, too charged up a bit, -- -- she raised one hand, pointing her fingers, and held it up in front of her mouth, and rounded her deep red lips into a circle: "-- -- Oooh -- -- goochee goochee goo, -- -- oooh, -- -- goochee goochee goo," she said and she reached out to tickle me. I'm very ticklish, -- -- extremely ticklish! The only thing I could do was tickle her back,   and was she ticklish too, -- -- more ticklish than I am. We bellowed, we laughed, we were terrified, we ran for our lives! Then, whammo, bam, down came the sugarcane slats on both sides, -- -- and we were covered beneath this pile of debris.

Afterwards, we crawled out from under this heap of junk, -- -- and again she gestured secretively to me, -- -- indicating that I was not to make a sound, while her eyes shone, and she said to me in a low whisper: "Let's go next door, next door, change rooms." We gathered up the odds and ends scattered around here and there, -- -- she asked me: "Oh good, a tea glass, should I take it?" We took it. Although our tea was completely spilled. "There're some melon seeds too, should we take them?" We took them. Even so, the only thing left of the melon seeds was an empty dish, -- -- not a melon seed left in it. "Will you help me look around for where my hat went to?" "It's on your head!" "Really! On my head!" She said, and started laughing out loud, "Is there another, -- -- is there another one of my breasts?" "What?" "Where did my other breast go to? -- --" **Oh!** -- -- found that too. So then we moved out, shifted location and changed to another room, switched like, see, you know, -- -- once more got settled in again all comfortable, -- --

Daybreak, -- --

(End of volume one)
January 6, 1974 -October 19, 1979.

NOTES

Page 4. Matsu (Ma Tsu) was a legendary young girl who performed miracles while living on the island of Mei-chou, off the southeast coast between Fu-chou (Fuzhou) and Taiwan, in the 10th c. A.D. In later centuries her spirit was credited with various miraculous successes in military engagements, fishing, and trade, winning a large following in the region, where she is worshipped as Holy Mother in Heaven (*t'ien-shang sheng-mu*) in Taiwan and Fujian, and Imperial Consort in Heaven (*t'ien-hou*) in Guangdong and Hong Kong.

Page 7. Wu Ta-lang, cuckolded brother of the heroic Wu Sung, who slays his sister-in-law after she murders Ta-lang in the classic narrative *Shui-hu chuan*.

Page 10. "Peach Spring Paradise" is an allusion to the utopia described in the writings of the poet T'ao Ch'ien (365-427), known to every schoolchild.

Page 10. "Clean Sweep" (men ch'ien ch'ing) is a play in mahjong, the term used also once in toasts, as in "bottoms up."

Page 16. Francis Bacon in *Novum Organum* (The Doctrine of Idols, 1620) presents four idols as illusions in possession of humans' minds, obstructing learning: Idols of the Tribe, the Cave, the Market-place, and the Theatre.

Page 22. Dostoevsky's *Notes from the Underground*, etc. were titles fashionable among the Western-oriented literary circle of Taiwan at the time.

Page 24. "Yellow River water comes from heaven" is a line from the poetry of Li Po (Li Pai, 701-62), as noted by William Tay, "Wang Meng, Stream-of-consciousness, and the Controversy over Modernism," *Modern Chinese Literature* 1.1 (September 1984): 15. *Niagara* (1953) is an American film starring Marilyn Monroe.

Page 39. "Soldiering in fatigues" in old army slang is "throw on tiger skin" (p'i lao-hu p'i).

Page 43. "Manhunt" is an allusion to the story "The Most Dangerous Game" by Richard Connell (1924), a piece regularly in schoolbook anthologies of fiction, and released as a film in 1932.

Page 46. "Su San sent to trial" (Su San ch'i chieh) is a scene from the opera *Yü T'ang-ch'un*. The scene, a popular favorite among Republican-era audiences, depicts the acquital of a prostitute wrongly accused of murder.

Page 52. "To read a man first read his face" is a parody of lines by Tu Fu (712-770) in his "Frontier Songs" (Ch'ien chu sai): "To shoot a man, first shoot his horse./ To capture rebels, first capture their chief." Tr. Ronald C. Miao in Wu-chi Liu and Irving Lo, eds., *Sunflower Splendor* (NY: Doubleday Anchor, 1975), p. 119.

Page 60. The festival of "crossing over" to salvation (*p'u-tu*), the Yü-lan-hui festival of the seventh lunar month (July, August).

Page 64. The poet Li T'ai-pai (Li Po) is indeed represented as a general in various Ma Tsu temples.

Page 65. Translated by Philip Yampolsky, *The Platform Sutra of the Sixth Patriarch* (New York: Columbia University Press, 1967), p. 132.

Page 66. "Such as this I have heard" (*ju shih wo wen*) is a formula in the Chinese translation of the Buddhist *Diamond Scripture* (*Vajracchedika*).

Page 69. "Twelve Thousand Miles of Outhouses" parses in Chinese as a parody of verses depicting the majestic scale of the Chinese empire.

Page 83. Popular religious art portrays the God of Wealth, Kuan Kung, with a dark, date-colored face.

Page 83. The Yuan shan Hotel, or The Grand Hotel, has for decades been the most famous hotel in Taipei.

Page 85. "The Faults of Ch'in" by Chia I (second century BC) has for centuries been standard school textbook reading on the material excesses and moral weaknesses of China's first empire.

Page 89. The stele of the Yen family Temple was composed by Yen Chen-ch'ing of the T'ang dynasty in ancient clerical script (li shu).

Page 90. A "captain in the army" in the Chinese text reads "san ken yu t'iao" or a "three stranded fritter," an allusion to the shoulder insignia worn by captains.

Page 106. This is an allusion to a line from Li Yü's (937-978 A.D.) tz'u poem *"Lang t'ao sha"* (Ripples Sifting Sand: A Song), translated by Daniel Bryant as "Flowing water, flowers falling, and spring gone all away" in *Sunflower Splendor* ed. Wu-chi Liu and Irving Yucheng Lo (New York, 1975), p. 304.

Page 107. "Moonlight Mansions" is lifted from a line in a tz'u poem, "Shui tiao ko t'ou" (Prelude to Water Music) by Su Shih (1037-1101), translated literally as [the moon] "lowers itself to the decorated door" in Kang-i Sun Chang, *The Evolution of Chinese Tz'u Poetry* (Princeton, 1980), p. 188.

Page 113. P'eng-kan is a large variety of tangerine grown in southern Taiwan.

Page 115. "Courtyard deep deep who knows how deep" is a well known line appearing in poems by Ou-yang Hsiu (1007-72) and Li Ch'ing-chao (1084-1151): "T'ing-yüan shen shen shen chi hsü."

Page 123. "A lump of woolen yarn" suggests an armband signifying mourning.

CORNELL EAST ASIA SERIES

For ordering information, please contact:
Cornell East Asia Series
East Asia Program
Cornell University
140 Uris Hall
Ithaca, NY 14853-7601
USA
(607) 255-6222.

8-93/.2M cloth/.5M paper/BB

CPSIA information can be obtained
at www.ICGtesting.com
Printed in the USA
LVHW090349301219
641964LV00009BA/69/P